A BROKEN REALITY

A Novel

Rob Kaufman

For My Number One Fan,
Always, Forever and Beyond…

This is For You.

1

Danny Madsen had been missing for four days, and hope was fading faster than the weak sunlight giving in to the cold night ahead. Worse, there'd been intermittent periods of snow and sleet throughout the day, creating slick surfaces on unlit county roads and leaving behind asphalt without traction or boundaries.

Like every other evening since the boy's disappearance, the approaching dusk put a damper on the search effort. Each was another day past the critical "48-hour window," another night for Jesse Carlton to fight back tears of frustration as he crawled the icy streets of Hingham, Massachusetts, in his silver BMW, looking for the ten-year-old boy the Amber Alert described over and over as white with blond hair and blue eyes, weighing fifty-six pounds and standing about four feet six inches. When last seen, they'd always add, he was wearing a bright blue North Face coat, blue corduroy pants, Nike sneakers and a backpack with the name "Danny" stitched into the left shoulder strap.

Danny's description echoed in Jesse's head as he made the right off of Main Avenue onto Forest, which passed the hundred or so square acres of conservation land. He didn't need the Amber Alert to picture Danny. He'd recognize him the instant he saw him since he'd known the boy from the day he was born. Jesse had long been best friends with his parents, Becky and Don, and Danny had become the son Jesse and Melissa tried and tried for but could never have. They'd become so close to the Madsens, in fact, that they'd purchased a home up the block from them, sight unseen, when Becky and Don told them it had come on the market. It was apparent to all of them that the less distance between the families, the more fulfilled their lives would be.

It was this honorary parenting of Becky and Don's only child that had Jesse driving the streets and highways in and outside of every neighboring town for the past four nights—pursuing leads he'd overheard cops discussing at the Madsen home, following up on hunches he'd get after scouring the Internet for clues from past abductions. Each evening as he began his search, Jesse prayed he'd be the one to bring Danny home safe, sound and emotionally intact.

Jesse knew his nightly searches were pointless, but he could no longer bear pacing the floor at home or sitting in the Madsen's cop-filled living room waiting for another bullshit tip, another clue that led nowhere but deeper into heartache. Melissa spent her nights comforting Becky while Don worked with the police to pursue every potential lead. Jesse's need to do something, anything, forced him into his car each night with dissipating hopes and, by the way things had been going recently, unrealistic dreams.

The last person to see Danny was the school bus driver who watched him jump down the vehicle's steps four days earlier, just three blocks from Don and Becky's. And that clue was as solid—and as clear—as mud.

Jesse turned off the radio and clicked on the high beams. The pavement was pure white from the newly fallen snow, and there wasn't another car anywhere to be seen. In front of him was blackness; behind him was blackness; on each side, nothing but blackness. How did he expect to see anything out here, let alone find a scared and freezing kid? He didn't know, but it didn't matter. This was the only action he could take that made him feel like he was actually doing *something* to help.

The yellow light poles every 300 feet or so did nothing but offer a blurry glow that barely reached the road. And now that a smattering of snow had started again, the soft crunch of flakes beneath the tires filled the silence with an eeriness that sent a strange tingle sliding up Jesse's neck.

On either side of Forest Avenue lay the Terrence Ford Conservation Land, acres and acres of brush, swamp and trees with a few neighborhoods dotting the outskirts. Since the homes were hidden behind the dense thicket and prodigious pines, they were usually invisible to Forest Avenue drivers. Tonight though, even in the deep blackness of this night, he could see their pinpricks of homey yellow light, which, like the rickety poles lining the road, was nothing he could see by.

As he passed the two-mile marker, his phone rang, jolting him from his concentration. The display on the dash showed Melissa's cell. He took a calming breath and pressed the button on the steering wheel. "Hey, babe."

"Where are you?" Melissa sounded almost panicked, her voice trembling.

"What's wrong? What happened? Where are *you*?"

"I'm at Becky and Don's. They just got a call from Agent Rivera...hold on."

He tried to be patient, but after a few more seconds of muffled voices he couldn't hold back. "Missy!" he yelled and banged his fists on the steering wheel. "For Christ's sake, what did Rivera say?"

"Sorry, Jesse. I'm just getting more details." The muffled voices he'd first heard faded away as though she was moving into another room. "Someone just called the hotline from somewhere out in Hingham. It was an older woman who lives—"

Jesse felt like his heart skipped a beat. "I'm in Hingham! Where in Hingham, Missy? Where?"

"Oh my God, Jesse. Wait, I wrote it down." His pulse pounded against the side of his neck as he waited for the crumpling of paper to stop and her words to start again. "Okay, the woman lives on Tower Road off Route 228, on the east side of that conservation area."

He brought up the GPS and frantically searched for 228. "I'm like five minutes from 228—five minutes. I'm literally on the other side of the woods." His voice was shaky. "I'll put Tower Road in the GPS."

"She says she saw a boy fitting Danny's description running past her house a couple of hours ago. She didn't call right away because she wasn't sure."

Jesse let out a shout of frustration. His shallow breaths quivered in his throat. "Shit, it's starting to sleet," he said. "I'm on Forest right now. It runs parallel to Route 228. I'll turn around and work my way toward Tower to see if I can meet up with one of the units."

"Jesse, please be careful. I don't want you getting stuck in the middle of nowhere."

"This isn't nowhere, Missy—it's Hingham," he said with a sigh, knowing there was nothing he could say to help quell her anxiety. She was a worrier, plain and simple. It was something he'd become accustomed to and had learned to be patient with, but tonight his nerves were too raw, his patience too thin.

"Jesse, sleet means ice. Ice means slippery. Slippery means…"

"Missy," he snapped. He bit his lip and took another breath. "I'm going to turn around and head back toward 228." He gazed into the darkness to his right, wishing there was a road that cut through the conservation area. "Once I get there, I'll give you a call. Until then, sit tight. This could be the break we've been hoping for."

"Oh God, Jesse. I hope so. Please be careful. I'll wait for your call. I love you."

"I love you, Babe," he replied, making sure to sound as composed as possible as he disconnected.

Jesse was once again alone, the soft muffle of the car engine filling the otherwise empty silence. Keeping safety in mind despite his own anxiety to find the boy safe, he made a careful K-turn in the middle of Forest Avenue. The tires slipped a bit on the icy road, so he let up on the pedal allowing the car to straighten itself out. When he faced south, he stepped on the gas again and drove as fast as he could without completely losing traction.

Jesse could see the lights of Hanover Mall through the melting snow on the windshield. The liquid dripping down the glass made it look as though the lights were dancing, shimmying back and forth to the steady beat of the tires crunching the ice beneath him. He glanced at the speedometer: 25 mph. If he could keep up this speed, he'd be back at the intersection of Forest and Main within four minutes.

A faint smile crossed his lips as he remembered finding Danny's favorite Spider-Man action figure in the back seat earlier that week; Danny must've dropped it the day Jesse helped out Don and Becky by picking him up from rehearsal for his school's play. The toy had been right in the middle of the seat, and he wondered if he could reach it—maybe it would change his luck, somehow attract Danny to him.

Jesse reached back, fumbling around, trying to reach Spidey. Nothing. He leaned further and slid his open palm along the seat. Still nothing. Angling backward as far as he could, he patted the floor mat behind him in hopes that the figure had slid during a turn.

No luck.

A quick glance showed the tiny superhero jammed into the corner of the back seat. Spider-Man was tonight's lucky charm; the idea felt right, and it would help him find Danny. It was a superstitious and even desperate move, but doing things by the book had so far turned up nothing.

"Gotcha!" he cheered when he snagged the action figure's foot. He turned back toward the road to see a black figure stumbling out from the brush in front of him. In less than a second, the headlights shown on the figure's face—it was Danny.

Horror seized Jesse by the throat and he gasped as he slammed on the brakes. The car went into an immediate spin, flying directly at Danny whose eyes went wide in the headlights. Jesse felt a thud against the back panel of the car. He screamed, the view from every window only blurred streaks of light. He tried to focus, to spot Danny somewhere in the whirl of his surroundings. But the boy was gone. He screamed again, his cry now muffled by the airbag exploding against his face. He squeezed his eyes shut, feeling the BMW skid off the side of the road and nose-dive into a shallow ditch filled with snow.

As the car lay on its side, ruined engine still ticking, Jesse could barely hang on to consciousness. Images and sounds swirled through his head: the screech of metal dragging along the pavement, Danny's face hitting the window, the sickening thump as the car smashed sideways into the little boy's body.

"It didn't happen," Jesse whispered. "This is a dream," he panted. "Just a dream." He repeated the words again and again until the weight of his eyelids became unbearable and he closed his eyes, allowing the sound of his sobbing to lead him gently into his own personal darkness.

* * *

As Jesse's mind struggled for something good to latch on to, memories of fifteen years earlier floated to the surface.

"Her name's Melissa and she's beautiful," Don announced from three bar stools down.

Jesse took a sip of the martini he'd been fantasizing about all day. It was colder and tastier than he'd imagined. The speakers behind the bar blared something dubstep, forcing Jesse to take a breath so he'd be able to yell above the din. "You'd better watch it," Jesse joked, gesturing toward Becky sitting on the stool beside Don. "You don't want your wife thinking you're looking at other women."

Becky smiled and shook her head. "I'm not worried," she said, gently poking Don's chest. "This man knows he already has the best woman around."

Don kissed her cheek and saluted like a five-star general. "Absolutely. She's correct. I have the best woman around."

Becky's poke turned into a slight punch. "Don't be a smartass, *honey.*" She turned to Jesse. "By the way, *I* was the one who thought of you as soon as I was introduced to Melissa at the library. She seemed so smart and beautiful, and you've been going from woman to woman for so long that…"

"Okay, then," Don interrupted. "Let's not go there right now. Why don't we get a table where it's quieter and we can tell you more about Melissa? Then you can decide if you want to meet her."

Jesse grabbed his martini. "Lead the way, Matchmaker Madsen!"

The maître d' led them to a small, circular table close to the center of the restaurant. On the linen tablecloth sat four place settings of elegant bone china, as white as the covering beneath them and as refined as the lustrous flatware surrounding each dish. In the middle was a crystal vase filled with roses that appeared freshly cut, with tendrils of clematis winding through the blooms.

Jesse smirked as their maître d' pulled a padded chair out from the table for him. "Hmmm...this is kind of fancy for just the three of us. I'm more used to barbeque, plastic forks and paper plates."

"Nothing but the best for you, my old friend," Don replied, ignoring Jesse's typical sarcasm.

Jesse sat down, slid his chair toward the table and cocked his head. "Something's not right here. What's up with you?" He glanced over to Becky, who immediately started reading the menu. "Why this place? What's going on?"

Before Don had a chance to respond, their waiter approached, introduced himself and began to remove the extra place setting.

"Not so fast there, *garçon*," Don said, tapping the table. "We might have a fourth."

Jesse choked on his drink. "No! What? You're kidding me. She's not joining us for dinner." He looked at Becky, who glanced up for only a second before returning to fiddle with her menu.

"I don't see the problem," Don said nonchalantly.

"Don, look at me!" Jesse gestured toward his wrinkled suit jacket and not so fresh shirt. "I've been working all day. I'm not prepared to meet anyone, especially not someone as much of a knockout as you say this woman is."

Don waved him off. "*Please*, Jesse. Like you *ever* look bad. You look like an underwear model, but with better hair." He patted the top of his own thinning crew cut, shaking his head in defeat. "You have nothing to worry about...at least with your appearance."

Don and Becky shared a laugh, but Jesse wasn't listening anymore. He was too busy straightening his tie and sliding his palms along the front of his shirt to press out the lines. It didn't matter how many people told him how handsome he was or how lucky he'd been to have been blessed with his beautiful mother's genes; when he looked in the mirror he simply couldn't see what others saw.

Jesse glanced at Becky, who was watching his every move from behind her menu.

"Becky, you should know better. I might expect this sort of surprise from my oldest and not-so-dearest friend Don, but not from you. You're more level-headed than this." He used his fingers to comb back the sides of his hair.

Becky raised her head and stared directly into his eyes. "Have I ever done this to you before, Jesse?" she asked, letting her menu fall to the table.

"No, but…"

"And if it doesn't work out, I'll never do it again. I promise." Becky looked around the room as though there might be hidden microphones surveilling their conversation. "What I *will* do is tell you that she told me she's finally gotten over a bad breakup. So the last thing I want is for her to get hurt."

Jesse shrugged his shoulders and sighed. "Okay." He took another sip of his martini.

"No, *really,* Jesse. Please be kind to her. I really think she's perfect for you and might actually be the one who—"

"I get it, Becky. I do." Jesse glanced over at Don and was about to ask for backup when he noticed his friend's attention focused on the dining room entrance. He followed Don's gaze to catch sight of one of the most impressively beautiful women he'd ever seen. Jesse couldn't help but stare as she approached the table.

She had a modest swing to her walk, like the shy version of a runway model, with a black sateen pencil skirt carefully hugging the outline of her hips with each perfect step. Her white, sleeveless silk blouse swayed with the pulse of her gait, and a pleat-neck keyhole introduced just a touch of her cream-colored skin. *Aphrodite*, a voice whispered from somewhere inside his head.

When Becky stood to greet her, Jesse awoke from what felt like a trance. He turned to Don, whose crooked smile raised a rush of anxiety inside him.

"She's a beauty, huh?" Don whispered, now also standing to greet Melissa. "Remember what Becky said, Jesse. Don't hurt this one."

Jesse didn't have time to respond before Don was hugging Melissa and turning her toward him.

"Melissa, this is Jesse. Jesse, Melissa."

"Hi," Jesse stuttered, reaching out his hand. "I'm Jesse."

She took his hand in hers and smiled wickedly. "Oh! Is that what Don meant by 'This is Jesse?'" Her hands were cool to the touch, and soft, like a light brush of nighttime ocean air. He looked to the floor and shook his head.

"I'm sorry," he said, searching for a reason behind his sudden inability to think or speak clearly. "I'm just a little bit..."

"Of a loser?" Don chimed in.

"Don, stop," Becky interrupted. "Please ignore my husband, Melissa. He and Jesse are very old friends and they often revert back to childhood." She gave Don a look of reproach. "Now, let's sit down and get you something to drink."

For Jesse, the rest of the evening was surreal. As the hours passed and Melissa kept choosing to talk to him—to *him*—it became apparent that beauty was just one of her magnetic features. She gave off an almost palpable allure, not only while she talked, but also while she listened, an invisible frequency arousing in Jesse the feeling that they were always meant to meet, a mutual yearning to discover one another from the inside out.

When dinner was over, Jesse slapped Don's hand away from the leather check holder, then grabbed it and slid his credit card inside. "This one's on me," he said. "As a thank you for introducing us." He threw a timid gaze toward Melissa.

"Ahem," Becky cut in. "None of this would've happened without my most beneficent influence."

Jesse turned to her. "Don't worry, Becky. Santa Jesse has you on his permanent 'good' list."

Melissa stood and kissed both Becky and Don. "I have an early morning. Thank you very much for a wonderful evening." She turned to Jesse, touched his hand and gently kissed his cheek. "And goodnight to you, Jesse. It was such a pleasure."

Jesse smiled and watched her walk away. After a while, he noticed that Becky and Don still existed.

"You're in trouble," Don said, tapping the top of Jesse's hand with his index finger. "I can see it in your face. You're smitten."

" 'Smitten?' " Jesse swiped at Don's finger. "Who uses that word anymore?"

Becky folded her napkin and placed it purposefully on the table. "Seriously, Jesse, please be kind. She's becoming a good friend and she's such a wonderful person. She's been through a lot and deserves only good things." She placed her hand over Jesse's. "No joke—promise me."

Jesse squinted, trying to get one last glimpse of Melissa as she walked out of the restaurant. When the door closed behind her, he turned to Becky. "I solemnly swear that I will never, ever hurt that woman."

Jesse shuddered from his own words, not only because he'd never before made such a commitment, but because he wasn't sure he'd be strong enough to keep it.

* * *

As he slowly regained consciousness, Jesse found it difficult to open his eyes, like duct tape had been stretched over his eyelids. He turned his focus to the commotion beside him: the scraping of boots along pavement, the groan of steel and road machinery, a man somewhere above him repeating his name.

"Jesse...Jesse," the man pronounced sharply, but without shouting. The voice sounded familiar, but Jesse couldn't connect it with a face. "Jesse...can you hear me?" A slight tap on his cheek. "Mr. Carlton? Jesse?"

Jesse tried to speak, but his mouth dribbled only mumbles. He tried with all his might to open his eyes, and when the lids finally lifted he had to immediately close them. The red and blue police car flashers were overpowering, and even with his eyes shut he could still see them against his eyelids. He turned his head to the other side, away from the lights, the noise and the voice. When he reopened his eyes, he blinked to clear his vision and found himself gazing into darkness punctuated by the unnatural strobing of color.

Now he could feel that he had been placed on a stretcher with a thermal blanket wrapped around him. Still cautious of the bright lights, he slowly turned to the voice that continued to repeat his name.

"Jesse, are you okay?"

Although the hood from the man's parka covered most of his face, Jesse could finally make out his profile. "Agent Rivera," he said, then remembered Melissa's phone call telling him about a woman who had seen Danny and then — after that — it was a blur. He tried to jump up but the safety straps across his chest held him down. He felt a sharp twinge on the right side of his rib cage. "Danny! Did you find Danny?"

Rivera swept the hair from his eyes and placed his gloved hand on Jesse's chest. "Not yet. But we're still looking for him. Right now, you have to take it easy and rest. We're going to get you to the ER. One of my guys just picked up your wife and they're on their way to meet you at the hospital." He pointed to Jesse's car. "In the meantime, they're getting your car out of the ditch so they can tow it to Jeb's service station. Not sure you'll be able to drive it again. It's close to totaled."

"Melissa said you had a lead. Some woman on Tower Road who said she saw him."

Rivera shook his head. "Hasn't panned out yet. But we're working on it." He leaned over so their faces were only inches apart. "How'd this happen, Jesse? Was there another car? Something in the road? Did you see someone?"

Jesse winced. An almost intolerable pain from within the center of his head spread into his eyes. He closed them and tried to think back to the moments before the accident. His mind was like an empty barrel—bare, hollow, nothing but echoes. He remembered hanging up with Melissa, turning the car around, the snow turning to sleet and then...nothing. *Shit.*

"I can't remember. It's a blank. I think I skidded on an ice patch or something. I'm just not..."

Rivera patted Jesse's chest. "Don't worry. It'll come back. Could be a concussion or something." He nodded to the paramedic standing behind Jesse. "First we get you some head scans, make sure you're healthy, and then we pick your brain some more. Right now you go to the hospital and I go back to the search. I'll circle back with you later today."

As they wheeled Jesse along the wet road toward the ambulance, he peered into the sky at the bright, blinking stars mired in an ocean of black. How did he end up in a ditch? Why was he in an accident? He could remember everything about driving, looking for Danny…

I must've fallen asleep, he thought. *It's dark. I've been up for days looking for Danny. Yeah, I must have passed out at the wheel from exhaustion.*

But deep down he knew that wasn't true. Maybe he had a concussion like Agent Rivera had said, but he remembered the call with Melissa, seeing the mall and observing the neighborhoods through the conservation land. Only a few moments were missing. That didn't sound like a concussion to him. It also didn't feel like he'd fallen asleep at the wheel, something he had never done before in his life.

Maybe it was nothing and the shock of the accident just kept a memory from forming. *It happens*, he thought before slipping back into unconsciousness, *but I don't think that's what happened to me.*

2

At first, Agent Antonio Rivera of the Boston FBI field office liked this quiet bedroom community. It seemed a bit more easygoing than the venues of his usual, big city cases, until Danny Madsen's disappearance had reached the five-day mark. That's when human nature took its typical course, hysteria pervaded the local neighborhoods and the blame game reared its ugly head. Not to mention a media frenzy that met the likes of any urban community in which he'd previously worked. In addition to top brass and the local police department, every citizen of the town wanted answers and all eyes were on him.

Danny's Amber Alert had been extended from the standard twelve hours to two entire days, but it expired without one significant lead. Then, yesterday, a call came in from someone who thought she spotted the boy running down her street. Rivera marshaled personnel from Rockland PD—Daniels and Washington, impressive young detectives already working the case when he was sent in—who dispatched officers to search the neighborhood for any sign of Danny. They found none, but the tip brought out Jesse Carlton, who crashed while looking for Danny out near the conservation land. Jesse was going to be all right, but his expedition was all for naught. Danny was still missing.

After word got out there was a possible sighting, the media had pretty much demanded a press briefing, and there would be one in fifteen minutes—but what was there to say? He would have Sergeant Washington give the city police perspective. She was made for the cameras, a sharp black woman who had, the year before, solved a Rockland murder that stumped (and embarrassed) officials with twice her experience. Maybe she would have something to add that would satisfy the public.

Rivera's cell phone rang. He looked down at it and grimaced. No matter what he said, his wife was not going to be satisfied. Briefing in fifteen or not, he knew not to let her go to voicemail. He picked up with a cheerful "*Mi corazón*," rolling the "r" like a purr, something she used to find endearing when they'd first dated. "I was just going to call to say hey."

"Keep it, *mentiroso*. You promised you'd be home early today." Rivera stayed silent. "If you really want to say *hey* to me, or to Tonio Junior, who only recognizes you from a photo on the wall, then say hey *in person* for a change."

Rivera closed his eyes. She had been mad yesterday, and the day before, but this was another level of pissed off. "Honey, the Bureau wants me here until the boy is found. Come on, you know how a missing persons case goes."

Silence, and then, so calmly it made Rivera feel icy, Maria said, "You think I don't know how 'a missing persons case goes'?

Remember, oh, I don't know, *Benji?* I know how missing persons goes, Antonio!"

"That's what I said, Maria. I can't do anything for Benji now, but I'm trying to keep these people from going through what *you* went through, what your sister went through. I just need another couple of days, a week, tops. Maybe I can keep *this* mother from mourning her stolen boy."

Maria let out a sigh that sounded like ocean waves over the phone's mic. "You have a boy yourself, you know, who'd like to see his *papá* once in a while. These weeks-at-a-time jobs, Tonio, it's not fair for the FBI to make you take them. There's got to be single agents available, or ones without kids. What about Maurice? Nobody is gonna marry him!"

Rivera barked a laugh, caught off guard by his wife's humor—and incredibly relieved, too. He looked around the room and saw a couple of the local cops had glanced up at his inappropriate laughter. He waved a hand in apology and returned his attention to the phone. "Not going to happen. He's in Fraud, anyway. Listen, honey, I've got to go talk to the cameras—let Tonio watch if he wants."

"No. That kidnapping stuff scares him to death."

Rivera looked at the first-grade school photo of Danny that was clipped to his case folder. "Me, too," he said.

* * *

The Rockland Chief of Police assembled the press in the department's conference room and provided a general outline of the case to date. He recapped who Danny Madsen was, when he was taken, what he was wearing and other points of description. After that, he introduced Rivera as the case's lead federal investigator, to get everyone up to speed on the latest developments.

Rivera stepped up, thanked the Chief and spoke solemnly to the media in the room, at first reading from a typed sheet: "At about 5:30 yesterday, the Rockland Police Department received an anonymous tip reporting that a boy matching Danny Madsen's description was seen running through a residential area of the city a short time earlier. Units were dispatched to search the area. Due to the weather conditions and nightfall, the search was suspended until first light this morning. Police in the neighborhood are currently going door to door in an attempt to find further witnesses or, we hope, Danny himself. That is all there is to say right now."

A hand went up politely. Rivera nodded at the reporter to proceed and she asked, "In what neighborhood was Danny spotted?"

"We cannot identify the *exact* place or the identity of the person calling in the alleged sighting at the present time. However, we are asking people within the Hingham area surrounding Plymouth

County location to keep an eye out for Danny or anything that might help us with this case."

A reporter he recognized as Rosalyn Pepper, the Rockland stringer for Boston 25 TV news, spoke up. "Agent Rivera, do you see any similarities between Danny's disappearance and the kidnapping and murder of your nephew, Benjamin Alvarez, two years ago?"

Rivera grimaced but tried to avoid any other visible reaction. Pepper had no idea what she was talking about. Benji wasn't ten years old, like Danny. He was fifteen and involved with a group of Los Angeles kids that didn't understand the consequences of stealing and reselling drugs from gang members. Benji wasn't abducted after getting off a school bus. He'd been tricked into thinking the Vatos Locos "invitation" was the start of his initiation and then killed to set an example.

Rivera had used every possible local and FBI resource to no avail. The gang's actions were too clandestine and swift. When Benji's bloated body washed up on the shore of the Santa Monica Bay, Rivera had to change his duties from an FBI Agent to a grieving uncle and pillar of support for his wife and her sister—a woman who still blames him for not finding her son in time.

The room was flooded with shocked murmurs. Rivera thanked Heaven that Maria wasn't allowing Tonio to watch this briefing. He didn't care for this Rosalyn Pepper—or most reporters for that matter. However, media outreach was vital in missing persons investigations. He said as evenly as possible, "The, um, cases are completely different. Benji was five years older than Danny and, well, visiting places of which his parents were unaware. Nobody knew where he had disappeared from. It made finding him much more difficult."

"So difficult that you found him only once he was dead, and you never did find his abductors or killers, is that correct?" Pepper said with an astonishing lack of sensitivity. "I'm sorry to dredge up unpleasant memories, Agent; I'm asking because my viewers would like to know why the FBI would send someone who failed to find his own—"

"*That's enough*," Rivera snapped so sharply that a few people in the room gasped. "The FBI Kidnapping and Missing Persons Division is working to find Danny. The National Center for Missing and Exploited Children is working to find Danny. And the entire Rockland Police Department is working to find Danny. This effort is more than me, Ms. Pepper, and you know perfectly well that I was not the lead in Benji's case. I tried to find him…" He took a moment to collect himself, anger at the reporter mixing with renewed sorrow at losing his nephew. "I tried to *save* him…but as an ordinary citizen, as a member of a family out of our minds with worry. Again, Ms. Pepper, the Danny Madsen disappearance is about Danny and his loved ones, not me."

The room was utterly silent. Rosalyn Pepper chewed her lip, feeling the disdain of everyone around her. Finally, she said quietly, "Thank you, Agent Rivera."

Rivera took a deep breath and surveyed the room. "If there are no more questions for the FBI?" There were not. "Please let me turn this over to Rockland Police Detective Sergeant Shari Washington, who will brief you all on the renewed search."

Washington patted Rivera on the arm as she took the lectern. Rivera took his place behind her and next to the Chief of Police. *What in the hell was that?* the Chief asked with a glance. Rivera could do nothing but shake his head. This boy's disappearance had undoubtedly disturbed the small community, and things would only get more strained if they didn't make a break in the case soon.

The detective reiterated where the tip came from, what areas were being searched and the next steps they'd be taking in the investigation.

A reporter's hand went up. "So, no sign of Danny was found?"

"That's correct," Washington said with obvious regret. "So far, there is no change in the status of the search. We continue to—"

"Most abduction cases that aren't solved in the first forty-eight hours never get solved," interrupted a fat man with a serious

Boston honk. "Amber Alerts usually don't last a day if nothing turns up."

Washington didn't flinch. "That's not a question. Also, we don't know for sure that this was an abduction. We are gathering together all of the facts before—"

"In seventy-five percent of child abduction cases," the gadfly continued, "the victim is murdered within three hours. Here's my question: Why the hell aren't you doing more to find Danny Madsen? Is it because he's white?"

The room broke into loud murmurs and Washington's jaw dropped. Before she could say anything all of them would regret, Rivera stepped between her and the microphone and barked an order to the patrolmen at the back of the room. "Get him out of here."

As the man was whisked out ahead of the uniformed officers, Rivera stepped up to the lectern and said, "Ladies and gentlemen, tensions are running high. Crackpots are coming out of the woodwork. The family is doing its best to keep things together. The community needs to do that, too. We need everyone to remain calm and let us do our job, which is to find Danny and bring him home safely."

"But the authorities now have *no* leads, is that correct?" another member of the press asked sharply. "Not even a *theory* you can share on where he might be? Does the FBI have *any* idea where Danny Madsen might be right now?"

Rivera measured his next words carefully, because he wasn't just talking to a reporter or viewers on television and the Internet. No, he was very likely talking to the person who had plucked Danny off the street between the school bus and his home five days earlier. "No, at present, we do not. But someone does. And we are going to work day and night and personally follow up on every lead or bit of information, no matter how small, until we find Danny."

He looked directly into the news camera lens and said with barely veiled anger, "Until we find *you*."

3

"Charles, come here and give your ol' Daddy a hug."

The eight-year-old boy, dirty and wearing an unwashed t-shirt like every night before bed, felt a glimmer of hope as Daddy put out his meaty arms and beckoned him over. He stepped around bits of a broken liquor bottle and built up speed, readying himself for the stink of whiskey and sweaty armpits, when—*BAM* — he ran directly into the man's balled up fist. With a phlegmy laugh, his father further drove his clenched paw into the boy's chest, right into his sternum. In white-hot pain, Charles fell to the floor and curled up, too shocked to cry, and knowing anyway that if he did cry, Daddy would start kicking him and telling him to man up.

His mother, as always, remained silent. She no longer bothered to say, yell or do anything anymore. When Charles could open his eyes, she had already been sent to the kitchen to get his father more of whatever he drank that always made him so mad. Charles continued to focus on just trying to breathe.

Eventually, Daddy said with disgust, "Get off the floor, faggot. Get out of my sight."

At first, Charles couldn't move; maybe Daddy broke something again. After a few more seconds he realized that although he couldn't stand, he could crawl across the carpet toward his bedroom. But he'd taken too much time to figure out what to do and Daddy stood wordlessly and kicked him in the stomach hard, like he was punting a football in the Super Bowl.

Charles gasped in terror and pain and did everything he could not to throw up. Lying on his side and hugging his stomach, he caught a glimpse of fleas hopping in and out of the carpet. He lifted his head to avoid a stray one from getting inside his ear. Although he could barely breathe, he was glad Daddy didn't break any ribs, because he would never let Mommy take him to the hospital again after the last time, when the police hung around asking questions. Daddy got madder than ever about that and had to find ways to beat him and Mama without leaving bruises or breaks that might show up on X-rays. It was one of the only things in life that Daddy had ever set his mind to and actually found a solution for.

* * *

Thirty years later, as he chased Danny Madsen through the almost pitch-black conservation land, Charles's mind reeled, wondering why this boy was running away from the loving treatment a boy could have only wished for. Danny had promised to be his best friend forever, and then he escaped out a window. What was he trying to escape from? Friendship? Tender loving care?

Charles couldn't figure it out, but when he caught Danny, he wouldn't punish him. No, he would just bring him back to the house and make sure Danny felt loved and protected. He would put bars on the windows if he had to in order to keep out the bad people and protect his new best friend.

He tripped over tree roots and large rocks that forced him to slow his pace. Why didn't they slow down Danny as much? Sure, the boy was slimmer and faster, but Charles was taller than Danny; he should be able to jump over roots and stumps with more agility. The problem was, his chunky legs, belly fat and sedentary video-gaming lifestyle kept forcing him to take short breaks so he could catch his breath. Sure, his long legs should've covered more ground with each step, but his unhealthy habits held him back from catching up with the kid.

Every now and then, he'd get so close, close enough to hear the boy's panicked breathing and an occasional cry for help.

Help? Charles wondered. *What kind of help does a boy with a loving home need?* Danny must have been extremely confused. But he wouldn't be for long. When Charles got him back home, he'd do whatever it took for Danny to understand he was where he should be. He'd make him Kraft Macaroni & Cheese—not that generic crap Charles's Daddy made Mommy buy—and get him his own Tom Brady football, Celtics basketball and anything else he wanted.

Still, he began to panic: if Danny made it to the road and got a car to pull over, he might be so confused that he could make it look like Charles did something wrong. He supposed that if loving someone so much, *so* much, was a crime, then he was guilty.

But unlike the crime Danny's parents committed—letting a vulnerable boy walk home alone from the bus stop every day— bringing a boy like Danny into a good home with everything he could ever want was *not* a crime. People might think that it was, though, and so Charles knew he had to stop Danny before it was too late and he ruined both their lives.

"Danny!" he yelled. "*Danny!* C'mon, buddy! I have your coat! You need to put your coat on! We need to go back!" But the boy didn't stop and neither did Charles's overwhelming rage. He kept his arms outstretched in front of his face to avoid the hanging branches and overgrown brush. His panic doubled, they were now only a hundred or so yards from Forest Avenue. If Danny made it to the road, Charles would completely lose control over the situation and whatever happened next would be up to fate.

It started pissing down tiny bits of ice. *Damn it to hell.* Charles could hardly see his own hands, which burned from the New England cold—he had rushed out of the house, like Danny, without wearing any cold-weather gear. He didn't even have time to think about grabbing a flashlight. How was he going to…

My phone! How could he have not thought about this sooner? He pulled it from his sweatpants pocket and flicked on the flashlight app. The light was weak and didn't allow him to pick up his pace, but now he could see a few more feet in front of him. He'd have to hope the boy would fall, get caught in brush or just give up. Maybe even freeze to death before he could reach Forest Avenue and signal any cars.

Freeze to death, his mind echoed. *My Danny, dead?* He had to stop again, black blooms of oxygen deprivation sprouting before his eyes. If Danny died, it would be terrible…but at least he would never again have to feel unloved. And Charles could find another best friend, one who would appreciate what he was doing for him.

But Danny wasn't dead and wouldn't need to die if Charles could reach him in time. He forced himself onward, and could finally see the running figure silhouetted against the reflections of the ice-slick road.

"No, Danny, *stop!* I mean it this time, Danny! Come on! We have to go back before they see you!" But he wouldn't stop, and the words fell out of Charles's mouth as Danny stumbled out onto the road: "Don't make me punish you!"

Why did he make me say that? WHY, Danny—

A car—a BMW, the kind Charles had always planned to get when he became rich—hit its brakes and went into a whirling skid. It caught Danny with a rear side panel and launched the boy like a rag doll back into the woods, toward Charles. Danny's shoulder hit a thick tree trunk, turning his body sideways and forcing him to land awkwardly bent, his head planting first with a *crack* that Charles could hear from almost twenty feet away.

"Danny!" Hastings screamed. By the time the boy's body lay motionless in the woods, the BMW had already skidded fifty more feet along the road before its nose slammed into a snowy ditch.

When everything went quiet, Charles quickly but stealthily stepped to where the body lay. He turned the phone light onto Danny, knelt down, put his ear to the boy's nose and placed his hand against the boy's chest. Nothing—Danny was dead—and the chest felt soft, like the sternum and ribs had been smashed into tiny pieces.

Feeling that, helpless fury flooded his brain. *I didn't do this*, he immediately told himself. *I didn't do anything but love him.* He looked up at the steam rising from the wrecked BMW.

They did this.

He stood and carefully made his way to the road, making sure no rescue vehicles or witnesses of any kind were within sight, especially since the car had ended up right under one of the streetlights. He crept out onto the shoulder and got near enough to the wreck to see there was a single person outlined against the inflated airbag—a man—unmoving and unconscious. He edged further onto the road so he could see the license plate, which read: LCKY123.

"Lucky," Charles murmured, his breath visible as he let out a bitter chuckle. "Not for long, you murdering son of a bitch."

He wouldn't cry for Danny, not until later, not until LCKY123, whoever he was, had paid for what he'd done. If the driver wasn't dead, Charles would have to make sure the cops knew exactly what happened. It would be the only way justice would be served and Danny's death wouldn't be in vain.

But Charles wasn't yet sure how he'd make that happen. What he was sure of was that he couldn't let the cops find Danny. If they did, they could possibly find his DNA on the boy, or fibers that would lead them back to his house. Evidence had to be destroyed and Danny was the most significant piece of that evidence.

He stepped back to where the body was rapidly cooling. "Why, Danny? Why would you do this to yourself? Why'd you let the bad man hurt you? *Why? Goddammit, Danny!*"

The temperature was plummeting even further and Charles knew if he stayed squatting where he was for another thirty seconds he wouldn't be able to straighten his legs. He had to move quickly, so he scooped up Danny and tossed him over his shoulder like an injured soldier, his lifeless, dangling arms and legs banging against him just out of sync with Charles's gait. Finally, they came to what he judged to be the perfect spot.

"You should've just stayed in your room, Danny," Charles said aloud as he slid Danny off his shoulder and down his arm until he hit the ground with a dull *thump*. "I'm sorry, buddy, but you asked for this. You basically *asked* that son of a bitch to murder you."

It gave him no pleasure to scold the boy, who had suffered enough already, but it did make Charles feel good to remind himself of the two people solely responsible for this tragedy: Danny and LCKY123.

He was still holding Danny's bright blue coat, something that could help him find this spot later. He tied the sleeves around the trunk of a skinny tree right next to the body. "I can't bring you back home. Too dangerous." A gust of frigid wind hit his face and he shivered.

"I'll come back tomorrow and give you a real burial. I promise." He knew he'd have to bury Danny not only to honor him, but to also reduce the chances that anyone would happen across the body anytime soon.

As he prepared to leave, he shined the flashlight in a circular pattern around the wooded area in which he stood. He had chased Danny all the way through the conservation land to Forest Avenue, not paying any attention to where he was headed or what path he'd taken. Then he'd carried the body a good distance back into the thick woods, not thinking of anything but getting far away from the road.

With alarm, Charles looked side to side, not exactly sure where he was. And he needed to know the precise location if he was going to be able to return and bury Danny. He *had* to bury him, he'd made his friend a promise.

He clicked off the flashlight to let his eyes become accustomed to the dark and search for a landmark that would help him get his bearings. Through the trees on his left, he could barely see the pulsing red beacon of a cellular tower. But what direction was it? He didn't get to be a Boy Scout—Daddy railed against their "queerbait uniforms"—so he didn't know how to read north from moss or trees or whatever, if that was even a real thing.

And then he felt the cell phone he was grasping. The thing had a compass on it. Not only that, it had Google Maps! Since he could see the flashing light on top of a cell tower, he knew he was standing within 500 feet of it. So, even out here in the conservation land, he knew he would get a signal.

He pulled out the phone, opened the app and said as distinctly as he could, "Directions to 12 Lynch Lane."

As if Lady Luck herself had laid out his path, a yellow line came up on the map leading from the spot in the featureless green woods directly to the safety of his house. He enlarged it and then clicked "save" so he'd have the exact route back to where he'd left Danny. Through the bursts of wind, he could hear the phone speaking to him. "Turn northwest for three-quarters of a mile, then proceed to the highlighted route." He smiled when he saw the street on which he'd emerge was just two blocks from his house on Lynch.

Another sound came from somewhere far in the distance: sirens, emergency vehicle sirens, traveling Route 228 and no doubt headed for the crash of the unlucky LCKY123. He had gotten out of there just in time. Smiling again, Charles shook his head at how well, other than Danny getting killed, all of this was going.

He said in amusement to nobody in particular, "Proceeding to the route."

But as he turned the flashlight back on and began picking through the woods, his smile vanished like a snowflake on a warm windshield. Visions not only of the friend he'd been forced to leave dead in the middle of the woods, but of the murderer who had made all of this necessary stirred the anger inside him. Whoever he was, the killer would be punished. If not by the police, then by Charles Hastings himself.

* * *

During the slow journey back through the woods toward his house, tears formed in Charles's eyes as he thought about how Danny had entered his life.

With Danny, it was supposed to be different. Even though he was rarely at fault when things in his life went wrong, Charles admitted to himself that he'd made mistakes, especially some of the times he'd made friends with youngsters to liberate them from what must have been sick, troubled homes.

There had been a regrettable incident a couple of years earlier when Charles picked up that Billy kid in Brookline. The little snitch had forced Charles to take drastic measures to keep him from calling 911 on the cell phone he'd secretly stowed in his jacket. Even after Billy was dead, the boy still tried to get him in trouble by almost getting seen inside the car as Charles transported him to somewhere safe. He sat the boy up in the front seat and even put a baseball cap on him as he tried to find an unlocked dumpster in the middle of the night.

After that, Charles didn't think he'd ever be able to trust someone new. When he could no longer bear the loneliness of having too much unshared love in his heart, he became best friends with Stevie from Framingham. But that didn't work out, either, and he cried the entire two-hour drive back from disposing of the body.

But Danny, he could tell Danny was special from the start. Charles knew it would be a huge risk taking in a new best friend from a town so close to his, but he'd spotted the boy a month earlier playing in the schoolyard with classmates during recess, and it immediately felt right.

It was just pure, blessed chance that he was driving his work van past the playground of Jefferson Elementary when he saw Danny standing atop the deck of a tunnel climber attached to a huge play system. He was playing tag with some classmates and the kid who was "It" was obviously after Danny. Charles stopped the car across the street and watched intently. He could see Danny's seriousness, how determined he appeared to reach the bottom of the structure without getting tagged and becoming the next victim, the next fool to desperately chase others around the schoolyard. He immediately felt a connection with Danny, cheering aloud inside the van as the kid faked out his pursuer, reversed his direction and made his way down the curved slide to the base of safety.

Charles had no doubt that he and Danny were alike in many ways. So many ways, in fact, that they should be friends, *best* friends, once he was able to show Danny all their similarities. He spent the next few weeks following the boy, finding out where he lived, learning his routine and trying to determine the best way to get him alone. He wanted Danny to understand that destiny had intervened the day Charles made a wrong turn going to an in-home service call, and they were meant to be in each other's lives. Once he had Danny to himself, he'd be able to explain everything to him; to show him the room he'd set up for him: the clothes, toys, games and even the puppy he'd bought for him. It would be his way to prove to Danny that their friendship, and whatever developed after that, would be Charles's number-one priority.

Then, less than a week ago, it was finally time to make things happen. The yearning inside Charles for someone he could love and who would be guaranteed to love him back—a new best friend—had filled him to the top. It was time to act.

He'd been through the plan a thousand times in his head. And it was a good plan, a solid plan. But he'd built his confidence while strategizing in the shower or at his kitchen table. Right now, as he sat inside his van on Chester Street behind a row of giant hydrangeas waiting for Danny's bus to show, he could feel that confidence begin to wane. He heard the bus' brakes squeak the vehicle to a halt and his hands began to tremble ever so slightly. *Shit.* Daddy always said he was weak, but *he was not weak.* He tightened his grip on the steering wheel and glanced at himself in the rearview mirror. It was now or never.

Charles turned around to the pup in the back seat. "Showtime, Bandit!"

He got out of the car and glanced up and down the street. It was as empty as every other day he'd scouted the area. *Perfect.* He walked to the other side of the car, stepped up to the sidewalk, opened the back door to the car and leaned in. Bandit sat up in his oversized bed, wagging his tail.

"Just a few more seconds, buddy, and we both get to meet our new pal."

When Charles heard the boy's footsteps approaching, he pushed himself back so he was standing behind the van's open rear doors.

"Excuse me," Charles said. The boy was better looking up close, the blue color of his eyes something Charles didn't know until that very moment. Their clarity and innocence almost took his breath away. He had to *focus.* "Um, what's your name?"

"Danny," he said cautiously. "What's going on?"

"Hi, Danny"—what a great name that was!—"do you happen to know anything about puppies? I just got one and I think he's sick."

Danny stopped and looked up and down the street. Charles could read the suspicion on his face—the schools all said don't talk to strangers, blah blah—but that's what Bandit was for. What kid could walk away from a puppy?

"What's wrong with him?" Danny asked, shuffling from one foot to the other but still not moving closer to the back of the van. He grabbed the strap of his backpack and pulled it to a more comfortable spot on his shoulder.

"I'm not sure. He's whimpering. When I touch his stomach, he cries. I'm not from around here, so I'm not sure where the closest vet is. I stopped here just to get out and check on him. I'm not sure what to do."

Danny inched nearer to the door and peered in. "What's his name?" Still on the sidewalk, Danny crouched to get a better view.

"Bandit," replied Charles, backing away and opening up room for Danny to come closer. Danny twisted his body to see better inside the open doors but kept his distance from the opening.

"Aw, Bandit, you're so cute," Danny said with a smile, his trepidation melting away, and stepped closer to where the puppy sat in the back of the van. "You don't feel good, huh?" Now he stepped right up and petted Bandit on the head.

One last time Charles glanced up and down the street. No one. Nothing. He had to make his move. With his gloved hand, he grabbed the chloroform-drenched cloth from the bag inside his coat pocket, leaned over from behind Danny and in one movement held it over his nose and mouth and shoved him into the van.

Danny struggled with more intensity and strength than he had anticipated, and as Charles worked to hold the cloth over his face with one hand and close the van doors with the other, Bandit jumped out and hit the asphalt running. For a split second, Charles considered trying to grab the puppy, but he couldn't risk Danny staying conscious and possibly shouting for help.

Once the boy was out cold and secured in the back of the van, Charles climbed into the front and looked in the side mirror. Children in the street had already crowded around Bandit and were trying to pet him.

"Well, that worked out great for everybody," he said with a smile, starting the van and making sure to obey every single traffic rule on the way home.

* * *

It took three days before Danny stopped resisting or trying to scream for help through the duct tape.

He sat on the bed, his knees tucked beneath his chin. Charles gently removed the tape from his mouth but kept the cable ties around his hands and ankles.

"Can we talk, Danny?"

"Where's my mom and dad?" Danny said without hesitation.

"That's something we can discuss later. For now, look around," he said, moving his arm in a circular motion as though introducing the next amazing act at a three-ring circus. "This is all for you. The games, the toys, the Patriots posters. Even Bandit was for you. But he ran away so we'll get another puppy. Whatever you want, you can have."

"I want to go home." Danny's eyes filled with tears. "I want to go home."

Charles rolled his eyes and moved closer to Danny. He wrapped his arms around his shoulders and rocked him back and forth on the bed.

"You *are* home, Danny. This is your new home." He waited for a response but heard nothing but sobbing and sniffling. "Your parents actually asked me to take you."

"No way they would do that. Take me home."

"They would do it and they did do it." He shut off the light and stood at the door. "You need your rest, so I want you to sleep a little bit now. It's almost midnight. Then tomorrow I'll show you around the house and we'll have breakfast. You need to eat. You need to keep your strength up."

As he closed the door behind him, Charles could hear Danny start to weep. "They wouldn't give me up," he cried. "They wouldn't give me up."

Danny's parents *had* given him up. They hadn't watched out for him like good parents do and now someone who would take care of him *for real* was in charge. Danny would recognize that soon enough. Until then, Charles would wait as long as he had to. There wasn't any rush.

* * *

When Charles walked into Danny's bedroom the next day, he found Danny lying on the bed, eyes wide open, staring at the ceiling.

"Good morning," Charles said hesitantly.

"I have to pee," Danny said flatly.

"All right, no problem."

Charles sensed resignation in Danny's voice. So instead of handing him the urinal, Charles grabbed the lock-back knife from his pants pocket, pulled out the blade and cut the cable ties around Danny's wrists and ankles.

Danny rubbed his sore wrists as he stood and slowly walked around the room as though he were testing the fit of new shoes.

"Let me show you where the bathroom is."

After Danny came out, Charles led him to the living room and sat next to him on the couch. He pointed to the stack of DVDs strewn across the coffee table. *Toy Story, Raiders of the Lost Ark, X-Men, Star Trek.* Charles had researched the highest-rated children's and sci-fi movies and bought them all. Anything to keep Danny happy and wanting to stay in the house with him.

Danny leaned over and seemed interested in the DVDs.

"Why are you home? Don't you have a job?" he asked.

Charles tightened his lips and forced a smile. "Sure I do. I fix computers, freelance, like a hired gun." He made a little shooting gun with his fingers, but he could see Danny was unimpressed. "Hey, you like computers, right? All boys like computers."

"I like going on the Internet," Danny said, then looked at Charles with what appeared to be enthusiasm. "Hey, can I?"

This was great! Danny was feeling comfortable enough to want to play Angry Birds or whatever his favorite game was! "Sure, just let me—"

You stupid bastard, Daddy's voice interrupted in his head. *You're gonna let that kid get online so he can email his parents, land your worthless ass in prison?* "Oh, wait, the Internet is, um, *down* right now," he said warily. "Maybe later."

Danny's enthusiastic eyes quickly narrowed in suspicion. "I thought you fix computers."

"No, I do! It must be the cable lines. It's the storm. A tree probably fell on them and they're down."

"Whatever," Danny said. He glumly gazed at the DVD in his hands.

Charles could hardly believe it. *Whatever?* Was that acceptance? Indifference? Was Danny disappointed that he couldn't go online, or that his plan to contact the outside world had failed? "W-What does 'whatever' mean, Danny?"

The boy shrugged. "It means *whatever*, Charles." It was the first time he'd used his name since arriving and although his tone seemed harsh, Charles felt encouraged.

"Okay, Danny. I just didn't understand what you—"

"Whatever means *whatever!*" he shouted, almost screaming the words. Danny threw the DVD across the room and jumped off the couch. He rubbed at the tears filling his eyes as he moved to stand directly in front of Charles. "If this is where I'm supposed to be, *fine!* If this is where my mom and dad want me, *fine!* Just leave me alone. I want to be by myself!" He ran to the bedroom and slammed the door, the *crack* reverberating throughout the house.

Charles hated this part, but he took a moment to remind himself that there was nothing to worry about. They got all mad and pissy at the beginning, but they always came around when they realized that there was no one else in the world who cared about them enough to keep them forever. Eventually, they understood, even if it was too late.

After taking time to let Danny cool off and come to his senses, Charles set two bowls down on the living room coffee table and walked back into the kitchen to get some paper napkins and plastic forks. Danny hadn't left his room all day and Charles was hoping that the idea of a bowl full of macaroni and cheese while watching a DVD would entice the boy to open the door and join him for dinner. He hadn't wanted to barge in or use force to get Danny to come out. He wanted the boy to choose on his own, and after the promising conversation they'd had earlier that afternoon, Charles knew it was only a matter of time.

That's when he heard the sound of crashing glass.

His first impulse was to escape out the back door of the kitchen, since the cops must have figured out Danny was there and were about to break down the front door. But when he didn't hear any voices or scuffling, he raced back to the living room to see everything exactly the way he'd left it. He quickly made his way to the hall and put his ear up against Danny's bedroom door.

"Danny?" There was no response. "Danny? Buddy? You okay?"

Still nothing.

He grabbed the doorknob, turned and pushed, but there was something in the way. He pushed harder. "Danny! Open the door!" The door opened slightly, enough for Charles to see the legs of a desk chair that had been set beneath the knob.

"*Shit!*" Charles cried, pushing against the door with all strength he could muster. "Shit!" he yelled. "Danny!" With one last thrust he hit it hard, cracking the door and leaving long slivers of wood dangling from the jamb's hinges. It fell flat onto the floor, with Charles almost landing on top of it. He looked wildly around the room.

Then he saw the hole that Danny had made by prying the boards off the window and smashing the glass.

"No. No. *God, no.*" He spun around, grabbed Danny's coat and his own hoodie, and scrambled out of the house.

He ran to the sidewalk, almost slipping as he tried to stop. The street was empty, but it was the dinner hour, so he had to make sure he wasn't moving too quickly. Otherwise, he might look suspicious, especially if someone had seen Danny running. There was no indication of what direction Danny had headed, but the conservation land was visible from where Charles stood. If the misguided boy was trying to find a place to hide, he would've headed for the woods.

Charles made an effort to walk casually but fast enough so that Danny couldn't get too far ahead. As he reached the corner and made a right turn, he saw fresh footprints in the quarter-inch of snow that had fallen an hour earlier, the size of a kid's sneaker — Danny's sneaker. *Yes!* Charles quickened his pace on the turn and immediately lost his footing on a patch of ice, falling hard on his back. Barely taking time to register the pain, he got to his feet and moved as fast as he could without attracting attention. The slip had cost him a few seconds, and he needed to be extra careful not to lose any more precious time. It was getting dark, and snow was starting to fall again, slowing Charles's effort to find Danny and bring him safely home— something that, in his heart of hearts, he knew was never going to happen.

* * *

And it didn't. The next day, as he followed the phone's map to the spot where he'd left Danny's body, Charles was still trying to figure out where it all went wrong. What mistake did he make? Had he always been such a lousy judge of character or was Danny just an anomaly, like Billy and Stevie? He shook his head to rid himself of negative thoughts and tried to focus on the task ahead of him.

Earlier that morning, he'd driven to Walmart and paid cash for a camping shovel, which he took home and folded up so it fit into his backpack. He needed to remember not to look suspicious, and someone walking into the conservation land with a big-ass shovel would definitely seem noteworthy. But he was pretty sure nobody saw him leave his house and enter the woods.

The walk seemed more arduous today than it did the day before. Chasing Danny, he had been running on adrenaline; on the way back, he had almost been insensate with at first relief, then sadness and anger. But now, going back to bury his friend was a chore he was required to do. He didn't give a shit anymore about his promise. It was just too risky to leave a body lying out in the open, even in the middle of the conservation land. There were joggers, even in this weather, and he didn't want his carelessness or arrogance to land him behind bars. Before he'd left the house, he swore to himself that he'd hold back any feelings of confidence or smugness until the body was buried and he was back home. Then he'd check to see if the police had arrested the driver of the LCKY123.

But that was later. Right now, he needed to get Danny into the ground before anyone found his body. He switched off his phone's password protection so that the phone would stay on while he held it in front of him and followed directions directly to where he left Danny.

When he reached the location, a shallow but even layer of snow obscured the body, making it look so small, so matter-of-fact. It was just *there*. In Charles's mind, this made it easier to deal with: what lay in front of him was just a thing to get rid of.

The ground was hard as hell, and for a few seconds Charles feared it would break the shovel, but eventually the rocky soil yielded just enough for him to dig. Red with effort, his arms shaking from unaccustomed exertion after almost an hour, he was able to dig a hole wide enough to fit Danny's small frame and just deep enough to cover him.

The night before, Charles had envisioned a hole six feet deep, like graves were supposed to be. Now, however, he understood why serial killers' victims were always found in shallow graves. Even in summer with soft soil, it would give any regular person a heart attack to dig with a shovel more than a couple of feet deep. In winter, there was no way to go any further down than absolutely necessary.

Charles's arms were almost useless now and he kept in reserve just enough strength to fill the grave back in and chuck the rest of the disturbed soil into the trees. Danny hadn't weighed much, but there was no way Charles could lift him right now. Luckily, it was no problem to use his feet to shove the boy to the lip of the ragged hole. With the remaining strength in his legs, he pushed and rolled the body a couple of times until Danny flopped all the way in.

Charles checked that the body was deep enough for him to pack the dirt on top of him flat. He was about to dump the first shovelful on Danny when the thought came to him that people weren't supposed to be buried with their shoes on. He couldn't remember why they weren't or where he'd heard this, but he knelt down and removed the Nikes. He placed them inside the grave next to the body and had picked up the shovel again when it occurred to him that maybe he should take the sneakers, to throw them into a trash can far away from his house or the conservation land. He took the shoes out of the hole and set them on the ground next to his phone.

He stood there for another minute, looking at the rest of the clothes on the body. There was too much identifying Danny Madsen and with the way the cops did things with microfibers and whatnot, some sort of evidence might remain and lead them back to him. It wouldn't matter to them that the fibers or DNA got on Danny while he was still alive, that Charles had nothing to do with the murder. They'd still probably use them to make it look like he had killed Danny. Charles knew he had no choice but to take Danny's clothes away from the area and dispose of them more prudently.

He knelt down and stripped the boy's T-shirt off, then his corduroys and then, after a few seconds of internal struggle, his underwear. He laid the shirt flat and placed the other items inside it, then tied it up into a bundle.

The removal of clothing had made Danny end up facedown in the hole, and for this, Charles was glad. He didn't want those staring blue eyes watching him as he threw shovel after shovel of dirt and rocks over his head, his back, his legs. As Danny disappeared under the black earth, Charles spoke his last words to the boy he thought would be his best friend forever: "I'm sorry you did this to yourself, Danny."

As he tamped down the grave, a bright blue shape caught his eye and made him look up. Danny's coat was still tied to the tree.

"Aw, goddammit," Charles moaned. It was okay; he'd just stick the clothing bundle inside it. He went to the tree and untied the sleeves, pulled the coat away from the tree trunk and noticed there was blood soaked into the fleece inside. Danny's blood. With Danny's DNA.

Hmm...now that might *really* come in handy.

4

On the walk back from burying Danny, Charles felt a surge of jubilant energy, as though an electrical force was plowing through his entire body. He wondered if it might be because things had finally worked out in his favor. But just as he emerged from the conservation land onto the street a couple of blocks from his house, his jubilation turned to fear.

On the corner of the street's intersection with Lynch Lane, a police car was parked and two cops, their backs toward him, were talking to a lady Charles had seen many times getting her exercise by walking the neighborhood.

Holy shit. This had to mean the police were going door to door looking for Danny. A sweeping sense of triumph returned when he realized that he'd actually been saved by Danny running away; if the boy had still been in the house, he would have screamed bloody murder when the cops knocked at the door. Now, there was nothing for them to find...except Danny's backpack. But that was well hidden inside the oversized toolbox he kept in the woodshed. All he had to do was get the sneakers, shirt, pants and bloodstained coat inside the toolbox and lock it up before the cops reached his front steps.

He decided to walk up the street parallel to Lynch so he could pass behind his house, then cross over and come back up his block. But he had to act *now*, while they were still occupied interviewing the woman.

Jesus, I hope she didn't see anything.

After his first four steps he stopped in his tracks.

Shit! Another pair of cops was talking to Mrs. Potts, the chatty old woman who lived across the street from him. His thoughts were doing somersaults, unsure what to do or which way to go. But he didn't have a choice. He'd have to hope luck found its way back to his side and the cops were so busy listening to Mrs. Potts they wouldn't even notice him walking up the street behind them.

Never taking his eyes off the officers, he moved quickly across his backyard to the rusted, beat-up corrugated shed. He pulled open the door, dragging and scraping its bottom along the rocks and gravel that over the years had worn away pieces of its metal edge. As he walked inside, he was greeted by the stench of ripe mildew and rotting field mice, a smell to which he'd become way too accustomed.

As soon as he reached the toolbox, Charles grabbed the clothes and shovel from his coat and pulled the key ring out of his pocket to...

The padlock key was not on his key ring.

"Oh, come *on* already." He'd forgotten that he'd thrown the toolbox's new padlock key into the kitchen's junk drawer so if the cops ever ordered him to open the toolbox, he wouldn't have the key on him.

For now, he'd have to dump Danny's clothes and the shovel under some shit in the shed and pray the cops wouldn't want to sniff around too much. He'd have to return later with the key to hide everything—if they didn't arrest him first for a crime he didn't commit.

Just as the police across the street were finishing up with Mrs. Potts, Charles made a beeline from the shed into the house. He took a quick shower and walked into the living room. Looking around as he dressed, he exhaled a breath of relief, grateful that he liked the same things little boys liked: video games, movies, the Patriots. Charles had bought a couple of things especially for Danny, but mostly, his house looked the same whether he had a friend staying over or not. There weren't even any clothes lying around, since Danny had repeatedly refused to tell him what kind of pajamas he liked. Charles silently thanked Danny again, realizing for the second time that day that by running away he had probably saved Charles from spending the rest of his life in prison.

* * *

The two policemen walked up the steps, rang the doorbell and, without waiting for a response, immediately knocked on the door. That annoyed Charles a bit, but no matter; he was feeling quite confident. He opened the door to find the heavy one writing in a spiral-bound notepad while the even heavier one snuck glances behind Charles's shoulder attempting to get a glimpse inside the house.

"I'm Officer Larsen," the smaller-sized cop said, "and this is Office Perry. We're asking people in the neighborhood about the Danny Madsen disappearance. You're familiar with it?"

"Yeah, of course. It's a tragedy," Charles said, then caught himself. "If he's dead, I mean. Still terrible either way, though."

"What's with the window on the side of the house?" asked Perry, pointing toward the plywood where glass should have been. "Somebody throw a rock through it or something?"

Hastings produced a smile, but not so big of one that it would make him appear happy at having to replace an expensive window. "Stupid thing. I was standing on the bed changing the bulb in the ceiling. I lost my balance and…well…I fell into the window. Knocked it out of the frame in one piece—I could've popped it back in if it didn't break into a million pieces on the ground!" He gave a rueful chuckle and waited for a response. Nothing. *Don't talk so much*, he scolded himself. *They'll think you're lying.*

Larsen scribbled on his pad as Charles finished by saying, "Luckily, I grabbed the inside wall and stopped myself from falling out."

"Luckily," Perry echoed without real interest, apparently just checking off boxes so he could go to the next house. Charles knew all he had to do was not seem overly memorable.

Larsen glanced down at his pad then back up to Charles. "Lady next door said she heard a crash and a man yelling." He bobbed his head left to right, angling for a view behind Hastings.

"Who? Mrs. Barnes?" Another forced smile. "She probably heard me yell when I hit the window. Then again she hears things anyway."

Perry stopped writing and tapped the pen against his bottom lip. "Hears things? What does that mean, exactly?"

"The old woman bangs on my door to tell me my music's too loud when I'm sitting here reading a book in complete silence." Hastings peered out the door toward the old woman's house. "She sees things, too. Told me last week she saw Mr. Potts from up the block go into her recycle bin and steal her soda bottles."

The officer waited for a moment, then said, "Yeah?"

Hastings shook his head. "Mr. Potts died three years ago."

"Three years," he repeated and scribbled something on the page with the older note. "Anyway, Mr. Hastings, have you seen or heard anything that might be related to the missing boy? And really, I mean, *anything*: somebody you don't recognize walking around the neighborhood, strange sounds at night, parked cars that don't belong around here, anything you can think of that could be helpful in finding Danny Madsen."

Charles did his best impression of wracking his brain to think of something that could help, gosh, anything at all. As he narrowed his eyes and stared into the sky as if some detail was *almost* appearing in his mind, he congratulated himself on this little pantomime. It was the perfect way to use up time. It was also good because Charles knew he needed to keep his talking to a minimum and get them to forget him and his house as quickly as possible. So at the end of his fake mental exertions, he merely shook his head, feigning regret at not being able to help. "I got nothing. Can't think of a single thing. I'm really sorry." His stomach was clenched in anxiety. Were they going to buy it, in spite of the Barnes woman and her big mouth?

Perry peeked behind Charles one more time. Charles tried not to show any particular expression at all.

He stepped to the side and swept his arm like a spokesmodel on *The Price Is Right*. "Want to take a look around?" He held his breath, hoping this bluff would keep the two policemen, obviously on a tight schedule, from feeling like they needed to check inside the house.

The officers glanced at each other, visibly considering the offer, and then shook their heads. "Not necessary, Mr. Hastings," Larsen said as he flipped the notepad closed. "It is 'Hastings,' correct?"

Charles nodded, hoping the cop's confirmation of detail was just a formality.

Perry handed him a business card. "The hotline number is on there. If you hear or see or suspect anything out of the ordinary, please call right away."

"Will do." Hastings slithered back into the doorway as the officers walked down the steps. "Will do."

He closed the door and leaned against it, letting out the breath he hadn't even noticed he was holding.

Holy hell. That was way too close.

It was excruciating to wait the nearly ten minutes it took for the cops to move two more houses down the block so they'd be out of view of Charles's backyard. But as soon as they had, he whipped open the junk drawer, grabbed the padlock key and hurried out to the shed.

He grabbed Danny's clothing, which now had cobwebs and leaves stuck on them, and put them on a rickety table already cluttered with old framed photographs, board games and books swollen with moisture and blackened with mold.

He inserted the key into the expensive Bulldog lock he'd bought just before bringing Danny home. It looked like polished silver compared to the dusty and weathered toolbox, and the key slipped in and turned smoothly.

He eased out the creaky main drawer, wincing at the screech of rusted metal on metal. He laid the shovel inside and stuffed in the bundle of clothes next to it. He pushed the complaining drawer shut, replaced the padlock and suddenly realized what he had right in front of him: *evidence*.

The same evidence he was hiding was *precisely* what he would need if the murderer didn't come forward and Charles had to take things into his own hands. The coat and sneakers Danny was wearing the day he went missing? There would be no way for the killer to deny what he'd done once Charles created a connection.

He locked the padlock and placed the toolbox on the floor against the backside of the shed. Before turning to leave, he waved his finger at the toolbox as though berating a small child.

"We're going to need you in case of emergency," he said. "So don't you go anywhere."

I'm talking to toolboxes now. What a life. That made him laugh out loud.

And it felt good.

5

Except for the sliver of light where the two silk drapery panels met, the bedroom was completely black.

Becky Madsen sat on the edge of the bed, rocking back and forth, waves of Valium, sleeplessness and inconsolable worry making her head spin and stomach turn. At times she thought she might vomit, but she didn't care. Other than her continual rocking back and forth, she couldn't move. Why would she? Where would she go?

Over the more than two weeks that had passed since Danny disappeared, the hole growing inside of her had become so deep and tender, she figured if she tried to stand she'd have a heart attack anyway. So she remained where she was, not knowing or caring about the time of day, when her next meal would be or who owned the muffled voices resonating outside her bedroom door since the moment she awoke that morning.

She could only focus on remnants of the nightmare, the same horrific dream she'd had every night since Danny went missing. It started with the telephone ringing and the adrenaline pumping through her veins. She stood in the kitchen watching Don speak into the phone, waiting for him to turn around with a giant smile revealing tears of joy. But instead he'd turn away from her and continue the conversation with a whisper and rounded shoulders.

Without warning, she'd be standing inside a dark, unfamiliar room. *Cold.* Everything inside and outside of her was cold. She'd tremble and shiver uncontrollably. The floor, the walls, the air...*cold.* And somehow she knew, wherever Danny was, he was just as cold. His hands, his hair, his forehead, his cheeks, cold as ice. She longed to touch him, slide her arm beneath his head and lift him so that his nose was tucked deep into the crook of her neck. *My baby is so cold. Why is he so cold?*

Closing her eyes within the dream, she'd hum Danny's favorite lullaby. The room changed to another, one that was empty and pure white. Hands clawed at her as she tried lifting herself onto a metal table, fingers pulling her coat sleeves, and she fought them off with slaps and screams. And then her legs would become useless and she'd sink to the floor, green and white linoleum tiles like those inside a morgue. Was that where she was? A morgue? At that point everything would fade to black and she'd shudder, realizing she was about to wake into the real nightmare.

The dream fragments ended there, but today the sense of loss was more profound, more palpable. Danny was no longer just missing but now completely gone from this world. A chill spread its icy tendrils through her as if the fingers of death were gripping her soul. It was like a sign, something telling her it was time to stop searching because her boy would never be found alive, if he was ever found at all.

In days not so long before, she'd shake her head in silent sympathy while watching news reports of sobbing parents attempting to describe the pain of losing a child. *Thank God that's not me*, she'd think to herself. Reading an article by a mother who lost her daughter to cancer, trying to explain how the death of a child goes against the natural order of things—*thank God that's not me*.

But now it *was* her. She pulled the terrycloth robe tightly around her and squinted in an attempt to see through the darkness of the room. For a split second she wondered if she'd made the whole thing up. Maybe she'd been dreaming! Yes! That must be it! Losing Danny had always been a fear and now it had turned into a nightmare, a lucid dream from which she was trying to wake. She studied the back of her left hand that sat upon her knee, turned it over and slapped herself across the face.

"Wake up!" Becky told herself, the sting of the blow barely making it into her consciousness.

The room remained dark, the pain within her boring deeper. She raised her right hand and slapped the other side of her face.

"*Wake up!*" she screamed. But again, nothing changed. The room, the pain, the dread, the weakness in the core of her being that spread to every inch of her body. They were all still there no matter how many times she slapped herself, no matter how many times she screamed Danny's name.

She continued to strike herself, even after the bedroom door flew open and Don ran over to the bed. He grabbed her hands and pushed them into her lap until she stopped struggling.

"Becky!" He cradled her head and gently brought the side of her face to his chest. "Baby, shhhhh..."

Not having the strength to pull away, she let him hold her, though it didn't soothe her in the least. As a matter of fact, it made her feel more tense and irritable. It made her want to dig her nails into his chest, claw her way through and come out the other side where she'd be in another cosmos, running with Danny across an endless field of green, the sun shining, the sky as crisp, clear and blue as sapphire ice. But her arms hung limply from her shoulders, her hands resting on her lap. She knew there would be no running through fields, no beautiful skies, no sapphire ice. Not now. Not ever.

"What can I do for you, Beck?" She didn't respond. He held her closer. "Alex and Lynn are making lunch and it should be ready any minute. I want you to eat something."

Until that moment, she'd completely forgotten that her brother had flown in from Ohio last night. When Alex had stepped out of the cab, a frigid panic ran through her veins when she didn't see his son Dylan, just a few days younger than Danny, standing with him. Once Lynn and Dylan appeared from the other side of the cab, Becky felt relief along with an odd sense of envy. *A son should be with his mother*, she'd said to herself. She continued the chant all night long until she fell asleep, as though the words themselves would eventually bring Danny back to her.

"We'll get through this together, Beck. I swear." Don's voice was tight with emotion. Becky could tell it pained him to speak those words, but she couldn't find the strength, or the will, to help him. "We can't give up. We still have hope. I know it doesn't feel like that right now, but we have to try to believe he's okay. Hope is all we have." Though the emptiness Becky woke up with this morning told her they didn't even have hope, she kept it to herself.

"Where's my brother?" she asked, her mouth resting against Don's chest. Her voice trembled and at first she didn't recognize who was speaking. "And where's Dylan? I want to see Alex and Dylan."

She knew she was grasping for security, a senseless peace of mind from knowing that at least one child in the family was safe. She would touch him and hold him, feel the warmth of his skin with her hands and face, the breath of life and soul missing from the body of her son who she had cradled in her nightmare less than an hour ago.

Where was he? Where was Dylan? She pulled herself up and walked toward the door, darting glances around the dark room.

"Where are they? Where's Alex and Dylan?" She attempted to catch her breath.

Don stood and walked toward her. She held up her hands in defense. "No. I want to see Alex and Dylan. Now! Do you understand me? I need to see them now!" Her breathing grew more shallow and quick, her voice loud but hollow. Don edged closer. Becky kept her hands up. "Don, where are they? What happened to Alex and Dylan? Tell me now!"

She was screaming and on the verge of tears when Alex dashed into the room with Dylan tromping just behind.

"Becky," Alex said, trying to calm her with his voice. "It's okay. We're right here."

Becky let out a whimper of relief and opened her arms toward him. He fell into her embrace and she held him close as he began to sob. "I'm right here," he wept. "I'm sorry...I wish I could...I wish there was something..." She held him tighter and rubbed his back. As his older sister, it had always been her duty to protect him from harm and today wasn't any different. Though her head ached ferociously and her mind was on the verge of letting go, she consoled him using the vaporous fumes of energy she had left.

"Shhhh..." Becky whispered, unable to take her eyes off Dylan standing in the darkest corner of the bedroom. "It's okay," she continued. "Just you being here is enough. Thank you."

"Please don't thank me, Becky." He pulled away and held her at arm's length, wiping his tears on his sleeve. "Just tell me what I can do for you. Anything. I need to feel like I'm doing something."

Becky gently wiped Alex's tears away with her thumbs and fought to smile.

"Like I said, just having you here is doing something for me." She walked to the window, grabbed the curtain panels and slid them to the side to let in more light. The sun made her eyes burn and head pound harder. She turned to her brother. "Where's Lynn?" Becky snuck another peek at Dylan, still hiding in the corner.

"She's in the kitchen doing her thing. She wanted to make food for everyone...to make things easier for you." He looked at Don. "That's okay, right? Do you want her to stop? I know she can be...well…"

"Alex, it's fine," Don said, leaning back against the chest of drawers. A frame holding a picture of him, Becky and Danny at Fenway Park fell facedown onto the bureau. The slap of glass against wood made Becky jump. Don quickly grabbed the frame, stood it up and positioned it exactly as it was. "Lynn is doing more than she should and we appreciate everything. I can't thank the both of you enough."

Becky moved away from the door and sat on a corner of the unmade bed. She looked at Dylan and studied his face: the smooth forehead, the freckles covering the tip of his nose, the rosy cheeks flush with the heat of bashfulness. As they peered into each other's eyes, both unsure who should make the first move, Becky felt an ache deep inside her gut. She patted the bed as a gesture for Dylan to join her. He reluctantly came over, staring at the carpet as though he'd lost his best friend somewhere deep within the textured pile.

When he finally reached her and scooted up onto the bed, he kept his gaze on the floor. He was unusually quiet, and Becky knew he was in the midst of absorbing sounds, sights, and words that no ten-year-old should have to experience. She placed her hand on his knee and scratched his blue jeans with the fingernail of her index finger.

"You're Danny's favorite cousin," she said, her voice tightening with emotion. "You know that, right?"

Dylan shook his head emphatically but remained silent.

"He always said you were his best friend, too. So you're more than cousins." Becky stopped speaking and inhaled deeply, looking to the ceiling for strength. "You're more than cousins. You're friends. *Best* friends, forever."

Dylan spun around and grabbed Becky's waist. His whimpers and moans were the only sounds she could hear as she held his head in her lap and twirled her fingers around the curls of his dark brown hair. She began to sway, forward and backward, side to side, closing her eyes, imagining it was Danny's head lying on her lap, Danny's tears dampening her lounge pants. And then she started to silently pray that it was Danny she was touching, that it was Dylan to whom the unspeakable had happened and she was now consoling her son, stroking his hair, wiping away his tears.

Yes. Thank God it was Dylan and not Danny. She didn't think she could bear what her brother and his wife must have been going through, such a horrible thing happening to their own flesh and blood. She could never have been strong enough for that.

"It's okay, Danny. It'll be all right, I promise," Becky whispered, her eyes closed, her back and forth movement intensifying. "Dylan loved you and you loved him. That's what's important." She knew he couldn't hear her over his sobbing, so she leaned over and kissed the back of his head, hoping that would comfort him enough until exhaustion set in and she would put him to bed. Tomorrow was supposed to be a big day: spelling bee finals and auditions for the fourth grade's spring production based on Disney's *Beauty and the Beast.*

Danny had been practicing every night for the part of Gaston, reading lines from a script they'd found together online. In the privacy of his bedroom he'd speak the words to the invisible Belle he was trying to woo. Although Danny never admitted to it, Becky had heard a rumor that he had a crush on Megan Dettmer, the girl everyone knew would audition for the part of Belle and get it without hesitation from any of the final decision makers. She was the school star, an old soul way beyond her ten years, who knew how to work a room effortlessly and more productively than most adults three times her age. Danny's advanced character wasn't far behind Megan's, and Becky could easily imagine them as a Boston power couple within the next fifteen to twenty years— Megan a cinema superstar, Danny a high-powered attorney and Becky a loving grandmother tending to and pampering her grandchildren within the walls of the most sought-after brownstone in Beacon Hill.

But first things first. She would have to help Danny work past the loss of Dylan and get some rest. She wondered if she should call Mrs. Phillips, the school principal, and see if the school would offer Danny some leeway—who knows, maybe delay the spelling bee, or put off the play auditions for a week or so. That couldn't be too much to ask. Danny had always been a very sensitive child and dealing with Dylan's death would take him longer than most other children. And she would help him through it, one day at a time, one *second*, if that's what it would take.

As she thought about when she should call Mrs. Phillips, a buzz from out of nowhere began and grew louder and louder until it pervaded the core of her head. At the same time, something grabbed the back of her neck. She wriggled a bit, trying to escape both the noise and the tightening grip. When it became clear that the sounds she heard were voices and the vice she felt was the grasp of a hand, she jolted open her eyes.

"Becky, stop! Please! *Becky!*" Alex begged as he pulled Dylan from her clutches. "This is Dylan, not Danny!" He lifted the boy, who sobbed uncontrollably and buried his face in his dad's neck. Alex spoke softly into his son's ear: "It's okay, Dylan. It's okay." He gently bobbed the boy up and down and walked toward the door, where they quickly disappeared into the hallway.

Becky's outstretched arms were empty, her hands grasping at air. She stared up at Don in disbelief, struggling to find words to excuse her actions or make sense of her brief suspension of reality. But no words were uttered; only an obscure rattling came from deep within her throat.

Don sat down next to her, a Valium in one hand, a cup of water in the other. "I get it, I understand. Don't think twice about it. Let's just get you through this best we can." He brought his hand up to her mouth until her lips parted. He placed the pill on her tongue and handed her the cup of water. "And we will get you through this, love. I promise we will."

She took a sip of water. The pill scratched her parched throat as it made its way down. She swallowed again and again, pushing it as far as she could until she couldn't feel it anymore. "You keep saying that. You keep saying we'll get through this, but I don't see how," she said, and began to weep.

She stood and walked to the window. The sun shined, and the snow was melting ahead of the new storm they were expected to get, creating small streams flowing down the street to the sewer grates.

"Seriously, Don, how am I supposed to get up every day and not think about making him breakfast or picking him up from practice? How will I go to sleep at night without tucking him in? Kissing his forehead?" Her voice cracked. "There's no getting over this, Don. Not for me. Not today, tomorrow or any time soon. Unless you can tell me right now that he's on his way home safe and sound, stop telling me I'll get through this. I can't bear to hear it anymore."

Don didn't move. "Why are you saying this? I'm going through hell, too, but I'm not talking like he's never coming home."

Only a mother knows, she thought, and lifted her hand to stop him from saying anything more. He fell silent and shook his head. Then he said, "I'm sorry, babe. I'm sorry. I just don't want you to give up hope. I'm nowhere near giving up on Danny, and you shouldn't be either, for your sake, for my sake—for *Danny's* sake."

"Can you just leave for a bit? I need to be alone." There wasn't space for anyone or anything in this room but herself and her thoughts.

Don nodded and stood. Once he had left the room and closed the door behind him, Becky heard the soft grumble of voices from the hallway. The chatter of her concerned family had restarted, and although Becky was grateful for their concern, she wished the house were empty and she could stroll from room to room like she would on any ordinary day. She knew the people in her home cared, that they all had compassion and wanted to help, but they didn't understand. They couldn't understand. The chasm between her and them was too deep and too empty, an abyss so void of light and air that at times she found it hard to breathe.

Overwhelming fatigue washed over her. She closed her eyes and let herself relax, clenching her fists as she waited for the next chapter of the nightmare to begin.

6

Charles Hastings was pissed.

Almost two and a half weeks had passed since Danny was killed and the TV news channels were spewing the same headlines about a missing boy and the possibility that someone had seen him running through South Hingham close to the conservation land.

And that was all. No mention of anyone confessing to hitting and killing him with their car. Online police and accident reports noted the BMW crash but mentioned no names or possible hit and runs. Charles's anger quickly turned to rage: the son of a bitch who killed his best friend was going to get away with it. Where the hell was the driver of LCKY123, and why wasn't he confessing? He could easily say it was an accident and blame it on the sleet and slickness of the road. Why wasn't he coming forward? Did he think he could hide his crime forever?

Charles knew that he himself was in the clear. At first he wasn't sure that the cops who interviewed him believed a word he'd said. He figured they'd be back to check on his story and verify some facts. But that hadn't happened, and although he was overwhelmingly relieved, he was more determined than ever to make sure the guilty party paid for Danny's death.

How the hell do I get the cops on this guy's ass without giving myself away? Charles tapped his fingers on the dining room table, creating a sound like soldiers marching in a wartime parade. He tapped and tapped and tapped, hoping the consistent rhythm would form an idea, a way for him to take the license plate number and figure out who—

He stopped dead in his tracks, remembering he knew someone who worked at the DMV. His name was…Mike? Matt? No—*Mark*. From what Charles could remember, they hadn't parted on the best of terms. Did they have an argument? Did Mark screw him over somehow? He couldn't put his finger on what had happened, but at this point, it didn't matter. Charles would just have to act as kindly as he could to Mark and do whatever he had to because this was the guy who was going to tell him the name of the LCKY123 driver.

He picked up his phone and scrolled down until Mark's photo appeared. He noted that their last contact was from three years ago. Mark still had a beard in the picture, which Charles figured was shaved off because of the stitches they had to put in his jaw—

That's what it was! He now distinctly remembered trying to get Mark to understand that young boys made better friends than adults like him; in fact, he'd opened up to Mark like he'd never done with anyone else before. Mark didn't agree, to say the least, and said some really hurtful things that reminded him of Daddy. Charles had hit him with a four-pound iron skillet, right in the jaw, and threatened to kill him if he ever called him those names again—or if he told anyone what Charles had said.

He knew he was lucky he hadn't gone too far and killed Mark that night. Not that he would've cared one way or the other, but he wasn't a murderer, not like LCKY123. On the way to the hospital, Mark had seemed very clear on the subject and never told anyone what Charles said or who had dislocated his jaw. Charles remembered Mark wincing as he nodded emphatically at what he was warned would happen.

Now that Charles recalled their last encounter, he looked up Mark's office number on the DMV website. He'd become a supervisor a couple of weeks after they'd first met and had his own office phone. Charles decided to call that number rather than his cell which he would most likely ignore.

As it rang, Charles had to remind himself to be considerate about the whole iron skillet affair. *It wasn't my fault.* It was actually Mark's fault for refusing to be a *real* friend, but even those few times a few weeks after the incident, when Charles had tried to contact Mark, he'd sure acted like it had been Charles's fault.

"Mark Kellison," the voice said over the line.

"Hey, man, it's Charles Hast—"

Mark hung up.

Charles redialed immediately and would continue to do so as long as it was necessary. He'd go down to the DMV office if he had to.

After hanging up three times, Mark finally stayed on the line. But his tone was icy: "I can't believe you're calling me, you son of a bitch. And at work? What in the hell do you *want?*"

This wasn't sounding good at all. Charles would have to use his unique ability of reading people to his advantage. He once overheard the shrink at the facility called it a skill of "the high-functioning sociopath," and Charles used it whenever it was required to get his way.

Based on Mark's tone, Charles jettisoned Plan A of trying to get Mark to forgive and forget. *What now?*

He remembered that Mark was always struggling to make ends meet. It was obvious the day they'd met, when Charles was sent on an on-site call at Mark's home to fix his computer. The screen was stuck on an illegal gambling site, and it took Charles over two hours to get the system up and running properly. As he worked on the computer, Mark sat across the desk babbling about his past winnings, hot girlfriends, and favorite drinks. His trust and carelessness gave Charles access to files and data that he found of particular interest: overdue invoices, a negative checking account balance and notices from collection agencies. It was apparent his DMV job wasn't paying enough for his extra-curricular activities of drinking and gambling.

And now that knowledge was all he needed to immediately switch to Plan B.

"Hello to you, too, Mark. I'll get right to it: what I *want* is to give you a hundred dollars for a very quick favor."

"Go screw yourself," Mark snapped and hung up again.

Charles called him back and Mark picked up.

Mark answered the phone with "Five hundred."

"What?" Charles said with a laugh. The money wasn't a problem—he didn't really spend much anyway except for video games and stuff for his new friends. It was the suddenness of Mark's counteroffer that took him by surprise. "But you don't even know what the favor is!"

"You either want me to illegally restore a lost driver's license, or you want me to illegally look up somebody's information from a license plate number. And I bet it's the second thing, because knowing you, you'd drive without a license anyway."

Charles was astounded but played it cool. "Yeah. The second thing. I have a license plate number."

"Bring the five hundred to the clothing drop-off bins in the Panda Express parking lot by Hanover Mall."

"Isn't that like four miles from where you work?"

"Exactly. I have lunch at one, so be there at 1:15. And if I see a skillet anywhere near you, the deal is off."

"No skillet, I promise. Not even a spatula." Charles laughed at his own joke.

Mark didn't.

"Just give me the plate number, asshole."

* * *

At about 2:00 the next morning, Charles drove with purpose and even excitement. In his hand was the DMV printout Mark had given him that showed the registered owner of LCKY123: one Jesse Carlton, who looked just as smug in his license photo as Charles expected.

Driving north along Route 139 was tedious enough, but now midnight road crews blocked the road, again and again, to do what, Charles had no idea—and didn't care. He was on a critical mission, and this non-stop construction bullshit made him feel like his head was about to explode.

The clouds had started blocking out the stars and the full moon's light diffused through the night sky like a lamp's bulb through its shade. Every now and then a lone ice pellet would bounce off the windshield. The weather report forecast more wintry conditions, even possible squalls, but Charles was determined to get to the Carlton's house no matter what the weather, or the construction crews, tried to do to get in his way. He wanted to see the home of Danny's killer, the coward who took the life of an innocent ten-year-old boy and now refused to face the consequences. One glance at the den of sick Jesse Carlton would tell him exactly what his next move should be.

He hadn't been back to Danny's neighborhood since the day he'd encountered the boy after he got off the bus. The suburban street was well-lighted, making the entire backdrop of his first meeting with Danny look sinister instead of how he remembered it, which was beautiful and inviting. As he passed the spot where he'd parked and waited for Danny that day, he shook his head.

If only you'd trusted me, Danny. If only you acted like best friends are supposed to act. And now you're dead thanks to Jesse Carlton. Just like always, everyone's against me.

Over to the right was Danny's house. If it weren't for the cars in the driveway, he would've thought the house was empty. As would be expected in the middle of the night, there was no sign of life, no activity at all. The windows were dark, the blinds were down and the curtains drawn. For a moment, Charles felt a sense of superiority as he realized that he was the only person on the planet who knew the entire truth about Danny. He was the one and only human being who could walk up to that front door and lead them to a spot in the middle of a wooded expanse where their son now lay beneath soil and rock. Most importantly, he was the only one who could bring Danny's killer to justice.

He continued driving slowly along the empty street, glancing at mailboxes, garages and front doors as he searched for the Carlton's house number, 107. When he saw those three numbers illuminated by a yellow porch light, he pulled to the curb and looked in the rearview and side mirrors to make sure no Neighborhood Watch busybody was observing him. He shut off the van and shifted over to the front passenger seat to get a better sense of the house's size and if there was any way he'd be able to get inside.

Charles wiped away the mist his breath formed on the passenger window and tried to identify some promising points of entry. He eyed the large slider window positioned on the side of the house between the giant bay window and high, wooden fence to the backyard. *Possible.* Then the other slider that appeared to show through to the kitchen. *Another possibility.*

He slid back to the driver's seat and gazed out the windshield. Although the street was quiet and there was not a soul to be seen in the immediate area, Charles wasn't sure about trying to get into the house. He hadn't done enough reconnaissance yet, and any screw-up would send him to jail for breaking and entering. What if they had a security camera inside? He had heard about burglars showing their faces to a video camera they had no idea was there, and that was all the evidence the court needed. Charles knew he wouldn't make it in jail and would end up telling the police everything about his relationship with Danny. Even though it was all above board and he didn't do anything wrong, he worried they'd focus on him instead of

Jesse Carlton. He had to take small steps and strategize each move; otherwise, he could end up in a shitload of trouble.

Besides, he thought, he didn't necessarily *have to* enter the house to intimidate Jesse Carlton into confessing. There had to be something he could do to let this killer know there was someone else who knew what he had done that night. Some way to scare the devil out of the man who probably thought he'd be able to hide his secret for the rest of his life.

He slid down in the seat and crossed his arms, his gaze falling again onto the slider on the side of the house. Charles stared without really looking at anything, trying to think of what he could do to shake up Jesse Carlton while also bringing the cops closer to finding Danny's killer.

When it finally hit him, he threw his head back against the headrest, closed his eyes and smiled.

"You're a genius, Charles," he said to no one but himself.

7

"I'm just about hanging on, Manny," Melissa whispered into the phone. "I can barely get Jesse out of bed."

She leaned back on the glider chair and swiveled around so she could see out the door of her home office. As she did, their Siamese cat, Minx, leaped from the floor onto her knees and circled around three times before finally nestling in her lap. The warmth of his body felt good on her legs, and she scratched the base of his chin, hoping to entice him into staying there a while longer, at least until she was off the phone.

"I still don't understand why you waited so long to tell me you were having such problems, Melissa. I thought you said he was getting better."

Melissa rolled her eyes. "Manny," she sighed. "you're my co-counsel, not my therapist. I've already overloaded you with work by being out so much. I didn't want to make things worse. Plus, I really thought Jesse just needed a few days to get back to himself. The doctors said it was a slight concussion at first, and then they said he just needed to rest. But he's barely gotten out of bed. He gets these terrible, terrible headaches and just can't seem to get through a day without pain or bouts of crying."

"Did you call the doctor?" Manny asked. A wave of relief ran through her once she heard the concern in his voice. She was worried that her absence and relinquishment of cases would put a strain on her position at the firm, but it seemed, as of right now, Manny was more worried about Jesse than their clients.

"Yes. The doctor said sometimes people get anxious and depressed after a concussion. He said it's the injury combined with the body's reaction and chemical changes which should most likely straighten itself out over time."

"Wait—he had a concussion or he *didn't* have a concussion?"

"I don't know, Manny. If he had one, they say it was really minor. But he's showing all these emotional signs that point to something else. At this point, the doctor prescribed amitriptyline to help him sleep and to work on his mood."

"And? Any change?"

"So far, nothing." She moved her fingers from Minx's chin to his cheek, directly behind his whiskers, and relaxed even more as the cat's purring made her feel more peaceful and in control. "He's still about the same. Seriously, Manny, I'm getting worried. Especially because he still can't remember what happened that night. It's like a blank spot in his brain. I've brought it up twice and each time I do, he gets this awful headache and just says he can't remember. I don't have the slightest idea what is going on inside his head."

"You know," Manny started, "I wonder if this could be a psychological issue. If the docs are saying he's physically fine, maybe the accident caused some kind of post-traumatic stress. Like when my wife had those panic attacks after the burglary at the house. She was actually diagnosed with PTSD. Maybe Jesse—"

She heard a sound and looked up to see Jesse standing in the doorway. Elated that he'd gotten out of bed of his own volition and actually donned a sweatshirt and pair of jeans, she jumped up from the chair, sending Minx flying off her lap. With catlike grace, Minx landed on the floor, let out his typical whine of annoyance and walked into the hallway as though insulted by her dismissiveness. Jesse chuckled, offering Melissa another flicker of hope. She apologized to Minx and kissed Jesse's cheek.

"Speak of the devil," she said, her smile feeling a bit out of place. "It's Manny." She pointed to the phone. "He's checking on you."

Jesse smiled and offered a slight wave. His voice was soft and low as if trying not to wake someone. "Tell him I say hi."

"Tell him yourself." Melissa held the receiver up to Jesse but he wasn't biting. He swiped his hand at the phone, turned around and walked down the hallway toward the kitchen.

"Shit," she sighed. "He doesn't want to talk right now. I'm sorry."

"No worries. Listen, I'm going to email you the information for my wife's psychiatrist, Dr. Bradley. Honestly, he's the best."

"That would be so great." Another wave of relief flooded over her. "And Manny…thank you for everything."

"Please don't thank me, Missy. Just hang in there. And call me if you need anything else. We're taking care of things here, so don't concern yourself too much with work for right now. Focus on Jesse."

Melissa placed the phone on her desk and took a breath, trying to get herself ready for Jesse's unpredictable mental state and whatever he was about to throw at her. Wanting to avoid confrontation for as long as possible, she picked up the stack of work folders sitting on her desk, hoping she'd find something she might have missed or a case that might need more research. But she'd already been up since before dawn putting the final touches on her current cases and her eyes were weary. She threw down the folders and looked around the room, pausing when her gaze fell on one of four photos sitting atop the antique credenza.

It was a picture of Jesse, Becky, Don and herself at the lodge atop Albuquerque's Sandia Peak. Almost five years ago the four of them decided to get away for a full week in New Mexico—not only to enjoy the beauty of the Southwest, but also to see if they had the capability to vacation together for more than a single weekend. As expected, it was smooth sailing from day one, and on the plane ride back there was the unanimous decision to make Santa Fe an annual getaway. The trip had helped strengthen their friendship and Melissa felt it solidified a relationship between herself and Becky that was more like a sisterhood than friendship.

She moved her eyes to the frame standing next to the Sandia Peak shot, a photo of Danny sitting on Jesse's shoulders at a Fourth of July fireworks show over Hingham Harbor. Her heart skipped a beat, and she put her hand over her mouth, remembering how her biggest decision that day was whether or not to use paper plates. She shook her head in disbelief that today her biggest decision was whether or not to believe the boy was still alive.

"And now *this*," she whispered to herself, worried about if and when Jesse would recover from whatever it was he was going through. She started walking down the hallway toward the kitchen. "Just what we need."

"What?" Jesse stood at the kitchen island stirring cream into his coffee.

Another breakthrough: first getting dressed, now making coffee. It had been too long since Jesse had attempted even this small an act of normalcy, and Melissa was ecstatic. But she kept her reaction under wraps: *If you act normal, he'll act normal.*

"Nothing, just babbling to myself." She pulled out one of the stools from beside the island and sat down. "Manny sends his best."

Jesse swallowed his first sip of coffee without expression. "I'm sorry. I just didn't feel like talking with him right now."

"I get it," Melissa said. "I totally get it. One step at a time. I'm glad to see you up and around." She rubbed his arm and pinched the thermal shirt he was wearing. "This is a good shirt for today, it's supposed to be cold. Do you think you'll be going out at all?" She scrunched her toes inside her slippers as if she were trying to avoid the eggshells she was stepping on.

"Not sure yet." Jesse took another sip of coffee and rubbed the scruff on his chin. "I will definitely be shaving today, that's for sure."

Melissa smiled and laid her hand on top of his. She heard a hollowness in his voice, a lack of strength that was never there before the accident. It hurt her to hear him like this, but she was determined to see the broken glass as half full. He was out of bed, walking, talking and actually thinking about leaving the house. That would have to be enough for right now.

"Bob called." Melissa waited for a reaction. Other than taking another sip of coffee, Jesse appeared unfazed. "He said everyone at the agency misses you terribly, but you are not to return until you're ready. He told me explicitly to tell you to take your time."

"I was actually thinking about going in today for just an hour or so." He took another sip of coffee. "My head doesn't hurt too much today and there are two campaigns that have deadlines coming up."

Melissa was taken aback, stunned that he'd go from two weeks of depression, most of that time spent in bed, to going right back to work the first day he showed any sign of improvement. Was this too soon? She rolled her eyes at herself, realizing she'd just been worried he wasn't doing enough. Either way, this was progress and she wasn't going to ruin it with her typical excessive doubt and worry.

"That's great!" She jumped off the stool, walked around the island and clasped her hands around his neck. "I actually rented a car for you last week—just in case you decided you wanted to go out for a drive or something. It's not your Beemer, but it'll do 'til you get yourself a new car."

Jesse slowly shook his head. "I didn't even think about the car. My mind has been..." He rubbed his temples with each hand; a look of confusion invading his face. "Actually, I don't know where my mind has been."

She hugged his waist and pulled his head onto her shoulder. She couldn't remember a time when he was this vulnerable, and it took all her strength to push down the lump in her throat.

"It's okay, Jesse. You've been through a lot. You need to just give yourself some time."

"And some vodka," he said.

They shared a laugh, and she looked at him with gratitude for this change. There was a spark of the old Jesse standing in front of her, the first glimmer of light she'd seen in weeks. Danny going missing had been hard on her, but it was nothing compared to how it had affected her husband.

"What are *you* up to today?" Jesse asked. "Any plans?"

Melissa bit her lip and glanced out the window toward the Madsen's house, the uplifting feelings she'd been enjoying over the last few moments quickly fading.

"I'm going to spend some time with Becky," Melissa said. She turned back to Jesse, his expression blank. "Then I'll probably come back and work from home. Waiting for you to get back."

Jesse touched her chin and gently kissed her cheek. "You don't have to babysit me, you know. I'll be okay."

Melissa gazed into his eyes and forced herself to hold back tears. Something wasn't right; there was more going on with him than just trying to recover from a bang on the head. Even the shape of his eyes had changed, the outer edges surrounding his brow drooping more than she remembered, his expression now holding a perpetual sadness and emptiness. It pained her to see him this way, and she prayed that the medication would take effect soon and he'd find his way back to the happy, animated, optimistic man she'd fallen in love with.

"I know you will, honey. I know you will." She hugged him as tightly as she could, all too aware that they were both trying as hard as they could to somehow believe the words she was saying.

* * *

Melissa watched Jesse turn the corner in the rental car before putting on her coat to go to the Madsens'. She'd wanted to drop off her files at the office before heading over, but Don had called a few minutes earlier to tell her that Becky had just gone through another breakdown. He said she'd mistaken her nephew Dylan as Danny and now refused to speak with anyone. He was talking so fast and low under his breath that she couldn't grasp the details of what had actually happened. All she could gather for certain was that Becky needed Melissa's help—and so did he.

She walked across and up the street with her hands in her coat pockets. Although the breeze was light, the air was absolutely frigid, stinging her face and forcing her to pick up her pace. Biting her lip, she shook her head slightly, still in disbelief that Danny was missing. His disappearance had turned the lives of so many people upside down. The mystery of what happened to Danny and where he might be was affecting her anxiety worse than anything she'd ever experienced. She shivered, trying to imagine what Becky and Don were going through. Would it be worse to never know, to never have an answer and keep hope alive? Or would it be better to get the call saying they'd found Danny's body, that this horrific mystery had been solved and put all the uncertainty to rest? Melissa exhaled a hard breath in an attempt to rid herself of the negativity. If she was going to help Becky, she had to be more positive, and thoughts about death were not going to help anyone.

As she approached the Madsens' house, she could see Don through the glass storm door. He waved and opened it, hugging her before she even had a chance to take her hands out of her coat pockets. She glanced over his shoulder to see Alex holding Dylan in a bear hug, gently swaying the boy back and forth. Red splotches covered Dylan's face and the tracks of tears on his cheeks made Melissa almost cry herself.

"Thank you for coming so quickly," Don said, helping her slip off her coat. He took her scarf and pointed to Alex. "You remember Becky's brother, Alex, right?"

"Of course," she said, walking over to the father and son and placing her hand on Alex's shoulder. She turned to Dylan and lightly wiped a tear stain from his face. "And I also remember this young person who has grown up to be such a handsome young man."

Dylan hid in the nape of his father's neck, turning crimson, no doubt with embarrassment.

"Hi, Melissa." Alex's voice sounded shaky and tired. "Thanks for coming. Becky's not talking. To anyone." He leaned his head away from Dylan and tried to keep his voice to a whisper. "We thought that you being her best friend and all...well, maybe she'd talk to you."

Melissa tightened her lips. "I can try, that's for sure. If it doesn't work, though, you might have to get the doctor to look in on her." She looked down the hallway. "First, let me see if I can help in any way. Is she still in the bedroom?"

Alex nodded and she turned to Don.

"Can I go in?" she asked.

"Of course," Don replied, walking her down the hall as though leading her toward a cell on death row. Other than a few slivers of sunlight streaming through the window at the end of the hallway, the corridor was dark, holding the sadness and frustration that had been moved in with the Madsens since Danny's disappearance. "Just a warning, Missy...she doesn't look good." He grabbed the doorknob and was about to turn it when Melissa grabbed his hand.

"How are *you* holding up?"

Tears filled his eyes and he swallowed. For a moment, she wondered if it had been a mistake to ask the question, but she could tell by his softened expression that he was thankful someone realized he was going through his own living hell. And since Jesse wasn't yet up to helping his best friend, she'd have to fill his shoes.

"I'm holding up." His voice trembled as he tightened his grip on her hands. "Thank you for asking." He was about to open the bedroom door for her but then stopped and removed his hand from the knob. "How is Jesse?" He slowly shook his head. "I feel terrible. I've been so consumed with Becky and Danny that I haven't even had the common courtesy to ask how he's been doing since the accident."

Forcing a smile, she looked into his eyes and decided Don had enough to be concerned about without her going into Jesse's strange moods and headaches.

"He's doing a lot better, thanks. He's actually going into the office today for a few hours. The doc says he's physically fit."

"That's good to hear," Don said. "It's nice to hear some good news for a change."

She kissed his cheek. "Let me try to get you more good news," she said, reaching for the bedroom doorknob. But as Don walked away, she could almost feel the morbidity seeping through the door. She closed her eyes and took a deep breath. "Positive," she whispered. "Positive."

* * *

Melissa shut the door behind her and saw Becky standing by the window. The air was stale and heavy, as if she'd walked into a room of an abandoned mansion. She took a few steps toward Becky, then stopped, not wanting to startle her from her semi-trance.

"Hi, Beck," she said softly.

Becky didn't look at her. "He's dead, you know," she said.

Melissa sighed. Not off to a good start. "Becky, you don't know that. How can you —"

"I know it," she interrupted. "I can feel it. I can even see it in my nightmares." She still didn't turn around, her gaze glued to an object in the sky that only she could see. "I just wish I knew where he was so I could hold him one last time. That's all I want right now. That's all I'll ever want again."

Melissa walked over to Becky and took hold of both her arms, turning her away from the window as gently as possible. When they were finally facing one another, Melissa looked into Becky's eyes and was taken aback by their glazed, rheumy appearance. She waited for Becky to return her stare but after a few seconds realized that wasn't going to happen. She could only hope Becky would hear her words.

"Becky, can you please just slow down for a minute and take some breaths?" She looked at the vials of pills on the bedside table. "Are you taking your meds?"

"I hate them. They're making me see things that don't exist, think things that have no basis in reality. I feel dead inside and scared of the world outside."

Melissa didn't know if that was how the meds Becky had been prescribed actually worked. If Becky was hallucinating or losing her grip, it could have just been because of stress. *Just?* She thought. *Yeah, it's 'just' the stress of her son vanishing, no big deal. Nice, Melissa.* "Maybe we could get you dressed and go out for a walk."

"I know what I did to Dylan." She pulled away from Melissa and returned her gaze out the window. "I mistook Dylan for Danny, and I made him cry. I'm sorry about that." She tightened the flannel belt of her bathrobe around her waist and crossed her arms. "But a walk won't take back what happened and it won't bring my son back to life."

"Becky, please. Stop this. Have you heard they have a specific area they're searching through, house by house, out by the conservation land? If Danny's there, they'll find him."

"*No!*" she snapped, with such uncharacteristic loudness that it made Melissa jump. "He's dead. I *know* he's dead. A mother knows when her child is breathing...and when he's not. You don't understand, *can't* understand. You're not a mother."

The words hit Melissa like a sledgehammer. But she kept on. "I just want to—"

"Please leave," Becky said flatly, the voice once again coming from someone she felt she'd never met.

Melissa waited for her to continue, for an explanation behind the request. But none came. Finally, she said gently, "Are you sure, Becky? We don't have to talk. I can just sit here with you."

Becky tightened the belt of her robe and closed her eyes. "I'm sure."

* * *

Holding back tears, Melissa left the bedroom and closed the door behind her. She inhaled deeply and let the breath seep from her lips while she tried to swallow past the lump in her throat. She gathered strength in her legs, pushed away from the wall and began to walk toward the kitchen where voices helped stir the silence. As she reached them, she forced a slight smile and made her way over to Dylan's mother. "Lynn, it's good to see you. Um…so how have you been?"

Lynn gave her a hug. "It's great to see you again, Missy. You look beautiful as always." She self-consciously ran her fingers through her bob cut. "Please excuse the way I look. I haven't stopped since we got here."

Melissa smiled. "If I could look as fresh as you do after 'not stopping,' my prayers would be answered." She looked at Don and wanted to kick herself. *Prayers about appearances when this man is praying his son is still alive. Jesus, Melissa.*

"That was a short visit," said Don, his tone still holding out hope.

"Too short," Melissa replied. "She asked me to leave. She didn't want to talk. And even when I suggested I'd just sit with her, she still wanted me to leave."

"Damn it!" Don shouted. "I don't know what to do for her anymore!" He pushed the sides of his head with his palms and squeezed his eyes shut. "The pills don't work. Sleep doesn't work. Talking doesn't work. I don't know what to do. I just don't."

Melissa had no idea how to respond to that, as she was in the exact same boat with Jesse. She said instead, "I have to get back to the house and get some legal documents to the office, but I'll check in later. Don, can you walk me out?"

When she and Don stepped outside, she gently took his hand and squeezed it, searching for the right words to help calm the thoughts which must've been clamoring inside his head. After a few seconds of silence, she realized those words were not forthcoming.

"I'm not sure why," Melissa started. "I really don't know why, but for some reason, Becky is convinced that Danny is gone."

Don's grip tightened. "What do you mean, 'gone'?"

She took a deep breath. "*Gone*, Don. She's convinced that he's dead." Saying the words aloud made her dizzy, and now she held Don's hand for her own support as well as his.

"Why would she think that?" He looked panicked, his eyes searching Melissa's for an answer. "Rivera has some solid leads, for God's sake. It could be the break we've been praying for."

Melissa touched his cheek with the backs of her fingers. "I know, Don. I know. I tried explaining that to her." She paused and peered out the storm door. Something moved up the block near her house, but she couldn't make it out due to the condensation on the window. She turned back to Don. "Honestly, I think the pills are making things worse. You might want to speak with the doctor about changing the prescription or dosage. If she's not leaving that room, if she's having episodes like she did with Dylan, if she's throwing people out who are only trying to help, then it's obvious the meds aren't doing what they should be doing."

"Thanks for the input. I'll have to talk to the doctor." Don kissed her on the cheek. "Thank you for coming. I hope she didn't scare you off."

"Don't be silly, Don. She's my best friend. And I don't scare that easy."

That last statement, she knew, was a lie.

The cold air felt good on her face. She took a deep breath when she heard the door close behind her. Her head was still spinning, and her anxiety had reached its peak, but she kept her composure as she strolled up the walkway toward the street. Her pounding heart said it all: the suffering inside the house had been choking her and the truth was, she needed to leave as much as Becky needed her to go.

8

If not for the ice on the sidewalks, Melissa would've run to her house as fast as she could, pushed open the door, slammed it shut and closed all the curtains and shutters—keeping the world, and all its inhabitants, locked out for eternity. Her emotions were all over the place: worry about Jesse, concern about the future of Becky and Don's relationship. And, of course, there was the biggest fear of all, the one that made her shiver from the inside out: that Becky was right and Danny was dead.

She held her coat closed tight and walked briskly along the block, across the street and up onto the grass apron that ran the length of their property. With her head down, she hopped off the apron and onto the plowed sidewalk, moving as briskly as possible to protect her face from the gusting winter wind. When she just about reached her house and finally looked up, she gasped and stopped in her tracks.

The side window had been smashed and a jagged opening, slightly larger than a baseball, was now in the center of the glass pane. Melissa darted her head from one side of the street to the other to see if there might've been any witnesses. There were a few cars parked up the road, but other than those, the street was empty. She tensed up, worried that something had happened to Minx or the sound of glass breaking had frightened him and driven him to hide in a place he shouldn't be. About to run into the house, she caught herself, realizing that someone might be inside. She stopped, reached in her coat pocket and grabbed her cell phone to call Jesse.

"Hey," he answered his phone on the first ring. "I was just about to call and tell you I was on my way home. Did you need me to—"

"Someone broke our window, Jesse. I think someone threw a rock or something through the side window." She'd been through too much to continue holding back her emotions and decided not to care how her tone affected him. She needed backup and she needed it now.

"Whoa, slow down. Someone threw a rock through *what* window?"

"The big slider window, the one in the downstairs utility room with the extra fridge." She still hadn't moved since she saw the broken window and the cold crept up her spine. She shivered. "I went to visit Becky and Don. When I came back, I saw the broken window and I called you."

"When did it happen? I mean, did you see it before you went to Becky and—"

"I have no idea when it happened, Jesse. It's on the side of the house you can't really see unless you're coming from up the block from Becky and Don's." She glanced back at the Madsens' house and thought about asking them for help. *They're going through enough, they don't need this.* She turned back around. "You didn't see it when you left this morning. I didn't see it when I left. Who knows? It could've happened while I was at Don and Becky's. It could've happened yesterday. It's on the opposite side of the house as our bedroom so it could've even happened while we were sleeping last night." Another shiver. She took a few steps closer to the house. "We can figure that out later. Right now I'm worried about Minx, but I'm scared to go in there."

"I don't want you going into the house. Just hang outside for a couple of minutes. I'm actually out on the road, I just picked up lunch. Be there in about ten minutes."

"Okay," she said, trying to sound in control. "Please hurry."

"I will. And Melissa, do *not* go in the house."

"Okay," she said. "Okay."

After they hung up, she paced back and forth, her anxiety level rising off the scale. Surely, if someone had been inside, they would have seen or heard her and run away.

She'd just check the door, see if anybody had tried to get in that way. That was all. She wasn't necessarily *going into* the house. She was just having a look to calm her frazzled nerves. Did Jesse really want her to stand in front of the house freaking out alone?

She would occupy herself and stay calm. Check the door. That was all.

She crept down the driveway, walked to the front door and tried turning the knob. Locked, just the way she'd left it. She glanced around to each side of the house, looking for footprints in the snow that might've led to the backyard. There were no signs that anyone had made their way around the back, and since the yard was enclosed by the six-foot wooden fence they'd installed last year, she was confident that no one could've gotten in through any of the rear entrances.

Sliding the key into the front door lock, she turned it and gently pushed the door open, inch by inch, until she was sure no one was hiding behind it.

"Hello?" she asked softly, her left hand holding open the storm door in case she needed to escape. "Hello?" she asked again, this time a lot louder.

Jesus, she thought, *like they'd actually answer.*

Other than the sound of her quickened breath, there was complete stillness. She let the storm door close and cautiously tiptoed into the kitchen. Everything looked in order. There was no sign of—

Something moved in the living room; she saw it in the corner of her eye and instinctively let out a blood-curdling scream. She almost turned to run out the front door before what she'd seen actually registered.

"*Minx!* God, you scared me!" She walked over to the cat and scooped him up in her arms. Minx buried his head in the crook of her neck and purred. "I know. I know. We'll catch the person who did this." She scratched the back of Minx's neck. "It's okay, sweetie."

Holding the cat, Melissa made her way into the dining room, still on edge as she tried to detect anything else unusual. Jesse would kill her if he knew she was inside the house, much less stalking around looking for intruders, but there was no evidence that anyone had gotten inside and she felt confident enough that she was completely alone. She cautiously made her way into the dining room and through to the living room. Everything appeared as untouched and neat as it did before they'd both left the house. Approaching her office, she took a quick glance into the powder room and hallway closet. Nothing. No one. A peek into her office, then the spare bedroom, and she let out a sigh of relief. All was clear. And although she felt just as sure that the upstairs was burglar-free, she decided to wait for Jesse to come home before investigating the second floor.

She walked down the main hallway and turned the corner to see the basement door closed. Pressing her ear up against the door, she waited to hear something, anything that would tell her she should take Minx and run outside. But there was not a sound other than the soft hum of the gas furnace. She placed her hand on the doorknob, slowly turned it, opened the door a few inches and listened carefully. Still, nothing.

After taking a deep breath, she opened the door fully and flipped on the light switch. She held on to the wooden railing and walked down the steps sideways, ready to run back up the staircase in case an intruder had been hiding down there. When she reached the bottom of the stairs, she took a quick glance around the room. The broken window and shards of glass littering the floor were the only things that seemed out of the ordinary.

As she crept further into the room, she noticed an odd shape in the corner next to the refrigerator: a large rock, resembling one of those making up the stone retaining wall in their front yard, sat on the floor. To the left of the rock was a deep gouge in the cement floor. To the right, a scratched and dented stainless steel freezer door. The rock must've landed on the floor, bounced up and hit the freezer door before rolling into the corner.

With glass crunching beneath her leather flats, she ran toward the stairs and held tightly on to Minx as she took two steps up at a time until she reached the door. She was about to close it when she heard the garage door opening. "Let's wait for Jesse," she said to Minx, still snuggling beneath her chin. "He'll know what to do. Once he's done yelling at me for coming inside."

She jumped at the slam of the car door. A few seconds later, Jesse was standing outside the house peering into the kitchen window. Melissa remained still, watching him look for her. When their eyes met, Melissa almost fell apart, the sudden expression of sadness and disappointment seeming to literally weigh down his face.

He shook his head in disbelief. "Honey, what the hell are you doing? Why are you inside? I thought you were going to—"

"Everything's fine. I checked downstairs and there's no one here." She went to meet him at the front door. "And if someone was upstairs, I think they'd have let us know by now."

"*Jesus*, Missy. Why would you do that?" Jesse shouted, now walking toward the open front door. "You couldn't wait ten minutes for me to get home?"

As Jesse entered the foyer, he threw his leather satchel against the wall and tossed his car keys into the ceramic bowl on the console table. He walked cautiously down the hallway toward the door leading to the basement, then stopped and turned toward Melissa.

"Please tell me you didn't go down there without me here," he said, his hand grasping the doorknob.

Melissa looked to the floor. "Okay, I'll tell you I didn't."

Jesse sighed and opened his mouth to speak when Melissa interrupted before he had the chance to start.

"The front door was locked and nobody was around. Whoever did this just threw the rock and took off." Melissa put Minx into her office and closed the door so he couldn't escape. "It was probably one of those punks who was speeding last week. The ones I yelled at and said I'd call the cops on."

"Which is exactly why we should call the cops!" Jesse grumbled, walking down the steps to assess the damage. Melissa followed closely behind. When he reached the rock, he kicked the toe of his shoe and turned around. "Do you see this? It's vandalism. How else are we going to get those punks if we don't call the cops?"

"We can't be one hundred percent sure it was them. And honestly, I think we've had enough cops for a while," she said, rummaging through one of the many boxes piled high along the wall. It was time to clean up this mess. "Plus, what are they going to do? Send the rock to an FBI forensic lab? I don't think they can even lift fingerprints off a stone like that."

Melissa stopped searching through the boxes and approached the rock, still unable to touch it as though its evil energy would flow up through her fingertips and into her soul.

"You see where that rock is from, don't you?" she asked.

"No. Where is it from?"

She ran back up the steps and into the kitchen. Jesse was right behind her as she looked out the window and pointed to the rock wall that bordered the driveway.

"It's one of *our* rocks—look!" She waited for a response from Jesse but got nothing but a puzzled expression. "I bet if we tried, it would fit perfectly in that spot. I didn't know you could even pull a rock out of that wall."

"Who goes around pulling rocks out of retaining walls?" Jesse finally spoke.

They looked at each other and said simultaneously, "Punk kids."

Jesse crossed his arms. "Anyway, I do think it's possible for them to get prints off a rock. We need to find out who did this so we can make sure it doesn't happen again."

Without answering, Melissa walked downstairs and continued searching for something to cover the hole. She located a section of tarp the painters had left behind a few years back, pulled it out and folded it in half a few times before tucking it under her arm. She then grabbed a broom, utility knife and a roll of duct tape from the garage before returning to the scene of the crime.

"Did you hear me, Missy?"

Melissa held the broom out in front of her. Jesse didn't take the bait. The day was wearing on her and she was quickly losing her patience. "I heard you, Jesse. For now, I just want to cover this window so that all the heat doesn't get sucked out of that hole. Then we can discuss whether or not to call the cops."

Jesse leaned against the island. "There's nothing to discuss. If we let whoever did this get away with it, they'll do it again. And again. And again. We need to find out who did it and why."

"Jesse, *please!*" She wasn't proud of herself for yelling, but she'd had enough arguing going on inside her head all day and didn't want to continue another fight with Jesse. "Can you *please* just let it be? I'm totally drained from my visit with Becky today and cannot deal with this town's faux police force." She took one step down and leaned around the door jamb so he could see her. "It'll be just like that time kids were keying cars up and down the block. Did they ever catch anyone? No. They did their canvassing, came up with nothing, then pretty much ignored all of our phone calls until our frustration dissipated. The same thing will happen this time and I don't have the patience for it." She sighed and continued down the steps. "I just don't."

Jesse shook his head, took off his coat and hung it in the hall closet. "I don't agree, but it doesn't look like I'm going to change your mind, so I'll stop." He picked up his satchel and walked into the living room. "I have to finish up some work anyway."

"Gee, thanks for your help," she said quietly enough so only she could hear her sarcasm. "I'll take care of the mess."

She threw her tools onto the floor, grabbed the utility knife and started to cut the tarp so it would fit over the window's gaping hole. Before anything else, she needed to make sure that nothing from the outside world could get in.

* * *

It took less than an hour for Melissa to cover the window and finish sweeping up the pieces of broken glass from the floor. When she was done, she looked around the room, feeling a faint sense of pride in how well she'd coped with the situation. Jesse might not agree; she hadn't heard a peep from anywhere inside since she and Jesse had their disagreement. She knew he was angry but right now she wasn't going to focus on that. It was up to her to get the house back to normal for both their sakes, and if she had to do it alone, so be it. Besides the broken window, cracked floor and dented freezer door, everything looked just like it did before she'd left to go to the Madsens'.

Except, of course, for the rock still sitting in the corner of the room. She'd swept on all sides of it, even wiped the floor around it, without once touching or moving it. It represented malevolence, something evil that had entered their home without permission, and she feared contagion if she touched it. For a moment she considered asking Jesse to get rid of it, but she figured he was curled up on the sofa trying to sleep off their argument. She was on her own.

She grabbed the yellow Playtex gloves from the cabinet beneath the utility sink and slipped them slowly onto each finger. Her breath was shallow as she bent down and lifted the rock with both hands, examining its shape, its light gray color with the shiny minerals causing it to sparkle in certain light. It wasn't as heavy as she'd imagined, but it was dense and weighty enough for her to speculate that only a man would have the strength to toss a stone like this through their window. The thought made her shudder, but not as much as what she saw when she turned the rock over. In crude block letters written in black marker was one word:

MURDERER.

* * *

The message on the rock had pushed Melissa so close to the edge that she thought she'd go over. But she couldn't, at least not yet. She had to take care of Jesse who collapsed backward against the kitchen wall when she showed him the rock. He had slid to the floor, where he still sat, holding his face in his hands.

She slid down next to him and massaged his icy hands in hers. "We'll get security cameras," she said, trying to get him to look at her and not the rock. "They can't do this to people. And why use that word? What does that even mean?"

Jesse nodded without looking up or uttering a word.

It seemed to her that *he* was the one who had gone over the edge, pushed by the assault on their house and their peace of mind. There was no doubt he had changed. Two weeks ago, it would've been *Jesse* comforting *her*, hugging her close and making her feel safe the way he'd always done over the past fifteen years. It would have been Jesse saying it was silly to involve the police in a minor act of vandalism. But now, it was Melissa doing the comforting, and it wasn't going well. It was more apparent than ever: Jesse needed psychiatric help.

Although Melissa initially hadn't wanted to involve the police, not for some stupid kid breaking a window, she changed her mind when she saw MURDERER scrawled on the bottom of the rock. She dialed Detective Washington's direct number, told her what happened and asked if she could come to the house as soon as possible. The detective immediately agreed. There was something more going on here than pure vandalism, and since she and Jesse had spent so much time with Detective Washington and her partner since Danny's disappearance, Melissa knew she'd be more than happy to help, especially if it might have ties to Danny.

"Washington and Daniels are on their way," she told Jesse, her tone like a mother reassuring her son that his father was coming home to take care of the bully down the street. "They said maybe Rivera will show, too, if he thinks it could be tied to Danny somehow. They should be here in a few minutes."

"Tied to Danny somehow? So, you think Becky's right? You think he's dead."

Melissa winced, his question more an accusation than an inquiry.

"No," she said quickly, then added, "not necessarily, anyway. But he could be, right? Maybe even probably? What do you think?"

He shook his head, obviously bothered. "I can't say, honey. But a rock that says MURDERER getting thrown through the window of the people closest to Danny's family seems like an awfully big coincidence. Maybe some crazy asshole, like that racist guy at the news conference a couple weeks back; maybe they think Becky and Don did something to their own son and mistook our house for their house."

"Is that what you really think happened?" She was trying to reassure him after his reaction to the stark message, but she wouldn't mind a little reassurance, too.

"I don't know," he said, sounding a million miles away. "But it didn't just say MURDER. It said MURDERER. Somebody's making an accusation. Who, we don't know. What the accusation is, exactly, we don't know. And who's being accused, we don't even know that."

Melissa glanced out the kitchen window. Dusk was approaching and she felt a chill crawl up her spine. Jesse was starting to rock back and forth. Why in the hell would someone do this to them, to *him?* Her husband had never hurt anyone in his life.

With Jesse swaying on the kitchen floor, not really there, Melissa felt more alone than she had since that horrible day her father was found in his car, parked in his reserved space at his office building's lot, dead of a heart attack at 49. When she'd arrived at her parents' house to console her mother, she found her in almost the same condition as Jesse, rocking silently, forward and backward, in the corner of the bedroom. Today, like that day twenty-some-odd years ago, she'd have to push aside her panic and take charge. There was no place to hide and no one else to do the job.

"Jesse." She gently gripped his arm. "Tell me, what's going on? Why did you collapse like that?" Silence. She glanced around the room as though the walls would utter the words she needed to make things right. "Honey, I'm scared, too, but we have to try to keep calm and think logically."

Jesse lifted his head. His eyes held a glazed expression, his face almost torn. "I don't know..." His voice quivered and he swallowed. "I don't know what happened. When I saw the note, it was like...like..."

Melissa grabbed his hand. "Like what, Jesse? Like what?"

He shook his head. "Like déjà vu, almost. Like I'd dreamed this whole thing before. I can't explain it." Jesse looked around the room, seemingly trying to get control over his spinning thoughts. "I'm sorry, Missy. I really am. I don't know what happened."

She cradled his head and pulled him toward her chest. "Don't apologize, Jesse. We're going to get you some help. I know it's not what you want, but we have to do something." She could hear his slow breath and feel its warmth on her neck. He wasn't arguing. That was a good sign. "Once the police leave, we'll make a drink, try to calm down and talk about next steps, okay?"

"Maybe I should get the gun out of the safe," Jesse whispered.

His voice was so soft Melissa could barely hear him, but she caught the word "gun." He'd bought the revolver four years ago, after a number of home invasions in the neighborhood, despite the fact that she'd fought him tooth and nail. He wouldn't capitulate: "Your life is too important to me," he'd said. She finally agreed after making him promise that it would stay in a gun safe in the back corner of the attic. They hadn't discussed the gun, nor had she seen it, since the day he brought it home and put it away four years ago. It surprised her that he mentioned it at all.

"No, Jesse. No gun." She shook her head. "It stays in the safe. You promised."

"It doesn't do us any good in the safe when we're in imminent danger. Our home is under assault, *we're* under assault. Plus…" He paused.

"Plus what?"

He didn't answer.

"Plus *what,* damn it?"

He let out a breath. "*Plus,* if anything bad *did* happen to Danny...I mean, if it ends up that... I mean, if we find out that someone really did murder him, I'm not holding back. *Whoever killed Danny is going to pay with his life.*"

Anxiety gripped her throat; for a moment, she wasn't sure she'd be able to breathe. She forced herself to take a breath and slowly exhaled to try to help calm the panic that was rising again. "What are you telling me, Jesse? You're going to become a vigilante and use your gun, the one you *promised* to keep hidden, and shoot someone? Kill them in cold blood? Is that what you're telling me?"

Before Jesse had a chance to respond, the doorbell rang, causing them both to jump.

"We'll talk about this later," she said. "Unless you want me to bring it up with the police."

He shook his head. "No need to get crabby about it. I'm just concerned, all right? I'm worried. And, just...I'm at my wits end and I'm babbling—"

"—like a fool," she said with a forgiving smile. She kissed him on the forehead. "Now, please go let them in. If we can't figure out what the hell is going on here, I'll be babbling right along with you."

* * *

Melissa felt nothing but silence and tension.

Although Rivera hid it well, she could still see the suspicion in his eyes. He leaned against the sink, his long black coat draped over his left arm, the rock grasped in his right hand. Without once looking at Melissa and Jesse, he analyzed the rock from all possible angles before finally placing it atop the granite counter. He folded his arms so tightly, it looked as though he was hugging his coat so that no one would steal it from him.

"I thought Detectives Washington and Daniels were coming," she said, her eyes darting out the kitchen window.

Rivera hugged his coat a bit tighter. "They were called out to follow up on a lead. I was on my way to the Madsens', so I figured I'd stop by here first and—"

Jesse's eyes widened and he spoke his first words since Rivera arrived. "Is there news about Danny?"

Rivera hesitated and peered around the room. Melissa observed him carefully. *There's that suspicion again.* She held herself back from calling him out on it.

"No. Unfortunately, no news." He cocked his head toward the rock on the counter and then looked to the floor. "But this act of vandalism concerns me."

With the tension growing thicker, Melissa sighed.

"Please say what you're thinking, Agent. I hope you know by now that you can be honest with us."

Rivera grimaced. "Well…why would someone take the time and effort to call you, either of you, a murderer? Has someone been harassing you? Might you know who did this, if you think about it hard enough?"

"Agent," Melissa started, "please tell me you're not even considering that Jesse or I had anything to do with…"

"With…? With what?" His voice was expressionless, exactly as it would be if he were conducting an interrogation.

"With Danny, for God's sake! What else would I be talking about?"

"But the note said 'murderer,' Melissa, not 'kidnapper.' Are you saying that Danny is dead? Do you both know something you're not telling me?"

Melissa felt lightheaded. She backed up against the cabinet and swept away the wisps of hair hanging in front of her eyes.

"She's not saying she knows Danny is dead, or alive, or anything!" Jesse said firmly. He reached around her waist and held her against him. "I mean, what else *could* that mean? She's wondering—and, frankly, I am, too—why there's an air of accusation around everything you're saying. As though we had something to do with Danny's disappearance."

"I'm sorry you hear accusation in my voice, Jesse. It's been a long day. Maybe my words didn't come out the way I intended. It's just odd that we have a boy from up the block missing for weeks now, no sign of him, and at the same time, a rock is thrown through your window by someone who claims one or both of you is a murderer. Do you not find that…a coincidence?"

"Jesus, Agent." Melissa had to work to keep her voice even. "You know how much we love Danny. And how much we love Becky and Don. You've watched us cry and suffer and feel their pain day in and day out. What's wrong with you?" She didn't even realize she was crying until she felt the tear run down her cheek. She swiped it away with such disregard her fingernail scratched her face. "And why the hell would I have called you tonight if we were hiding something? For God's sake, take your distrustful cop hat off for half a second and think like a logical human being."

"I apologize, Melissa," Rivera half-whispered as though in need of clearing his throat, then found his voice again. "But my job here is not to avoid unpleasantness or to make you or your husband feel comfortable. My job is to find out what happened to Danny

Madsen and, if possible, bring him home. I will investigate any lead—
every lead—until that is accomplished. So, I'm sorry it includes putting
you under the microscope, but you should understand that this
shows how serious I am about finding your godson."

Soberly, Melissa said, "Of course."

"And the psychology of why people who commit crimes call
the police to attract attention to themselves fills entire books. I don't
think you did anything or even know anything about what's
happened to Danny, but a guilty mind can force all sorts of behaviors
that seem to make no sense at all from the outside. Okay? That's all."

"Okay, Agent. Sorry for losing my cool," Jesse said, and put
out his hand.

Rivera shook it with a reassuring smile. "Totally
understandable, Mr. Carlton." He wrote down a few notes and
slipped his notebook back into his coat pocket. "I don't have the
resources right now to start an investigation into a rock thrown
through a window. But I will write up a report tonight and leave it
with the officer in charge. She'll send a team out here tomorrow
when it's light to check around the house, canvas the neighborhood
and see if they can find anything that might help make some sense of
all this." He started toward the front door, gliding his hand along the
rock as he passed it by. "It's the note that has me stumped, and
you're going to have to help me with that."

Melissa said nothing. She watched Jesse walk Rivera to the front door, reach for the knob and stop before turning it. He looked straight into Rivera's eyes. "It has us stumped, too, Agent. And it doesn't make us feel very safe in our own home."

Rivera patted Jesse on the shoulder. "I'll have a squad car stay around the neighborhood tonight. I really don't think you need to be concerned, but a few extra men in blue can't hurt."

"No, it can't," Jesse said with a grimace and opened the door. "Thank you for coming by."

Once Jesse shut the door, Melissa met him halfway down the hallway, where she wrapped her arms around him. She closed her eyes and breathed in the scent of his skin. She kissed his neck, hoping it would help bring back the man she'd fallen in love with. As though he'd been hit with a jolt of electricity, his head jerked back, and entire body became rigid.

He pulled away and walked into the kitchen. "I feel like drinking. A lot."

She didn't answer, knowing there wasn't enough liquor in the world to warm the blood that now ran like ice through her veins.

9

It took ten straight days of Melissa pleading with Jesse to talk with a psychiatrist before he finally gave in.

"He's one of the best trauma counselors and therapists around," she'd said from the opposite end of the living room sofa, her feet on the coffee table and legs bent holding her tablet. Jesse continued pretending to read the newspaper. "Manny said Dr. Bradley helped his wife Alexandra through one of the most difficult periods of her life. He supposedly helped save her life."

Jesse folded the paper and tossed it onto the side table. He shifted so he could stretch his legs across the sofa and knead Melissa's thigh with his sock-covered feet.

"I don't need my life saved, Missy. I just need some time. It's really not that long since the accident. The doc says it takes time for things to get back to normal." He leaned his head back onto the sofa arm. "And spring is finally showing up. Soon we'll be able to open the windows, get some fresh air in here and maybe even get away for a few days."

Melissa continued to look down at her tablet without saying a word. He could tell she was holding her tongue and decided that wasn't such a bad thing. He really didn't want to know what she was thinking.

"You're not the same," Melissa blurted out. It was something she'd been wanting to say for weeks but couldn't find the nerve until now. "And since the rock was thrown through the window, you've gotten even worse."

He sidestepped. "Well, maybe that's because they never found out who did it. It's like Rivera didn't really give a shit. I wonder if he told Becky and Don about the note. There was no way *I* was going to say anything to Don—"

"Damn it, Jesse! Don't change the subject. I'm talking about *you* right now!" She turned to look out the floor-to-ceiling living room windows. He could hear the struggle in her voice to hold back tears. She took a breath. "You know you've been different," her voice had softened as she peered into his eyes, "since the night of the accident. You know that, don't you?"

He stopped tapping his feet against her thigh. She was right. He wasn't the same. How could he be when every time he closed his eyes trying to remember that night he'd see nothing but a black, empty space? Or when his eyes jolted open at 3:00 every morning he'd be lying in sweat with the panicked sense that everything was closing in on him?

It was easier to deal with the emotions during the day, pushing them aside and shoving them beneath the responsibilities of work. It was when he'd lie down to go to sleep at night that was most frightening and caused a cold terror to run through him, the time when abstract thoughts and feelings would scream through the shadows, erasing the quiet and stillness of the darkness. Every night while getting ready for bed he'd wish for the slumber ahead to be different, that he'd wake up feeling just a bit more content and refreshed. So far it hadn't happened, and like Melissa, he was getting concerned, but he thought time was going to be his savior. Just a little more time.

The Xanax their GP had prescribed helped take the edge off the anxiety and allowed him to breathe easier, but the overarching problem remained: he still had the constant fear that he was losing something every day, a piece of his mind vanishing, fragments of consciousness falling away bit by bit. It all started with the inability to remember the moments leading up to his car accident. But now the anxiety of memory loss would spike into a panic attack, then fall back to the baseline dread. The constant churning of this emotional cycle was taking its toll.

"Yes, I know I'm not the same," he answered. "Maybe something got loosened up in my brain and needs time to get back to where it belongs. Honestly, I'm just a little off, that's all. Think about it—wouldn't it actually be weirder *not* to feel out of sorts with God knows what having happened to the child of our closest friends? Really, I'd like to hold off just another month or so. I really think the extra time would be—"

"Have you been on a scale lately, Jesse?" Melissa said to cut him off. "I don't even need to see what it says to know you've lost about fifteen pounds."

"Well, you did say my belly was getting a little mushy…"

"This isn't funny, Jesse." She swatted at his legs. "Something's not right. And since all the specialists have given you a clean bill of health, it means there's a psychological issue going on and you need to talk with someone. Otherwise I'm scared things are just going to get worse."

"And if I don't?" he tested her.

Without any emotion, as though he'd asked her what she planned to wear to work tomorrow, she responded. "Would you rather go through this alone?"

Jesse twisted onto his back and looked at her. She wouldn't return the glance and continued to tap on the tablet. He kept staring. Nothing. He felt a sharp wave of panic and took a deep breath. Melissa had tried time and again to talk with him about the night of the accident, but time and again he refused, trying to convince them both that when it was time for his memory to return, it would. But something held him back; a door slammed shut, not allowing his brain to do its job and recollect what had happened that night. Yet in spite of his silence she'd stood beside him, giving him a sense of security and comfort that up until now he never realized could be in jeopardy. *I can't make it through this without her.*

"Okay, fine. I'll go." Jesse surrendered and waited for the smile. Once it appeared, he was able to breathe again.

"Thank you," Melissa said, now hugging his feet. "You want me to go to the intake session with you, kinda give you some backup if you forget what to mention?"

He didn't even need to think about it—plus he knew it would make her happy to be there, and this was about *them*, not just him. Yes, he was the one with the memory issue and anxiety, but he wanted her to know they were a team, no matter what. "That would be great."

"Oh, good. If I'm there, I can make it easier for you to get a feel for what Dr. Bradley is like without worrying about forgetting anything. It's important you like the person you're going to talk with, or at least feel comfortable with him. And according to Manny, you will."

* * *

Based on the first three minutes in Dr. Bradley's office, Manny couldn't have been more wrong.

Jesse didn't like Dr. Bradley. He didn't like how hard the man tried to hide his Boston accent or how his full head of black hair, sliding into a gray, stubbly beard made him look like an aging Hollywood hunk. He didn't like how close together his small, beady eyes appeared or the bump on the bridge of his otherwise perfectly shaped nose. Most of all, he didn't like the fact that this South End, know-it-all, pretentious psychiatrist was going to try to dig into the recesses of his mind.

"Jesse?" the psychotherapist asked from the high-back chair positioned across from the sofa in which he and Melissa sat. "You still with us?"

Jesse turned to Melissa, then back to him, and nodded. "Yeah, of course, Dr. Bradley. Why would you ask that?"

"Please feel free to call me Roger."

Please feel free to stick your fake intimacy up your ass, Jesse thought, but said out loud, "Okay, *Roger*, why would you ask that?"

"Well, I just asked you if this is a convenient time of day for future visits or if afternoons are better. You didn't respond, so I figured you were thinking about something else."

Jesse took a deep breath and exhaled loudly. "I had to think for a second. I don't have my calendar implanted in my head. That's not a problem, is it?"

Dr. Bradley leaned back in his chair and wrote something on his pad. "Of course not, no."

It better not be, for two hundred dollars an hour. Jesse nodded noncommittally.

Roger smiled and placed his pad on the table between them. "I get it, Jesse. I do. Many people don't want to be here at first, and that can be for lots of reasons. I've personally had intake sessions where the client told me later they didn't think they really liked me, or the whole time we were talking they were thinking how they couldn't wait to get out of here and tell the world that they were never coming back."

If Melissa weren't sitting right next to him, Jesse would've sworn she was reading the doctor his lines through a hidden earpiece. She was the only one who knew him this well, and to hear these words coming from someone he'd just met was unsettling to say the least. But he wasn't even talking about *him*—he was talking about "people." Meaning maybe Jesse wasn't as hopeless a cause as he himself had assumed.

"I'm not really..." Jesse started. Melissa squeezed his hand again.

Roger said in a soothing tone, "You don't have to like me from the start. In fact, for the therapeutic relationship, you never have to *like* me or think of me as a friend. But for me to help you, I will ask you to *trust* me. I'm a medical doctor, a psychiatrist, as well as a psychological therapist. You don't have to want to hang out with your doctor, but you do have to accept that what a doctor does is trustworthy, at least as it relates to your plan of treatment. It's also important you know that whatever we do is done for your benefit only, not for the doctor's and not for the patient's spouse—at least not directly. Everything we will do in here is to help you and only you. Does that make sense?"

"You're good," Jesse smiled, his mind blown by his inner reaction to this semi-stranger. In less than forty-five seconds, Dr. Bradley—no, *Roger*, he would call him Roger—had managed to quell Jesse's anxiety and vaporize the anger he'd felt when he'd entered the office. He turned to Melissa, who hadn't said a word since they entered the office, and almost laughed aloud at the wide-eyed expression on her face. It was obvious she had warmed up to Roger as quickly as Jesse had. "Let's get started."

"I'm glad to hear you say that, but allow me to tell you a little more about the work I do. I use a customized form of Cognitive Behavior Therapy, or CBT. I deal with the here and now, what's going on today. Unless I feel it's required, I don't delve into your childhood trying to find the unconscious reasons for why you don't like a certain movie or you're overly attached to a blue blankie. CBT has been found to help you understand that *you* are in charge of what you feel and how you think."

Jesse let out a little laugh. "I don't feel in control *at all.*"

Roger laughed, too and said, "No...but you will. I'm not saying for a second that loss of memory or what have you are what a person would consciously *choose*. No, CBT helps its users break old habits that are keeping them from being as psychologically healthy as they can be. Anger, fear, guilt—we can work on all of these, and I have had more clients than I can count really get in touch with what's going on in their own minds. And change it, if they decide it needs changing. There are other avenues we can take if we find we're not making progress as quickly as we'd like, but I think it's the best place to start." He sat back in his chair and let out a big breath of air with a smile. "Okay, I'm done."

Melissa and Jesse sat still, awaiting whatever was to come next.

Roger grabbed his pad and reclined into his chair. "Okay, great. Now..." he looked at Melissa and studied her face for a few seconds. "Melissa, as I said on the phone the other day, unless I'm working with a couple on their relationship, partners typically aren't part of the initial session. However, I do feel this is a special situation, so while you're here I'd like to ask you a few questions. Is that okay?"

"Of course," she responded.

"Can you tell me why you called me to schedule this appointment rather than having Jesse call?" She squirmed a bit before crossing her legs. "By the way," Roger continued, "please know that is a question, not an accusation."

"Of course," she said again. "I called for two reasons. First, I was the one who talked to Manny Jacobson about you, so I felt you and I had a connection of some kind."

"I see. And second?" Roger asked, his expression exhibiting a silent knowledge of what was coming next.

Melissa looked at her hand holding Jesse's. "I wasn't sure Jesse would call."

"And if he hadn't called, how would you have reacted to that?"

"I guess I would've thought he was either too scared to call...or that he didn't think he needed help."

"I don't know if that's fair," Jesse interjected. "I mean, I *did* agree that I needed some help and that we should meet."

"No one's saying anything about your mindset with this. I pushed Melissa to answer because I wanted to know *her* attitude toward you coming here," Roger said, in a voice so calm it seemed he was almost whispering. "I just wanted you to think for a moment about whether it was mainly Melissa who wanted you to seek help or whether you wanted to be here."

Jesse was ready to disagree but the therapist beat him to the punch. "Okay, not that you *wanted* to be here, but that you felt it was *important* to be here."

The little joke relaxed them all and Jesse could tell Roger was someone he could work with. He stretched his arm along the sofa and let it rest behind Melissa's neck. She gave him a smile that told him she felt comfortable as well. The fact that he admitted to needing help gave him a glimmer of hope that talking with Roger could be the first step toward finding a piece of the person he'd been before the accident.

"So...what now?" Melissa asked.

"Now—if Jesse would like—he and I can get to know each other a little bit. How do you feel about that, Jesse?"

He felt good about it, and said so. "Should Melissa hang out in the waiting room?"

"That would probably be most helpful, if you're both okay with that."

They were. Whatever needed to be done, whatever Melissa needed him to do, Jesse told himself, he would do.

* * *

A few minutes into their session alone, Roger asked Jesse, "Why do you think you knew and then lost the memory of something in the accident?"

"Well...it feels like it?"

With a warm smile, Roger said, "Jesse, are you telling me it feels like it, or asking me? Of course, I know you're telling me, but don't feel that you have to blunt your statements here. Don't hold back, if you can do that, okay?" At Jesse's agreement, he went on. "Can you tell me about this feeling? What does it actually *feel* like?"

138

"Like something happened. Something that could help find Danny."

"I understand, but what I want you to do is tell me what it *feels like*. What signals are your body giving you that create this feeling?"

Jesse's throat tightened slightly and a few pinpricks of sweat formed on his forehead. What did his *body* feel like? Why the hell would *that* matter? Still, Roger was the doctor, so Jesse did his best to answer the strange question. "Um…the *feeling* is like my brain is cloudy in places. I mean, when I try to remember what happened that night on the road, it's like there's just nothing there. Like, you know when someone asks you a trivia question and you know the answer is somewhere in there, you just can't find it?"

"Yes, unfortunately," Roger said with a self-deprecating smile.

Jesse smiled back, but it wasn't because he was amused or feeling good. It was the kind of smile you gave a bully to keep him from beating you up, a nervous expression of desperation. But the doctor wasn't trying to beat him up or do anything but help him. Then why did he feel like he was swimming in a pool full of sharks?

"Jesse? Are you all right?"

"Sorry, yeah, I'm good," he said without meaning it, and continued, "Well, that's what I'm *feeling*. It's not like I just don't know or plain can't remember something that definitely happened, like what I had for breakfast last Tuesday. It's like I *do* know it, *I do* remember it, but I can't get at it through the cloud."

Roger scribbled another note, this one slightly longer than the first. God, Jesse wondered what he was writing. Maybe *CRAZY PERSON*. "Just a second." He stood and walked to his desk in the corner, where several folders lay. He opened one and brought it back with him to his chair, still reading as he sat down. He looked perplexed. "Jesse, I have your neuro exam results here. You didn't actually suffer any head trauma in the accident. Of course, your head was rocked back by the airbag inflating—but the airbag inflating is exactly what kept you from major head trauma."

"Well, no…but…" *Had* the doctors actually said the word "concussion" or did he and Melissa just assume that's what it was? "So, I didn't actually have memory loss?"

Roger looked up from the folder and immediately set it on an end table next to his chair. "No, not at all, let me be really clear about that, okay?"

This was weird. "Okay."

"What I *am* proposing—and I haven't done any kind of physical evaluation—is that the memory loss isn't from a *physical* trauma. Also, you should be open to the idea that there is no real memory loss, in that a physical memory was formed but then 'shaken loose,' if you will, by the shock of the crash."

"So…I'm crazy."

Roger smiled again, but his words were serious. "*No.* You seem mentally 'with it,' not 'crazy' in the slightest. And anterior retrograde amnesia—that's doctor-speak for short-term memory loss—from a *psychological* trauma is just as common, if not more so, than from a physical injury. That would also explain why you feel like something is blocking your memory of what happened. Because, if I'm right, something is doing exactly that."

"So, you're saying something happened that was so terrible, my brain won't let me remember it?"

"It's more subtle and complicated than that, but essentially, yes." Roger stood again and walked around the desk, pulled open a file drawer and took out what looked from the back like a photocopied list of some kind. "At this juncture, I feel your situation falls within the dissociative amnesia category, not any specific kind of mental illness or defect. Just the emotions associated with being in such a bad accident can spur a memory loss like this, and possibly others going forward."

Jesse winced from the feeling of an imaginary spider crawling up the back of his neck. "What do you mean 'possibly others going forward'? Am I going to start forgetting more things?"

"Please note the word "possibly", Jesse." Roger tapped his temple with the page corner of the photocopied list. "It's important to remember that dissociation falls on a continuum of severity. Think about when you get lost in a great book or drive down a familiar stretch of road and don't remember the last few miles. That's what I would call a mild form of dissociation. Midway on the spectrum would be dissociative symptoms that might display themselves as quote "stepping out of your body" and performing actions that deviate from your typical personality. A more severe form of this process might be something like Multiple Personality Disorder, which I'm sure needs no explanation."

"No, I've seen the movies," Jesse quipped. "So where am *I* on this 'continuum'?"

"Since this is our first session, I can't and won't make a definitive judgment. However, based on what I know, heard, read and seen so far, I'd say you're at the mild end of the spectrum."

Jesse let out a sigh of relief.

"For now, let's agree not to focus on what *could* be or what *might* happen. Let's also not frame this memory blockage in mental illness terms. If it turns out however that there *is* a psychopathic component to the problem, we have many ways to work with that as well, okay?"

"Of course, yes, yeah," Jesse said, but kept his eyes on the paper Roger held as he retook his seat. "What's that?"

"You've heard of word association, where someone says a word and then you say the very first word that comes to mind, no matter how irrelevant or silly it may seem?"

"Sure, everybody has, I think. But shouldn't I be lying down on a leather couch or something? This seems like a very shrinky kind of thing to do—sorry, no offense."

Roger laughed and said, "None taken. I like movies as much as the next guy, but they don't quite have their finger on the pulse of modern psychotherapy. That said, word association is an old tool, but one that often gives good results as a first attempt to access a patient's subconscious. And the subconscious is exactly where I think your lost memory is located…again, *if* there is any memory that's been lost."

"Okay, sounds good. Word me, doctor." They both smiled at that.

"All right. Keep your eyes open or closed, it doesn't matter for this exercise. I'll say a word and then you respond with the *first* word, no matter what, that enters your mind. All right?"

"Sounds good." Jesse leaned forward as though waiting for his number to be called at the deli counter.

"*Mother.*"

"Dead."

"*Father.*"

"Dead."

"*Head.*"

"Injury."

"*Water.*"

"Ice."

"*Hunger.*"

"Devour." *That's a weird response,* Jesse thought. *Oh, well.*

"*To part.*"

"Let go."

"*Pencil.*"

"School."

"*Dead.*"

"Danny. I mean, he's not d—"

"Don't worry about explaining. This is just what's in your head, so no wrong answers. Now: *Child.*"

"Danny."

"Okay, one more. *Sad.*"

Jesse froze. The word that came to his mind immediately was, once again, *Danny*. But this was getting ridiculous. Finally, he said, "Worried."

"Okay, very good, Jesse. Now, just a little bit more for this session—"

"Wait, Roger, what does that mean?"

The doctor looked puzzled. "I'm sorry, Jesse—what does what mean?"

"My answers. Danny, Danny, Danny. I think I might seem a little obsessed with Danny."

"Who wouldn't be, in your situation?" Roger put down the photocopied list, which Jesse had noticed he hadn't written any of his responses on, and bent forward slightly to meet his eyes. "Remember that the responses don't mean anything by themselves, Jesse. It doesn't take a psychologist to know that what might have happened with your best friend's son is first and foremost in your mind. I wouldn't have been surprised if you had answered 'sad' with 'Danny' as well."

"I actually was going to. That *was* the first thing that came into my head. But I didn't want to say it again. I feel…" He trailed off.

"How does that make you feel, Jesse? If you're comfortable telling me, I would like to know."

"I feel…guilty."

Roger kept his eyes fixed on Jesse's, blinking slowly and thoughtfully every two seconds or so. It was relaxing to look into them, which was no doubt the point of Roger doing it. Finally, the doctor said, "Feeling guilt when something bad happens is very common. But ninety-nine times out of a hundred, the person feeling it had nothing to do with anything even remotely associated with the event. Heck, many people feel guilty for 'letting' their loved ones get on an airplane that then crashes, even if they are a thousand miles away. Feeling guilty is okay, Jesse. It means you care."

10

Eight weeks, Charles Hastings thought as he sat in his van a couple of houses down from where Jesse Carlton lived. *Two months and this son of a bitch hasn't come forward. What's it gonna take for this guy to fess up already?*

Charles was getting more impatient by the day but knew that the action he was about to take would completely change things for the better. This morning was the vigil at Danny's school marking two months since his disappearance. The local Boston news stations had gone into detail about the event and Charles decided this would be the perfect opportunity to get the police to connect the dots between Danny and Jesse.

It was time to use the "emergency" stash he'd been hiding in the toolbox to his advantage. If being caught red-handed with Danny's bloodstained personal items didn't make the bastard confess, nothing would.

Charles rolled his eyes. Just about everyone responsible for Danny's death would be attending the vigil. Not only Jesse Carlton and his wife, but Danny's inattentive parents as well. The school's teachers and principal, the aides and even the boy's fellow students. They'd all let Danny down. If they'd only paid more attention to him and loved him more, Charles would never have needed to intervene and take him home. He pitied the boy and despised his family and so-called friends. Their obvious lack of care had resulted in Danny's death and Charles could do nothing but shake his head.

A bead of sweat rolled down his forehead and he cracked the driver's side window ever so slightly. He glanced in all mirrors and out each window as he waited for the couple to leave. The scene couldn't have been more perfect: the whole block deserted as everyone headed to the school so they could show their support for the Madsens. Charles pursed his lips and chuckled, thrilled that this chance had arrived and proud of himself for being smart enough to keep Danny's clothes.

His smile fell away when he saw the Madsens' Lexus LS pull up in front of the Carlton's house. In the front sat Don and Becky, who he'd seen on television displaying, as the newscasters had called it, "great bravery in the face of such tragedy." That was how the media was framing Danny's disappearance now: as a tragedy. Finally, after eight weeks, everyone appeared to be coming to the correct conclusion that the boy was dead. And so this vigil was more of a memorial. At long last, people were accepting the fact that Danny was gone for good—and that meant it was the perfect time to turn the heat on Jesse Carlton full blast. Danny's friends and family needed closure and Charles was the one who would give it to them.

Melissa briskly walked out the front door and up to the SUV. She gave Becky a kiss on the cheek through the passenger-side window, said a few words and then climbed into the back seat. After a moment, they drove off. Jesse remained in the house, his shiny new black BMW still sitting in the driveway.

Charles didn't like this at all. But he knew Jesse *had to be* going to the vigil, so he didn't allow himself to panic. Instead, he took in a deep breath through his nose and let it out through his mouth. And then another one. *I don't know what he's pulling, but I can wait him out. I'm a lot smarter than Mister LCKY123.*

* * *

Inside the house, Jesse Carlton cursed himself for his bad time management.

Since the accident, at least at work, he'd become an efficiency dynamo. The deliberate and intense focus helped him to avoid dwelling on Danny and the impact his disappearance was having on his two best friends. The problem was, once he left the office, all of the anguish, fear and guilt would flood him like a tsunami of emotion. There were times, too many times, when Melissa would find him just staring off into space.

Where were you? she'd ask, trying to seem light, but failing.

He'd always answer, truthfully: *I wish I knew.*

And now, as he searched for his keys, he found himself having another confusing and disconnected experience. The keys usually hung on the hook by the kitchen door that was connected to the garage, where he and Melissa always came in and out of the house. But they weren't on the hook or anywhere in the kitchen. His anxiety started to intensify until he remembered that when he got home from work yesterday, he dragged the recycling bin from the side of the house to the curb and then came in the front door.

He walked to the foyer and exhaled a sigh of relief when he saw his keys glistening on the hall table. He shook his head; he had plenty of time before the vigil to pick up his black suit from the dry cleaners. But he was still annoyed at himself. He'd wanted to help set up the vigil at the school with Melissa and the Madsens, but he hadn't managed his time well, again, and had to send them on ahead.

He swiped up the keys…and stopped.

In a silver frame on the table was an 8 x 10 photo of himself, Danny, Melissa, Don and Becky at Danny's tenth birthday party last year. It was one of his favorite photos and the lump in Jesse's throat grew as he gazed at Danny's wide smile exposing a missing front tooth. He remembered calling out "Danny, say Cheez Whiz!" right before the waitress snapped the picture.

A gray wave of sorrow crashed down on Jesse, throwing him into an explosive dizziness that almost made him vomit in the hallway. Agonizing guilt seized his heart —*I care, that's all. It means I care, like Dr. Bradley said*—and he stumbled to the sofa in the living room to fall face down into the plush cushions, barely making it before he blacked out.

When he awoke, he sat up on the sofa, both the nausea and dizziness having evaporated along with his consciousness. But shit— how long was he out? He looked at his watch. *Twenty minutes. Holy crap, it felt more like twenty seconds.* He only had half an hour left to get the hell out of there and pick up his suit at the dry cleaners. Now he'd have to get dressed in the car so he'd be able to get to the vigil a little early and help set up like he'd promised. He had to...Danny deserved no less.

* * *

Charles was very proud of himself for biding his time and waiting. Jesse Carlton had taken *forever* to leave. It was like he was putzing around the house and backyard to purposely torture Charles and make him sweat it out. Yet as agitating as the additional wait had been, he didn't abandon his original plan, constantly reminding himself that he didn't need Jesse to leave early. According to the news, the vigil was going to be two hours long, so Charles just had to be patient because he'd have more than enough time to complete his plan.

After what felt like hours, but was really only fifteen or twenty minutes since the wife left with the Madsens, Jesse finally walked out of the house, pulled the car out of the garage and left. Charles waited prudently for another five minutes before springing into action. He grabbed the garbage bag containing Danny's coat and Nikes and got out of the van.

Keeping his eyes straight ahead, Charles made a beeline to the garage. It was closed now, but he'd been using code grabbers and universal openers for as long as he'd been fixing computers. He had the door lifting open in less than a minute – another reason to pat himself on the back once he got home.

He zipped into the garage and scanned the area for the perfect hiding place. Two BMX mountain bikes hung next to a workbench that seemed fit for a professional carpenter. Tools suspended on brackets neatly lined the wall above the bench. Screws, nails, bolts and other hardware were contained in their individual plastic compartments housed inside an organizer with drawers and labels. Two plastic garbage bins lined with bags stood against the side wall. Garden tools hung on a track of clips that looked as though it had been customized specifically for this particular garage.

Jesus. This asshole probably spent more money organizing his garage than normal people spent on food. Jesse Carlton's priorities were screwed up, no doubt, so much so he thought he could actually get away with murder.

Charles forced the bitter thoughts from his mind; there'd be time for those later. Right now he had to act quickly and not give anything the chance to go wrong.

He needed a place where nobody would see the evidence unless they already knew there was something stashed there.

Right there! He moved to the back right corner of the garage, took the sneakers and coat from the bag and positioned them neatly between the snow blower and bags of ice melt, slightly hidden but easily findable to anyone who was looking for something that shouldn't be there.

When he was satisfied with their placement, he crumpled the garbage bag and made to dash out of the garage before stopping short and almost tripping over his own feet. Would leaving a pair of sneakers and a bloodstained coat be enough to make the cops suspect Carlton? He knew it would, of course it would, but would just suspicion be enough? He stood for a moment inside the garage, trying to think of something else he could do to seal the bastard's fate. He tried to think quickly, every additional second exposing him to more danger.

By the time he got back to the van, started it up and slowly cruised down the street, he felt satisfied. *Mission accomplished,* he thought with what he considered well-earned confidence. Once he was a few blocks away, he pulled out the burner phone he had bought just for this occasion. It was time to call the cops and lead them to the man they'd been trying to track down for the past three weeks.

* * *

Melissa Carlton had never before attended a vigil for a person she loved so dearly and it was not something she ever wanted to do again. While at Boston College she had gone to several candlelight observances mourning fellow students who died from gun violence or suicide, but those were acquaintances at most. She had never watched local and state dignitaries speak about someone she actually knew, someone she had held as a baby. Someone whose absence was sending her husband into a spiral of…

Of what? She asked herself as she drove back home. She glanced at Jesse, who was awake but slumped against the passenger door with his eyes closed. He was in the thrall of his headache, one of the extreme ones he'd suffered since the accident. She thought through every doctor they'd seen and gritted her teeth in frustration. Each one had said there was no serious head injury and simply sent them home to fend for themselves. If there was no brain injury, why would he have blackouts and sometimes just go dead with super-migraines? No one could give them a definitive answer and the mystery was feeding her anxiety like a slow-acting poison.

Goddamn useless doctors. She was glad they had Dr. Bradley, at least. So far he'd been able to keep Jesse from feeling completely alone with his worry and emotional pain about Danny. Jesse had always been a little closer with Danny than she'd been, maybe because he always wanted a son. When Danny was born, there was still hope that they'd have a little one of their own to be like a cousin to him, but after years of trying and thousands of dollars spent on fertility specialists, Jesse realized that Danny was going to be the son he'd never have.

Sometimes she wondered if it wasn't the accident causing Jesse's episodes but more the uncertainty of Danny's existence. Whatever it was, she knew that when they got home, Jesse would need to go upstairs and rest until the intense pain subsided. Fortunately, as terrible as the headaches were, they went away pretty quickly once he'd lie down in the dark and be able to relax his muscles. She figured she'd bury the bulbs they'd bought last week herself and wait for Jesse to feel better before deciding which plants would go into which pots. She'd stay out back and quietly putter around while Jesse recovered from his latest bout with pain.

She pulled into the garage and Jesse opened his bleary eyes. When he sat up and looked at her, the dark rings around them made it appear as though he'd just been pepper-sprayed. He blinked at the sunlight and spoke his first words since asking her to drive and going limp inside the car: "Let's never do that again."

"I know, honey. You need to lie down." She didn't need to phrase it as a question. "You go upstairs and I'll take care of a few things down here and out back. Just breathe out all the bad stuff and try to relax as much as possible. You've been through a lot."

"*We've* been through a lot. But I don't see you collapsing. I wish I could man up."

Melissa closed her eyes and counted slowly to three, breathing in and out with each number. Then she said, "This has *nothing* to do with manliness. Or, wait, maybe it does—and the 'manly' thing to do is take care of your wife. Which you can do by taking care of yourself right now. And stop worrying about being manly."

Jesse smiled. "Okay, okay. Going upstairs. Carlton out."

She smiled, too, as he got out of the car and went inside. He was a good man. She wished to God that Danny was still alive somewhere and would one day soon be coming home. But if he was already dead, then she wished that he'd just be dead and they could go on with their lives. She wanted to smack herself for thinking this, but the day after day pain, both emotional and physical, was slowly becoming unbearable.

She grabbed her cell phone and got out of the car. As she went around the house to the garden, she reminded herself that every day would get a little bit better. For now, though, she would tend the garden, relax a bit and—

No.

God, no.

No, No, NO!

Melissa covered her mouth with both hands, but it was too late to silence a terrified cry. She tried holding the rest of it in with the hope that she hadn't already jolted her husband out of sleep.

On the inside, though, she couldn't stop screaming.

Fragments of ceramic planters were scattered all over the deck, smashed to bits by someone who must have snuck into the yard while they were at the vigil. The pots had been struck so forcefully, there were shards of pottery on the steps leading down into the yard, some on the lawn itself and some reaching as far as the rain gutter almost fifty feet away from where Melissa stood.

She and Jesse had spent the evening before placing the planters and pots along the deck railing so the two of them could have some downtime together getting the backyard ready for summer. It was an annual practice and despite all the recent tragedy and sadness, they'd decided to keep the tradition going. It was one of the easiest ways to help bring some beauty back into their lives. And now that beauty was gone, obliterated by a nameless coward who, for the second time in less than a few weeks, disrupted their lives through a sick and vengeful act.

She glanced around the half-acre lot, watching for movement, looking for any sign of the perpetrator, but she was met with only silence and stillness. She took a few steps across the deck, the terra cotta rubble painful beneath her sneakers as she made her way to the sliding back door. To her relief, it was locked, so maybe whoever did this entered the yard by coming around the house and didn't go inside. *One less thing to worry about.*

She grabbed her phone to call the police—they'd have to take action now that their home had been vandalized *again*. Her fingers trembled as she searched for the police station's number she'd called during the rock incident. When she found it, she walked down the steps to the lawn and was about to press "redial" when she noticed something strange in the flower bed that ran along the length of the deck. She stopped in her tracks, ice pellets filling her veins.

With nothing yet planted, the bed was pure topsoil awaiting its future residents. Melissa stood directly in front of the deck so she could see the flower bed head-on. Once she took it all in, the phone fell from her numb fingers.

Within the flower bed lay a large piece of a broken wooden baseball bat.

But it wasn't just any bat. This was Danny's bat, the one they'd always had hanging on the wall of their garage. Jesse had kept the bat and Danny's catcher's glove and mask in the garage so that Danny could come over at any time and have everything he needed to play. Now, someone had taken the bat from the garage. How? The garage was closed and could only be opened by the remote or with numbers punched into the keypad. And it had been closed when they got home.

How they did it didn't really matter. At this second, what really mattered was why. But she didn't have an answer for that, either.

She was still shaking her head when she noticed that the bat fragment, the section that perfectly framed Danny's name, was pointed at her like an accusing finger. She gasped as she moved closer and the word written on the bat, directly beneath Danny's name, came into focus.

MURDERER.

It was the same message, in the same handwriting, that had been scribbled on the rock thrown through their kitchen window, the message that pushed Jesse so close to the edge she thought she'd lost him for good. And now she was worried that this episode might lead him back to the very same place. It was bad enough that he was about to have to deal with the destruction of his property again— she didn't want him staying up nights analyzing a cryptic message by some faceless lunatic who was somehow getting off by taunting them. She decided that if hiding this message would help him keep moving forward, that was what she would do.

She grabbed the piece of the bat, ran to the back of the yard and threw it deep into the boundary of hedges where she hoped no one could find it. Quickly returning to the flower bed, she stepped into the dirt and rubbed her sneakers back and forth, spreading the soil with both her feet, leaving the bed once again flattened and ready for planting. A wave of panic ran through her as she realized there might've been fingerprints, hair or some sort of traceable DNA on the bat that she just hid, potential evidence that might tell them who was doing this. Did she just throw away their only hope of finding their tormentor? *Holy crap. What did I do?*

The back door creaked open. Jesse stood in the doorway. "Babe? Everything okay?" His voice was choppy and hoarse; clearly she'd awoken him from a deep sleep. He squinted as if the light hurt his eyes. "I heard a yell."

"It's nothing," she said, but it was difficult to hide the wavering of her voice. "Go lie back down. It's nothing, really."

He didn't comply. Instead, he placed his hand above his eyes to shield them from the sun and slowly walked toward her. "Okay, tell me what happened."

She took a deep breath, dreading him seeing the scene for himself, but relieved she'd gotten rid of the accusatory fragment of baseball bat. "Someone broke all the pots we put on the deck."

"What do you mean, broke all the pots?"

"Look," she said, taking a step back and gesturing at the ruined scene. "I don't know. Someone snuck into the backyard and used a baseball bat—*Danny's* bat—to break everything."

Jesse's eyes grew wide despite the sunlight. His mouth fell open slightly.

"Where's the bat?" He almost choked on his words. "Where's Danny's bat?"

Melissa fought hard to hold back tears. "They must have taken it with them. There's nothing left but small pieces, almost splinters of the bat up on the deck." She watched him carefully for some kind of reaction. Did he believe her? "They had to have done this while we were at the vigil. The entire neighborhood was there, so who knows? Maybe everyone's garden was vandalized. Let's not assume it's just us." She paused, her heart leaping into her throat as Jesse stopped at where she'd found the bat lying in the soil. But he didn't linger, thank God. "The thing is, the bat was in the garage. The door was closed when we got home. But maybe they closed it—can you remember? Did you close the garage door when you left?"

Jesse looked lost. "I...I *think* so."

"No, honey! This is important—*did you close it or not?*" She hated having to use a harsh tone with him, especially in his condition, but it would make her feel a lot better if he had left it open. Kids that committed breaking and entering were much scarier than kids who were just vandals and liked to mess with people.

"I closed it," Jesse said with finality. "I remember."

Damn it. Tears burned her eyes and it felt as though the only thing stopping them from falling down her cheeks was what felt like a boulder in her throat. How she wished she could call Becky and Don for help. If this had happened a few months earlier, they'd be at her side within seconds. But it wasn't a few months earlier. It was now; it was today. The last thing she'd ever think of doing was to ask the Madsens for help on the day of their son's vigil.

She shook her head in an effort to push out her emotions and focus on the two things she had to do right then: swallow her tears and call the police. But as she picked up her phone again, she heard a knock at the gate, where two officers were already standing.

She turned back at her husband to see if he was looking too, but he was no longer standing beside her. In the few seconds she had turned the other way, Jesse had collapsed.

* * *

Once Jesse opened his eyes, it took him a couple of seconds before he realized where he was. He saw Melissa standing above him, looking down with worry etched into every feature of her face. He attempted to smile, to show her just a bit of confidence he didn't really feel. She wasn't buying it.

Behind Melissa stood two patrolmen, one who looked like a rookie and another who appeared old enough to be a few weeks away from retirement. Jesse couldn't tell if their expressions displayed concern or irritation, but at that moment he really didn't care. He was dizzy and on the verge of vomiting, so his focus was more about not puking than it was about the mood of these two strangers.

"Let's get you inside, sir," the older cop said as he offered his hand to help him up. "You look white as a sheet. Should we call you an ambulance?"

With the officer's help, Jesse was able to walk to the back door. The movement helped energize him and he could feel his strength returning. Although his head still felt as fuzzy as a bad hangover, as long as he didn't look directly at the bright sky, his nausea seemed to ease up and his legs became steadier.

"I'm okay," he said, trying to break free of the grasping hands. "I just need to sit down for a minute."

As Jesse sat on the sofa with the two cops watching over him, Melissa went to the kitchen to get him a glass of water. He could almost feel the younger cop's glare and the nausea started to resurface. Was this guy here to actually help or to simply go through the motions for the purposes of paperwork and protocol? Jesse was about to question his motives but caught his paranoia in time and bit his tongue.

Melissa returned with the water and handed it to him.

"Just take a sip, Jesse, please. It'll help with the headache. You could be dehydrated."

Jesse obeyed and drank some water which, to his surprise, helped revive him further. Melissa gestured for the officers to sit on the chairs opposite the sofa as she sat down next to Jesse.

"Are you okay?" she asked. "Should I call the doctor? I don't like the way—"

"Missy," he interrupted. "I swear, it was just the migraine. The light was too much. Add to that what those damn punks did and it hit me hard. I'll lie down again once we're done here."

A knock came at the door. The older patrolman answered it and Detectives Washington and Daniels stepped in, greeting everyone solemnly.

Jesse remained seated in fear that standing up would cause his head to throb. "Hello, detectives." He nodded to both cops and tightened his lips. "So, what happened? Who's doing this to us?"

Washington appeared confused. She turned to her partner, who gave the slightest shake of his head to show he was at a loss as well. "I'm sorry, Mr. Carlton—who's doing *what* to you?"

Melissa took her husband's hand.

"The vandalism," he said, his own perplexed expression matching Washington's. "Didn't you get Melissa's call? Wait…do you guys think the vandalism really *does* have something to do with Danny?"

Melissa rubbed Jesse's fingers with her own. "I never made that call, Jesse." She nodded toward the two patrolmen sitting across from them. "They showed up before I had a chance to dial the phone."

"Dispatch received a 911 call," Daniels said carefully, "but it wasn't from Mrs. Carlton. It was someone who called with a tip. This is the first we've heard of any vandalism since the window incident."

Jesse felt his entire body tense up. "A tip? From who? About what? About who broke all our pots with Danny's baseball bat?"

The tension in the room was palpable as all four police officers looked at one another, each with their own confused expression.

"You're not here about the pots," Melissa said. Jesse couldn't determine if she was asking or telling them this fact.

"No, ma'am," Daniels said to her, and then to Jesse continued, "Mr. Carlton, the Crime Stoppers Hotline is anonymous, so we don't know who the caller was other than an adult male who sounded white and had a local accent."

Washington said, "The message lasted less than seven seconds. However, its content was quite clear."

Jesse waited. "And?"

Washington said, "The caller said, 'If you want to know who murdered Danny Madsen, go to 107 Roseto Street.' That's all. Then he hung up."

"That's *our* address," Melissa said vacantly.

Jesse looked toward the ceiling, his eyes darting from one end of the room to the other. *This has to be a dream. No, not a dream. A nightmare. Becky, Don, Melissa, me. We're all trapped in a nightmare that just won't end.*

"We're aware of that, Mrs. Carlton," Washington said. "Do either of you have any idea why someone would accuse you of this?"

Jesse felt a sharp pain slice through the center of his skull, so intense he was sure he was going to pass out again. But Melissa tightened her grip on his hand with her own ice-cold fingers. He looked at the detectives, eyes bleary and nausea surging. "What the hell is going on? Who's doing this to us?"

"I wish we could answer that for you, sir," Daniels said. "Agent Rivera may be able to shed some light on this. He's on his way now."

Great. Just great. Jesse thought back to the last time Rivera was at their house and had put them on the defensive. It was obvious that he and Melissa were on their own with this never-ending nightmare. There was no help coming from anywhere or anyone—not the local police, not even the Madsens.

And definitely not Rivera.

Melissa took a deep breath and said, "About the pots—"

"Please hold that thought, Mrs. Carlton," Detective Washington said as she looked out the front window. "Agent Rivera's here."

11

Rivera kept the engine running as he sat in the Carlton's driveway and examined his surroundings. Other than the open gate leading to the back, nothing appeared out of the ordinary. He shook his head and rubbed his closed eyes with his fingertips.

Shit. Nothing was making sense. When he received the message about the anonymous 911 tip, he immediately realized the caller had referenced the Carlton's address. That fact alone triggered his hunch that this was a setup. But by who? Who the hell was trying to set up Jesse or Melissa or both…and why?

From day one of the investigation into Danny's disappearance, it was clear to him that the Carltons wanted nothing more than to see Danny home safe and sound. His feelings were verified the night he visited them after the rock had been thrown through their window, their words and actions proving innocence beyond a doubt. And now, the same unknown suspect was trying to incriminate them. Rivera's gut clenched. The caller had used the word, "murdered" in his message. That meant whoever was doing this to the Carltons was most likely the criminal who not only took Danny, but also the maniac who killed him.

He was about to shut the engine when his cell phone rang. He took the phone out of his inside jacket pocket. The display read: *Maria.*

"Hey, babe," he said, pushing the speaker button so he wouldn't have to hold the phone to his ear.

"*Mi amor.* How *are* you?"

"Busy. About to step into a meeting. Did you need something?"

"Yes, Antonio. I needed to hear your voice." Silence. "I think it's been about three days and I can't remember what you sound like. Plus, Tonio is asking if he still has a papa."

"Maria…" He pinched the corners of his eyes with his thumb and forefinger. "We've been through this before. Please."

"*Lo siento.* I just miss you."

"I miss you, too. Of *course*, I do. It's just…"

"Is it the Madsen boy?"

"Yes." He wanted to tell her more, but couldn't take the chance of any kind of information leak. He trusted Maria, but his paranoia about phone and vehicle taps wouldn't let him talk any more about the case. "Yes, it's about Danny Madsen."

"You don't sound like it's good news."

"Maria, you know I can't discuss it." Frustration started to kick in and his body tensed up. "I promise to be home for dinner. Tell my boy I love him and I'll see him tonight with a special surprise." *What surprise?* He wanted to slap himself for making such a promise.

"He's going to be thrilled!" Her voice had a much cheerier tone than when he'd first picked up, washing away some of his tension. "And so will I. I'm sorry to bother you. I know you're busy."

"I'm sorry, too. I love you."

"*Te amo,*" she said as he hung up and slid the phone back into his pocket.

He shut off the engine and inhaled deeply. For more than two months he'd put his family on the back burner so he could find a missing ten-year-old boy, driving down from Boston every time a lead came in or a news conference had to be held. He couldn't count the basketball games and teacher conferences he'd missed due to some dead-end tip or hunch from the local detectives, Washington and Daniels.

The goodnight kisses he gave Tonio as he slept had left Rivera empty. He missed the comfort of holding Maria's hand as they strolled the park or talked about the day's events while washing the dishes together. It was the longest eight-plus weeks of his fifteen-year career, and the worst part was that he had nothing to show for it. And now, the 911 call, this "big break," which he received word of by cell phone just as he was finally heading home, once again forced him to put his family on hold.

He pulled himself out of the car, walked to the front door and rang the bell.

Melissa opened the door. "Hello," she said gravely, stepping aside so he could make his way toward the living room.

Rivera saw Washington and Daniels standing on one side of the room and two patrolmen sitting across from Jesse on the other side. He nodded to everyone, an uneasy silence increasing the tension he'd already been feeling before entering the house.

Jesse stood as Rivera entered, extending his hand to shake politely, but then he wobbled on his feet and had to sit down again. "Sorry, Agent, not feeling so good."

"He passed out," the younger patrolman blurted. "Shock at the vandalism, we believe."

"Vandalism?" Rivera said in surprise, looking first at the local officers, then the detectives, and then Jesse and Melissa. "What, again?"

Washington took the lead and described the chronology of events: from the anonymous 911 call to the discovery of vandalism and the subsequent bagging of evidence.

"Agent Rivera," Jesse said after the recap, "you need to find out who is doing this. First the rock with *MURDERER.* Now the pots...and this call to 911." He held his head within his hands and closed his eyes. "You know this is some kind of setup, right? For some reason, a psychopath is trying to make *us* look like..."

Silence.

"Murderers," Melissa said. "Just say it. He's trying to make it look like we hurt Danny. Even *killed* him." Tears welled up in her red-rimmed eyes. "And he does it to our only safe place, our *home.* And to make it worse, he used Danny's bat! It's just not right."

"Let's see the pots," Rivera said. The two patrolmen led him outside and only when they stopped walking did he notice that Washington, Daniels and the Carltons had followed them. "How do you know it was Danny's bat?"

Melissa clasped her hands and he immediately sensed something was off. "I... Well, I saw splinters of wood up... up on the deck," she stuttered. "They looked like pieces of a baseball bat. When I checked the garage, I saw it was missing. Gone."

After a few moments analyzing the scene, he looked at the group of six standing behind him. "So that bat's gone and there wasn't any kind of message left anywhere?" He glanced at the flower bed Melissa had cleaned up. A small splinter of wood lay in the far right corner. The police all looked somewhere else, sheepishly. "You know, like the word, *MURDERER?*" Again, no one made a sound.

"My thought is— a tip comes in saying to go to the Carlton house for information on who might have killed Danny. There's no doubt in my mind this is the same nut who threw a rock through their window with *MURDERER* written on the bottom. It doesn't make sense to me that he wouldn't leave a similar message, don't you think?"

Washington leaned down and gingerly lifted the shard to look under it. "No, sir. No message anywhere."

Melissa slowly shook her head. Then she said, "Actually, there was."

Jesse turned to her, his mouth and eyes wide. His voice rough as if it was difficult to talk, he asked, "What are you saying?"

"Why didn't you tell us this *immediately?*" Washington demanded. "Where is this message?"

Rivera didn't need to add anything, since that was exactly what he was going to ask. But this stirred his confusion even more. What the hell was Melissa thinking? He knew she had nothing to do with the boy's disappearance, so why did she lie?

Her ashen face now flushed with red as she took in everyone's stare. She walked to the back of the yard and disappeared for a few seconds inside the fence of hedges. When she reappeared, she walked slowly toward Rivera and held out the bat as though volunteering a peace offering. "It was in the soil," she muttered. "I threw it out before Jesse could see it."

"*What?*" Jesse stepped back, almost stumbling. Rivera could tell it came out much harsher than he meant it to, but his distress was real. "Why? *Why* would you do that?"

Melissa looked directly at Rivera and pointed to Jesse. "Somebody's trying to drive him crazy! Whoever it is, they know how much Jesse loved Danny, and they're just trying to torture him. Torture *us!*"

After Daniels snapped on a pair of rubber gloves, he grabbed the bat from Melissa and cleared his throat. "Mrs. Carlton, you do know that destruction of evidence is a crime, don't you? The term is 'spoliation.' In spoliation of evidence cases, it's assumed that the evidence consisted of something damaging to the person who destroyed it. Did you try to hide this evidence because there might have been something damaging to you or your husband?"

Rivera rolled his eyes. There was no need for a lesson on criminal justice terms, and though he wasn't technically in charge of the city detectives, he didn't approve of Daniels questioning Melissa in front of all of these people, including her husband. He couldn't prevent it, but he could step in. "Detective, if you don't mind, I'd like to question the Carltons at the station, have it on record. You'd be there, of course."

It worked; Daniels and Washington nodded. "I was surprised, that's all," Daniels said. "Apologies, Mrs. Carlton."

She nodded without looking at him, tears now running down her cheeks. Her husband continued to stare at her.

"Melissa, Jesse, we'll do the interviews later," Rivera said, making sure his expression was one of understanding and not coercion. "I'm really going to need a logical explanation as to why you would throw away such a crucial piece of evidence."

Obviously Melissa regretted what she had done, but her reactions to his statements helped him realize she did what she did to protect her husband. But he had to be sure.

After suggesting the officers sweep the entire area for anything else the vandal might have destroyed, he got close to the Carltons and said quietly, "Melissa, I don't think you had anything to do with any of this. But I have to know: why *did* you try to get rid of the bat? You had to know it would be important in the case. Can you help me understand?"

Sniffing, Melissa looked at her husband. "I was worried about Jesse. I thought it might send him over the edge."

Jesse's reaction wasn't exactly anger, but it was close. "Y-you think I can't handle this? I can't protect you? Us? From some lousy kids with rocks and sticks?"

Except for the rustling of a squirrel thrashing through the bushes, there was silence. Then she said, "No, I don't."

The anguish on Jesse's face brought Rivera back to the times when Maria's sister would stop just short of blaming him for never finding Benji.

"Jesus, Missy," Jesse started, "I can't believe—"

"If it was just kids, then yes, of course, but it's not just that." Melissa's voice sounded choked with unshed tears. "They got into the garage without the opener. That was planned. And they wanted the bat, *Danny's bat,* not only to destroy our planters, but to write *MURDERER* on it. They want to mess with us. I don't know why. But losing Danny is making you lose your mind, too, Jesse. I didn't want them to push you so far that you won't be able to come back."

Jesse didn't respond, but he let her put her head on his shoulder and rocked with her for a bit.

Detective Daniels approached them. "The rest of the outside is clear, sir. Whoever did this did a clean job. I mean, as far as shoe prints and that. The vandalism was messy, obviously."

Rivera used great effort to keep from rolling his eyes again. "What about inside?"

"Inside the house?"

"Detective, for the love of..." His words trailed off into a ragged sigh, then he asked Jesse and Melissa, "Do you mind if they do a quick check inside the house just to make sure it's clear? *Some* investigators find doing so to be relevant." His tone was acid.

"We have nothing to hide," Melissa said confidently before her expression turned sheepish. "Um, I mean, please do whatever you need to do. The garage is where Danny's bat was, so they should probably look in there, too."

"Thank you," Rivera said, clearly annoyed. The owner of the house shouldn't have to tell law enforcement where to look for crucial evidence. They already had enough to contend with. He nodded to Daniels to get on it. "Maybe we can go back inside, too, have a talk about all this?"

After they settled in the living room, Rivera slapped his open notepad absently against his fingers. "I have to admit, right now, I'm at a loss. I'm not required by law to tell you this even once, but I don't consider either of you a suspect in Danny's disappearance or, if he's gone, in his death."

He watched them both let out breaths they apparently had been holding in since he started talking.

"*But* you might know something that you don't even realize you know. I think coming to the station and talking with me on the record might be extremely helpful in figuring out why someone is targeting you like this."

"Should we have…you know…a lawyer present?" Jesse's voice sounded less far away now, but still meek and worried.

"That's your right, of course, but, while I'm not required to tell you that you *aren't* suspects in an investigation, I must by law tell you before questioning whether you are a person of interest or an actual suspect. Again, you are not currently suspects or persons of interest in the Danny Madsen case. In my opinion, you don't need to go to the expense of an attorney, but you should absolutely do so if it helps calm your nerves about things. Remember, you can invoke your Fifth Amendment rights or decide you do want a lawyer present at any time. So, can I question you both tomorrow?"

Jesse and Melissa exchanged looks and nodded, first to each other and then at Rivera, both of them. Melissa offered a faint smile and said, "Thanks for taking this so seriously, Agent Rivera."

"It *is* serious, all of it," he said. "In the meantime, I would highly recommend getting a camera system installed. It's the best way to keep an eye on the exterior of your home and possibly find out who's doing this. The sooner you get it, the better."

"We will," Jesse said. "But could you somehow get a patrol car to pass by once in a while? We need cops checking out our house and this street. There's a lunatic out there and who knows what the hell he's going to do next?"

"I completely understand. I'll ask the locals if they can accommodate you. So, what time might you—" Rivera was interrupted by the doorbell.

"It's Becky and Don," Melissa said with a quick glance out the window. "Please let them in, would you, officer?"

As the older uniformed cop let the Madsens into the house and led them toward the living room, Rivera stood. He shook hands with each of them and said, "I wasn't able to attend the vigil, but I've heard there was a remarkable outpouring of love for Danny. How are you holding up?"

"We hadn't heard from you in a while." Becky's tone was hard, almost robotic. "And when we saw your car and the police car outside, we thought we'd come by and see if there was any news. You know, anything Danny's *parents* might be entitled to know."

Rivera slowly blinked. This was exactly what he'd wanted to avoid, the Madsens thinking they were last on the list to get news about their son. *Damn it!*

"I was just about to leave here and come to your house. The reason I came here first was because there was a 911 call—"

"Agent Rivera!" Officer Washington's yell came from the other side of the kitchen, by the door leading to the garage. "Agent!" she called again, this time much louder and with an air of true urgency in her voice.

Rivera headed for the garage with Becky, Don, Jesse and Melissa following close behind. He was about to ask them to wait in the living room, but knew that would be a waste of breath. There was too much emotion among the four of them to think they'd stay behind rather than waiting to hear what Officer Washington's yell was about.

"Over there," Washington said, pointing to the opposite side of the garage.

Rivera followed where the detective pointed. Shadows from the gardening tools hanging on the wall blurred distinction between light and dark. He squinted to help focus and when he realized what he was seeing, his blood froze: a child's bright blue North Face coat lay neatly folded in the corner. On top of the coat sat a pair of Nike sneakers.

No.

It's probably just a prank from those asshole kids, Rivera thought as he came closer. He could hear a mass of footsteps behind him and hoped it wasn't the parents. This kind of cruel taunting was designed to trouble innocent…people…

He stopped in his tracks, then squatted down, trying to obscure the items from view of those behind him. He looked closely at the jacket, not touching anything for fear of disturbing the scene. There was blood inside, the fleece collar turned up just enough to show it. Of course, he would have the department bag it and get it checked for a DNA match. It could have been Danny's blood or it could just be blood the vandals smeared on the fleece from God knew what.

But this was bad.

Very bad.

* * *

Inside, Don and Melissa helped Becky sit on the couch, while Rivera's ears still rang from her piercing scream. It had been so primal and full of pain, as if she hadn't just seen possible evidence of Danny's death but had helplessly watched her only child being murdered right in front of her. Jesse, on the other end of the couch looked almost as though the experience hit him just as hard. Melissa asked if she could get him anything, but he just shook his head, very slowly, his eyes unblinking and his mind no doubt full of horrors.

There was nothing Agent Rivera could do about that, but he could do his best not to make the situation any worse. He asked Washington and Daniels to take the bagged evidence back to the station and get the analysis started: DNA, fibers or hairs, dirt or other possible residue and contaminants. The uniforms stayed behind; Rivera didn't dismiss them because, frankly, he didn't know if the Carltons would voluntarily come in for questioning. Tomorrow wasn't going to be good enough, not with this most recent development. It would have to be today. It would have to be now.

He hadn't become a senior field agent for the FBI through a lack of diplomatic skill, however. After being asked if they wanted to go home—they didn't—the Madsens sat together on the love seat, and Rivera sat facing them all on a dining room chair the officers brought in. It was best that he sit, which avoided creating a feeling of distance between himself and all of them.

"Becky, Don, Melissa, Jesse…I believe all of you have been honest and upfront with me, and I'd like to now repay that courtesy to you," Rivera started. He would have to tread extremely lightly if he wanted the discovery of what seemed to be Danny's clothes to elicit more cooperation from the couples and not less.

All four of them nodded, each of their faces drawn from shock and fatigue. Rivera took a breath.

"Mr. and Mrs. Madsen, I'm asking you not to jump to conclusions about anything. Finding clothes that match Danny's doesn't mean they are actually his. This case has received a huge amount of media attention, and the description of what he was wearing has been on the news for weeks. The bat used to break Jesse's and Melissa's pots was reportedly hanging in the closed garage, so we know that the perpetrator was inside it at some point. It seems that whoever is vandalizing the Carlton's home is trying to mess with everyone's heads about Danny's disappearance. If you put these two things together, it suggests that having us find clothing that looks like your son's could be part of their sick game. The person or people who did this had the opportunity and the means to step up their hoax."

Becky wasn't going to be able to speak, Rivera could tell, but Don said, "So why didn't they just do this stuff at our house? We live less than a block away. Why involve Jesse and Melissa?"

"But," Rivera said cautiously with a compassionate glance at the Carltons, "they aren't trying to make you suspect yourselves. I believe, and this is pure speculation, of course, that this is being done to make you think your best friends had something to do with the disappearance of your son."

Don and Becky looked at Jesse and Melissa with alarm.

Quickly, he added, "I want to tell you that I don't think your friends did anything other than love your son. I think it's being done to hurt the Carltons, too. *Why*, I have no idea." He turned to Jesse and Melissa and said, "I'm hoping you will accompany me down to the station so I can formally ask you some questions about what happened here today and about the previous vandalism."

"We're persons of interest now," Melissa said flatly. "Aren't we?"

"You are. However, that does *not* mean the same thing as a suspect. You are not under arrest. But I do need to interview you both…separately, I'm afraid."

The Carltons looked at each other and said in unison, "All right."

Rivera nodded. "Great, thank you." He would have been left with no choice but to arrest them if they had refused, so he was greatly relieved. "You're entitled to have a lawyer present, of course."

"No, it's okay. We have nothing to hide," Jesse said, but Rivera noticed a twitch in the man's eye that revealed his anxiety. "We'll come now."

Rivera nodded a "thank you" and started walking toward the front door. "I'll wait for you outside," he said.

When he reached his car, he slid in the driver's seat and slammed the door shut. With a hard breath, he pulled the memo pad out of his shirt pocket, flipped it open and grabbed his pen to write himself a reminder that made his heart hurt:

Call Maria. Cancel.

12

As an FBI agent, Rivera was able to utilize the Rockland PD's personnel and facilities through the department's courtesy. They were only too happy to cooperate with the Bureau, since both authorities were on the same page: they wanted Danny Madsen found and his abductor identified and brought to justice.

Still, as well as the system had been working, Rivera was always aware of the fine line he had to walk. On one hand, he had to respect the jurisdiction of local or state police; but on the other, as part of the country's top criminal investigative agencies, he needed to be able to do his job. The on-the-record questioning of Jesse and Melissa Carlton was one of these times when both sides of the hand had to be played.

Of course, Detectives Washington and Daniels had every right to be in the room of their own HQ as local persons of interest were interviewed about a crime committed in their jurisdiction. And they'd made no effort to conceal their desire to hold the Carltons in custody until there was enough evidence to arrest them or let them go. But Rivera was just as plain about needing another twenty-four hours to obtain more facts. He would bet his career that the couple had nothing to do with Danny's disappearance, but gut instinct only went so far. The locals didn't need the FBI's permission to arrest anyone, but they had reached a compromise that allowed Rivera another day to sort things out before they moved ahead with charges.

His part of the compromise, however, was that from behind the two-way mirror, Washington and Daniels could watch his "interrogation." He'd have to ensure that Jesse and Melissa didn't think the line of questioning was as serious as it actually was; he needed them to be as relaxed as possible since this interview could mean the difference between them being persons of interest and becoming actual suspects.

When Rivera informed them he'd be speaking with them separately, looks of alarm shrouded both their faces. Originally, he had considered talking to them together, but that wasn't protocol, and to appease the local cops so they wouldn't slap cuffs on the Carltons prematurely, he knew he had to go by the book.

Since Melissa was the one who destroyed evidence and was first and foremost facing a potential obstruction charge, he decided to speak with her first. A couple of uniforms brought Melissa in, had her sit at the table in the center of the room and placed a bottled water in front of her. When Rivera entered a moment later and saw the water, he smiled inwardly—these cops knew what he'd learned long ago: when and how an interviewee drank their beverage could be a serious "tell." Rivera liked the tactic, but because of his belief in Melissa's innocence, he couldn't help but feel a pang of guilt.

He sat and offered Melissa a smile, but nothing more. She looked like hell and he wanted to provide a bit of compassion but held back, once again walking the thinness of the line. "Mrs. Carlton, I appreciate you coming down here to help me understand what's going on. Should we wait for your attorney before we begin? Will it be someone from your firm?"

"I don't need a lawyer, Agent." She addressed the mirror, figuring correctly that someone was watching from behind it. "Other than erasing the word *MURDERER* from the flower bed to protect my husband, I am innocent of any wrongdoing. There you go. I have nothing more to hide. I'm sorry I did it, but there was no malice or obstruction intended. We are the victims here. Period."

Rivera nodded in support; she must have felt devastated at the vandalism and took the first action that came to mind in order to spare Jesse more psychological damage. He decided that, even if those watching from behind the mirror didn't like it, he'd try to put her at ease.

"Mrs. Carlton, I'd like to share something with you. It's about a technique I use sometimes to put a little extra psychological pressure on those know-it-all punks who think they're too clever for law enforcement personnel." He smiled at her intrigued expression.

"It was time for finals at a local college and one of the math professors had four of these know-it-all punks in his class who had blown off the final so they'd have more time to study. They went back to class two days later and asked the professor if they could make up the test because they'd gotten a flat tire two days before on the way to taking the final."

"Okay," Melissa said cautiously, but with a crooked smile. It was good to see on her—Rivera felt confident she wasn't as anxious as she'd been when first entering the room.

"Typically, the only time the professor allowed students to make up exams were when they were too ill to attend at the regular time or they had to deal with something like a family emergency. However, he made an exception this time and agreed to their request. After giving them pencils, paper, even calculators, he set them in four different empty classrooms to take the test."

"So this is like the empty classrooms for Jesse and me?"

"Don't get too far ahead of me," he said and laughed dryly. "So, the professor goes to each classroom and gives each student the sheet of paper with the test questions on it, face down. He stands outside the closed classroom doors and says loudly, 'You may begin.' Each student then turns his paper over and there's only one question on it."

Melissa waited as Rivera drew out the suspense. Finally she said, "Come on, you're killing me! What was the question?"

"'Which tire?'"

After a second, it sunk in and she covered her open mouth with her hand. "That's brilliant."

"Isn't it? So, the point here—other than to put us both at ease—is that I don't think there's any disagreement between you and your husband over 'which tire.' I just need to get each of your perspectives on what's been going on without one of you possibly influencing the other's impression. Colors of things, makes of cars, even the presence or absence of certain people; a million studies have shown peoples' memories can be highly unreliable, especially when a potential influence is present. So I'm here with you by yourself to avoid that problem."

"Wow," she said, letting out a breath. She relaxed her shoulders and leaned forward. "That really helps. I'm ready when you are."

Rivera nodded and said, "You can stop the interview at any time... if you decide you want a lawyer, or anything else, okay?" She nodded, and he continued. "Now, can you walk me step by step through everything that happened after the vigil and before I arrived?"

Over the next fifteen minutes, Melissa outlined exactly what had happened that day: the solemn drive home from the vigil, Jesse's headache, the moment she first saw the vandalism, accidentally rousing Jesse, rubbing out the accusing word with her foot, anything and everything she could remember.

There were a few extra details, but nothing new that struck Rivera as significant. He had to admit, he was relieved. Her story matched, point by point, what she had told the uniformed cops, the local detective, and Rivera himself at the Carlton's home. "That's it, Mrs. Carlton—"

"I hope you'll go back to calling me Melissa, Agent," she said, obviously relieved at how the interview had gone. "Now that I'm not a suspect."

"You never were a suspect, Melissa." He wasn't sure if the people behind the mirror would agree. However, he was confident that, having heard her spontaneous, consistent relation of events, Washington and Daniels wouldn't think to consider her anything more than a person of interest now. "Would you ask your husband to come in? The interview shouldn't take any longer than yours did, about fifteen minutes or so, okay?"

That might be the truth, Rivera thought, but he also knew it could end a lot differently for Jesse than it had for Melissa.

* * *

Rivera was already seated when Jesse entered the room. He was hoping that having Melissa send him in, rather than Rivera "summoning" him, would help ease Jesse's tension a bit and also keep at bay his obviously ever-increasing anxiety.

Rivera was concerned, on both a professional and personal level, that Jesse seemed to be unraveling more and more each time he saw him. The man was a successful ad executive, had an adoring wife and was lucky enough to possess best friends who stood by him even in their darkest hours. But there was something haunting Jesse, an emotional slide he recalled Melissa saying had started the night of the accident... an accident Jesse still couldn't remember. And to make matters worse, he was now being psychologically hunted by a tormentor who had remained a mystery for too long.

Rivera hoped he could close the man's growing fissure before he cracked completely, at least enough to get to the bottom of what was going on. The boy's clothes in the garage—if they were Danny's—were the closest they'd come to a real lead. Now, he needed Jesse to keep his shit together in order to make that lead pay off.

Rivera's phone bleeped and he read a text from Detective Washington confirming that the jacket and shoes had been picked up by FBI courier and were headed to the lab in Boston. DNA tests were being expedited. He should have the results within twenty-four hours.

"Agent." Rivera looked up from his phone to see a pale and wavering Jesse Carlton step into the room. "Close the door?"

"If you would," Rivera said with a smile that he wished was honest. The man looked even worse in the twenty minutes since he'd last seen him. *Qué pasará, Jesse?* he wondered, doubting the weakening man could even tell himself what was eating away at him. Right now, though, Rivera couldn't worry about Jesse's mental condition; he needed to find Danny and would do whatever it took to get there. "Please have a seat, Mr. Carlton, this shouldn't take long."

Jesse sat and stared unblinking at the big mirror positioned on the wall behind Rivera. "Who's back there?"

That caught Rivera off guard. It was a question usually asked by punks and paranoids, not middle-aged men who weren't even under arrest. "You don't need to concern yourself with that, okay? I just want to ask you a few questions regarding the incident at your house, the same questions I just asked your wife—"

"Those detectives, Washington and Daniels, that's who's back there, right? Maybe other people I don't know. Definitely a video camera." Jesse gave a meek wave to the mirror. The manner in which he spoke was completely different from what the words themselves seemed to indicate. His tone wasn't smug, like he was showing off his intellect, and it wasn't challenging, as though he was protesting at being watched. It was more …resigned, somehow. Like, *Okay, I have assessed the situation.*

Rivera had seen this many times during interrogations in which the subject knew he was going away for a long time and nothing could be done about it, so there was no need to fight or get defensive. Since Jesse was neither under arrest nor officially a suspect, however, his behavior was very strange.

"If we could just proceed, Mr. Carlton, you should be out of here in no time." Rivera asked the same preliminary question he had with Melissa. "First, should we wait for your attorney to arrive before we begin?"

Jesse snapped out of his daze, which, as odd as it seemed, made him appear calmer. His eyes widened. "What? Do I need an attorney? I thought this was just asking about what happened?"

"It is. It's protocol to make sure   "

"Am I a suspect?"

"As far as I'm concerned, Mr. Carlton, at this time, you're a person of interest. That means we feel you may have pertinent information of some kind. You are *not,* and I repeat, are *not* a suspect. A suspect is someone we believe has committed a crime. I hope you understand the difference between the two and that there's no reason to feel stressed."

He could almost feel Washington and Daniels peering through the mirror behind him, itching to put Jesse in cuffs and report their progress to their bosses and the media.

From the look on Jesse's face, Rivera half expected him to start challenging his statement; to accuse the FBI and police of lying in order to trap him or make him admit to something that never happened. Unfortunately, Rivera's instincts held true. Jesse began calling out to the mirror in agitation, "What do you people *know?* I don't care if I'm a suspect or not—maybe I *should* be a suspect! I want to know what happened with Danny, goddammit—*what do you know?*"

"Mr. Carlton! *Jesse!* Please…calm down." He placed his hand firmly on the table and waited for Jesse to notice it. "Jesse, we need to know what *you* know. That's why you're here. That's the *only* reason you're here. If you were a suspect, I'd be legally obligated to tell you so before questioning you. So, listen: *you are not a suspect at this time.* Okay?"

Jesse turned his attention away from the mirror. If he was trying to get arrested and ruin his life, Rivera thought, it wouldn't take much more of this erratic behavior for the local detectives to make that happen. Jesse took a deep breath and sat back in his chair. "Okay. Sorry. Yes, okay."

"Thank you. Now, please answer me clearly: do you want your attorney present?"

"No."

"All right, then. If you change your mind at—"

"I guess you'll know if I'm guilty of anything," Jesse said, pointing to the mirror. "And they'll know too, especially because—"

Oh, for the love of Christ. "Please stop with that, Mr. Carlton. If you change your mind about the lawyer, tell me immediately. Now…let's leave that guilty talk behind us. Okay? All I want to do is to hear what happened today from the end of the vigil until I arrived at your house this afternoon."

Jesse blinked a few times. "What did Melissa say about it?" he asked. "I haven't even had the chance to ask her that question myself."

Rivera almost started to tell him the "which tire?" story, but quickly realized Jesse wouldn't find it amusing. Quite the opposite, in fact. Instead, he said, "I'm not concerned right now with what your wife told us. Let's talk about when she called you while you were in the bedroom. You were lying down because of a bad headache, correct?" He figured he'd just start in the middle of the events, whatever he needed to get the man talking about what actually happened.

"I don't think she meant to call out to me, Agent," Jesse said. "I heard what sounded like a scream, actually the end of a scream. It was when she'd seen what those assholes had done to our garden. To *us*…to our home."

Rivera kept a reflexive sigh to himself. He didn't need Jesse getting caught up in the emotions related to the incident and risk another break down. "Just the facts, Mr. Carlton, okay?"

Jesse nodded. "Sorry, yes, of course. What were you asking?"

Rivera cleared his throat. "Okay, so what was your thought when you heard your wife's call or half-scream or whatever the exact sound was?"

Jesse seemed unsure how to answer. "I mean, I ran down to her. It was instinct, she's my wife. No offense, Agent Rivera, but what kind of question is that?"

Rivera put his hand up in a "none taken" gesture and said with a reassuring smile, "Sorry, I was unclear. Of course, you immediately ran down. No, what I mean is your mental reaction: were you surprised when you heard her? Or did you suspect what had happened?"

"I was taken by surprise, of course." He considered the question further for a moment. "I mean, once I saw the pots were smashed, I immediately assumed it was those goddamn kids again. Am I missing something? Why are you asking that?"

None of your business, Rivera thought reflexively. *You're answering my questions here.* "I'm just establishing that you have been through a lot and your mind might have gone to that place automatically, like you were expecting some sort of vandalism to happen again."

"Ah."

"What I'm trying to establish is how the vandalism plus what we found in the garage might be affecting your mental state. Basically, I'm wondering if someone is playing mind games with you and why they might be doing something like that."

"That's the question of the century, Agent," Jesse said emphatically. "Whoever's doing this knows what happened to Danny—the coat and the shoes prove it. My therapist says I feel guilty about what happened to my godson, and that it's completely natural for me to feel personally responsible." Jesse looked down at the table and started picking at the label on the bottled water. "Dr. Bradley is the only person who knows that. Maybe *he's* the one doing this to me." Jesse pushed out a feigned laugh.

"Do you think that's the case?" Rivera asked, knowing the answer.

"Of course not," Jesse replied. "I'm not sure he's strong enough to even *lift* a baseball bat."

That made them both smile.

"Well, based on my experience, I'd say your therapist is one hundred percent correct about the guilt aspect and feeling responsible. However, we still aren't sure that the items found *are* Danny's or if some bad actor is simply trying to screw with your head."

"Okay, right. But it's like this person or these people, whether they're involved with Danny's disappearance or know who is, are just trying to get their thrills. Like they know I feel responsible about him missing and want to make me suffer."

Rivera smiled, but not too much, as he said, "Maybe a rogue gang of psychology majors are vandalizing your house."

Jesse actually laughed this time, which Rivera thought was a positive sign, but then turned serious. "They're like stalkers, like the bullies in high school who find your weak spot and keep sticking the knife in and twisting it." Jesse slowly shook his head back and forth. "I just don't get it."

That was interesting. Washington and Daniels behind the glass might find it a stretch, but it made sense to Rivera that someone who knew how guilt affects a trauma survivor might use that emotion to torture Jesse psychologically. But *why* would someone do that to this poor guy? From what he and the others had told Rivera, Jesse didn't have any enemies, and it would take a lot more than mild dislike from an aggrieved coworker to bring on these kinds of stunts. If the items supposedly belonging to Danny were fake, then Jesse's tormentors were really turning up the heat. There had to be a reason why someone would take the time and effort to single Jesse Carlton out for this particular brand of psychological abuse.

During Rivera's first weeks at the academy, a statement had been drilled into his head by just about every mentor he'd met: *If someone takes an action, they take that action for a reason. Once you figure out the reason, you can find the suspect.* Even crazy people had their reasons, even if it was just that they were crazy.

This case didn't smell crazy, though. It reeked of revenge, Rivera thought, although he had no idea whose revenge it was or what it was in retaliation for.

If the DNA on the jacket turned out to be Danny's, however, the situation would be totally different. For one, he'd probably no longer be able to keep the locals from charging Jesse with murder. But, assuming, as Rivera did, that Jesse Carlton had nothing to do with the disappearance, then these vandals were more than just thugs. They had Danny's clothes. That meant either they were abductors and probable murderers, or they knew who was responsible for Danny's disappearance and, most likely, his death.

"Go out on a limb with me here, Jesse. Why would anyone choose *you and Melissa* to do this to? From what you've told me, you two don't seem to have any enemies at all. Give me your perspective, don't hold anything back, even the smallest thing. Why would someone do this to you and your wife, commit character assassination at the very least and possibly try to pin a murder on you?"

Jesse seemed taken aback by Rivera's question, which made the FBI agent wonder, *Hasn't he asked himself this before?* The whole "punk vandal kids" theory had stopped at *MURDERER*. And now, with the coat and sneakers, it was something much more than that. Rivera was more interested than ever how Jesse might answer.

"Maybe I should ask it this way: why did they choose to torment *you* rather than the parents who live half a block away? It would seem like this person, or these people, could twist the knife into Danny's parents even more cruelly than they have done to you."

Something plainly popped into Jesse's head, and his lips twisted in a way that showed he had never considered it before. After a moment, he said, "Maybe they think I did it."

Rivera could feel Washington and Daniels's eyes piercing from behind the mirror into the back of his head.

"But since I didn't do it and they can't prove it, they do this bullshit." Jesse smiled despite himself. "Pardon my French. But maybe. I don't know."

Rivera waved it off. "No, this is good, just say what you think without holding back. Sometimes you know something subconsciously, but you don't realize it consciously until you hear yourself say it. So, let's say they think you had something to do with Danny's disappearance or, God forbid, his death. Why might they think that? Don't hold back, like I said. Just free-associate, maybe there's something you saw or heard or thought that your brain won't give up on its own."

"Free association? I thought that was only something psychiatrists do with patients."

"Shrinks *and* FBI agents. And we do it for the same reason. Sometimes your brain wants to talk but can't, not with all the everyday psychological shit on top of it. Pardon *my* French."

Jesse laughed at that, thank God. Rivera didn't want to do anything to knock him off the stream-of-consciousness path he was asking him to follow. Jesse would say anything vital as his brain went on automatic, but there *could* have been a person who said something telling at the office or something he saw but never consciously took notice of.

Yet Jesse hadn't responded to his last statement and Rivera was getting impatient. He knew he had to tread lightly while also being insistent. "Just *go*, Jesse. Why would someone do this to you and Melissa, specifically? Let's say they really do think you had a hand in these crimes—*why* would they think that?"

Jesse shrugged. "Honestly, I have no idea."

"No, think of *something*. It doesn't matter how off the wall or impossible it is. Just start guessing."

"Okay..." Jesse took in and let out a deep breath. Rivera could see he really was searching his brain for something to throw out there. "Maybe they saw me help him practice baseball in my backyard the day before he was kidnapped. It was in the snow, but he really wanted me to pitch to him so..." He cleared his throat and blinked back tears. "So, he could be ready for Little League tryouts this spring."

"Of course," Rivera said with real empathy, remembering all the things Benji would have done if he hadn't been murdered. "Keep going, if you can."

"Um...same thing with school the week before he disappeared. I drove him one day when he missed the bus and Don and Becky had already gone to work. I was working from home that day. Maybe somebody saw him in my car and knew I wasn't Don, so they think I'm the kidnapper."

These were really good guesses, Rivera thought, even if they probably weren't the case. Some of this could also be behind the heavy guilt Melissa told him Jesse was carrying. Maybe this would help with his therapy, if nothing else. He made sure Jesse could see him write on his legal pad, *WITNESS MISUNDERSTANDING?* He hoped that would encourage Jesse to continue, and it did.

"Maybe it's somebody who knows Don or Becky and also knows I'm their really close friend. Some amateur vigilante read in a book that family friends are sometimes the kidnappers and started testing us to see if we would confess under pressure." He paused, gazing at the ceiling as he thought. Finally, he said, "That's all I can think of, Agent. Weak sauce, I know."

"No, not at all, Jesse, seriously. These will be very helpful—"

A polite knock came at the interrogation room door. Rivera stood and cracked it open to scold the uniformed officer standing there with a manila envelope in his hand. "Don't you know not to interrupt a goddamned interview?"

The officer said quietly, obviously trying to avoid Jesse hearing him, "I'm sorry, sir, but the DNA test results are back on the Danny Madsen items, sir. I thought you'd—"

"Excuse me just a minute, Mr. Carlton," Rivera said, staying formal so the uniform wouldn't gossip to others that Rivera had become overly chummy with a possible suspect. He stepped into the hall and shut the door behind himself. "They only took it to Boston two hours ago. How can it be done already?"

"Apparently they fast-tracked it, sir, and faxed the results to us. Excuse me for asking, but isn't that a good thing?"

"Yes, of course it is. I'm just surprised." He took the envelope in which the officer had placed the printed results, no doubt after taking a look at them so he could tell the entire squad room.

The truth was that he wasn't pleased someone above him had put the Madsen DNA test ahead of every other in the Boston office. The fact that they did it immediately upon receiving the samples by courier, then *faxed* the results in a breach of security protocol, meant his higher-ups wanted an immediate arrest for the sake of the media. The extreme fast-tracking showed they were hoping for a match between Danny's DNA and that in the blood on the items which resembled what he'd been wearing when he disappeared. Since the results were faxed, they must've gotten what they'd been hoping for.

He opened the envelope and pulled out two forms. The first showed the result of the lab test, and it was as he had feared: POSITIVE. The second form was an order to arrest Jesse Carlton for the kidnapping and murder of Daniel Donald Madsen.

Rivera closed his eyes and leaned against the door. Protocol was pushing his next step down his throat: if the boss said to arrest someone, the agent did it. It wasn't some backwater police department where the rules were bent all the time; the Bureau had its reputation for a reason. Still…Rivera just didn't think Jesse or Melissa had anything to do with Danny's disappearance or the clothes they'd found. He felt like he was *this* close to a breakthrough, making things add up. Getting the person who really did abduct and probably kill the child.

More than that, even, he knew Jesse Carlton was a decent man, a good person who loved Danny with all his heart and would be devastated if people thought he had anything to do with the boy's demise.

So there he was. On the one hand, he had been ordered to arrest a man whose innocence was clear in Rivera's mind, one whose arrest would send him into a downward spiral he might never recover from, even once exonerated. But on the other, he *had* been ordered to arrest Jesse no matter his personal feelings.

He needed some time. With sudden clarity, he found a way to get some. Proper etiquette included conferring with the local detectives before making a federal arrest in a case within their jurisdiction. That, he calculated, would take half an hour or more before the matter was fully explained and settled. He could even ask the department's captain to join the conversation, which could add some more time. Rivera would decide the exact procedure to take Jesse into custody, talk it over with Boston just to make sure they didn't also want him to arrest Melissa Carlton. All of this could last two to three hours...if he did it right.

He cracked open the door and said to Jesse, "You probably want a bathroom break by now, right?"

Jesse said, "No, I'm good. We're almost done, aren't we?"

"No, it's still going to be a while." Rivera gave him a significant look, then subtly jerked his head toward the two-way mirror. "Why don't you come out here and have a break while I talk with my colleagues?"

Jesse stood and joined him in the hallway. "They want me to arrest you," Rivera said quietly, hoping Jesse could hear him above the din of the police station. "But you're not under arrest yet. Here's what you need to do: Walk out of here, very casually, and go straight to the Madsens'. They're your best friends, it's right by your house, and you are over there all the time anyway. It'll take the Rockland PD more time to locate you there than if you went home, but being there won't make it seem like you knew anything or were trying to run. Contact your lawyer on the drive over. Now take Melissa and get out of here. For God's sake, don't panic and *don't leave town*. I'm going to work on convincing these guys that you aren't a fugitive from justice."

Jesse had gone completely ashen, but his expression showed he understood how big a favor Rivera was granting him. He nodded and moved to leave, but before he did, he said, "Agent, why are you doing this for me?"

"Sometimes I have to listen to my gut and not my boss. This is one of those times. Now go make plans for what happens once they do find you and bring you in—lawyer, family, whoever will need to take care of things if you're in jail waiting for arraignment, okay?"

"All right. Thank you, Agent Rivera, thank you for everything."

He nodded. "*Go.*"

With that, he watched Jesse walk down the hallway and stop in front of the chair in which Melissa sat. Leaning over, he whispered something that drained all the color from her face and gently took her hand. As they walked past almost a dozen police officers toward the exit, she turned to Rivera and subtly nodded. He closed his eyes and massaged the lids as long as he could without passing out from exhaustion.

Now came the hard part.

* * *

Rivera tapped on the door to the observation room and entered. Detectives Washington and Daniels were leaning against the wall opposite the two-way mirror, discussing something quietly. As Rivera entered, they cut their conversation short.

"Agent," Washington said, "with all due respect, what the hell was that?"

"Detective," Rivera echoed, "with all due respect, that the hell was trying to help a frightened man who rightly feels persecuted by the circumstances surrounding the discovery of his godson's bloody clothes in his own garage."

"What we *believe* are the kid's clothes," Daniels corrected.

Rivera held up the envelope. "*Are* the kid's clothes. Just got the results back from Boston."

Washington blinked. "*Already?* Well, hot damn! I guarantee it shows we have our killer." She shot a look into the interrogation room. "Once Carlton gets back from his 'break', we'll take care of him." She glared at Rivera. "You didn't already put him in lockup, did you? This was supposed to be our collar, or a joint one at the least."

"Not cool, Agent Rivera," Daniels said.

Not cool? Daniels was young, but he wasn't *that* young. Rockland wasn't a tiny burg by any means, but good detectives in smaller departments like this tended to get headhunted by better departments in bigger cities or go federal. At the start of the case Rivera noted that since these two were still in Rockland, they either weren't experienced enough to move up the ladder or they just weren't good enough.

"Detectives… seriously? Carlton's been in the bathroom for two minutes. When would I have had the time to lock him up?"

"Yeah, you're right. Sorry," Washington said, her ire being stoked by Mr. Not Cool. "Just want to make sure the FBI knows it's not snatching this collar out from under us."

"Take it easy, please, both of you. Nobody's snatching anything."

Rivera made a slow, distracting display of pulling the DNA results from the manila envelope and held them out to the detectives in a way that meant they had to cross the small room to take them. He would draw everything out as long as he could; Jesse Carlton needed every second Rivera could give him. They would find and arrest him by dusk, but maybe, with the chance to prepare, his attorney could help him evade jail even for a night and avoid losing the remaining thread of sanity holding him together.

If Jesse had kidnapped and killed Danny Madsen—and the evidence was damning, whether Rivera felt it was planted or not—then justice would eventually be served. Arrest, trial, incarceration, even execution. No one was getting away with anything. But if his intuition of Jesse's innocence was correct, nothing would be lost and quite a lot might be gained by Jesse having these few final hours of freedom.

"As you can see," Rivera said, "the lab shows a match with Danny Madsen's DNA. So, whoever placed the coat and shoes in Jesse Carlton's garage knows what happened to Danny—"

"We know what happened, Agent," Daniels said. "And I bet there's an order to arrest Carlton right now inside that envelope."

Damn. He tried to play it off by reaching inside and looking at the Boston office order as if it were the first time he'd seen it. "You called it, Detective," he said, and handed the order to Daniels. "They don't say anything about including the local PD in the arrest, though. Maybe they want me to just bring Carlton in under federal jurisdiction. I guess I'll go—"

"Whoa! Excuse me, but that's bullshit," Washington said heatedly, exactly as Rivera was hoping she'd react instead of calling his bluff. He didn't really have anything after *I guess I'll just go* since he didn't actually want to head out to arrest Jesse, and he certainly didn't want to explain quite yet that he had let their "perp" leave the station. "This is a joint collar, damn it. We're gonna talk to the Chief right now. I don't care if he has to chew some FBI ass—we're not afraid of you guys. And all due respect, Agent Rivera, but don't you dare even put the cuffs on Jesse Carlton until we're in that room."

Rivera had to remember to look nonplussed even though this was working out better than he could possibly have hoped. They'd need time to deal with the Chief, get their strategy together, develop a statement and then contend with the rest of the bureaucracy that came between their politics and the solving of this crime. That would take at *least* an hour.

Not wanting to upset the perfectly balanced situation, Rivera said only, "I won't do anything with Carlton until I hear back from you. But, man, the Bureau really wants this collar for itself, I can tell you that."

Daniels struck a more diplomatic tone, probably because he felt the department had the upper hand for the moment: "We appreciate you holding off, Agent. We've just worked really hard on this case and want to build public trust regarding how we handled it."

"Of course. It's cool," Rivera said, using Daniels's word on purpose. "I'll grab a bite while you talk to the boss, if that's okay?"

Satisfied, the detectives scurried off to find the Chief and make their case. Rivera immediately went to the squad room and, just as he had hoped, spotted Larsen and Perry fishing for donuts.

"Hey, guys," Rivera said, "nice work on the Madsen case. I'd like to talk to you about some of the info you gathered the day you canvassed the neighborhood where Danny might've been spotted. I know it's a little early, but I'm thinking about getting some dinner…maybe that new buffet up on Seventh. My treat?"

"You bet," they both said.

Rivera smiled and shook his head as they headed toward the exit; he'd never seen these two men move so quickly.

13

Don Madsen wasn't sure why such a small sip of bourbon brought tears to his eyes. Was it the heavy bite dragging along the back of his throat? The vaporous aroma of Tennessee smoke filling his sinuses? Or was it more likely the fact that this was the first time in months he'd sat on his living room sofa without police, FBI, friends, Becky or his son by his side?

He took another slug and swirled the bourbon inside his mouth, hoping to catch the last bit of flavor before the effects of the alcohol smothered the liquor's richness and the overwhelming sadness that clung to him like a cancerous shadow.

The house was quiet except for the random sounds coming from the kitchen – Becky washing the two dinner plates, the two glasses, the two sets of forks and knives. They were two now, a couple, just like they used to be. But they weren't like they used to be. They never would be. Never could be. The past was a blur of surreal circumstances and hopelessness, the future an unknown journey through days, weeks and years of just trying to get by. His hope that Danny was still alive had weakened, and Becky's insistence that she knew her son was "gone" only added to him nearing surrender. Until there was proof that his son was dead, he'd hold on to that sliver of hope, but it was thin as a single thread trying to lift a wrecking ball.

He closed his eyes and took another sip of bourbon. In the darkness before him he saw nothing but his son's face – Danny's giant smile after hitting his first home run in the Little League playoffs; the dirt on his cheeks, with traces of tear stains, after he'd fallen off his bike and needed ten stitches in his knee; the blue twinkle in his eyes as he watched his mother open the Christmas gift for which he'd saved his allowance all year – the gold necklace with the letter "B", the one piece of jewelry she never took off. He specifically remembered the look of tranquility as Danny lay sleeping with a slight smile that allowed a proud father to know that his son was happy, content and most likely dreaming of his life as a movie star, a doctor, a baseball player or whatever it was he'd set his mind to that week.

Don's eyes jolted open when he felt Becky's finger softly glide across his cheek. She wiped away the tear and kissed the side of his face.

"I know," she said. She tossed the dish towel she'd brought in from the kitchen onto the armchair and reached across the back of the sofa to rub his shoulder. "I know."

They sat in silence for a moment. She took the glass from Don's hand and took a sip as they both stared at the photos on the wall. He wondered if the same question tearing through his mind was also in Becky's: what should they do with the photos? Should they keep them on the wall? Take them down? It pained him just to consider the question.

He turned to Becky and was going to ask her about the photos when he noticed wrinkles around her eyes that months ago hadn't existed. He'd have traded every snapshot he'd ever taken to erase those lines and have Danny back, sitting between them and smearing mud from the Little League field on their couch.

She took a sip of bourbon and handed him the glass. "I'm not sure where to go from here," she whispered. "And I really don't want to discuss it. I just wanted you to know that I'm lost inside." She hugged him closer. "And I know you are, too."

Don took a large swig from the glass to push down the lump in his throat. There were probably groups for people like him and Becky, people who had been through the same sort of tragedy and might be able to lead them through the maze of unfamiliar emotions and fears. But he wouldn't bring that up. At least not yet. If she wasn't willing to talk with *him* about her feelings, there was no way she'd be open about those things with strangers.

He could feel the darkness start to enfold the two of them and knew it was time to change the subject.

"I wonder what's happening with Jesse and Melissa. They've been with Rivera for hours already. I thought we'd hear something by now."

Other than her arm tensing up and her breathing getting more shallow, Becky showed no response. Don figured she was lost in thought and might not have heard him. "What do you think? Jesse and Melissa have been with Rivera for—"

"I heard you, Don."

Don placed the glass on the sofa table and turned toward her. "What's wrong?"

"Nothing."

"Becky." He took a breath. "Becky, what is it?"

"Nothing."

"Beck, tell me."

Becky rolled her eyes and slid toward the far side of the sofa. "He's been your friend since you were five years old. I don't want to say anything that would hurt you...or him."

"Yeah, you're right. We've been friends forever and he's like a brother to me. But *you* come first. Period. If there's something on your mind, I need to hear it. Now more than ever we need to be open with one another."

Becky let out a sigh. As she bit her bottom lip, Don could tell whatever she was holding back was a heavy weight. And the longer she waited, the more certain he was that he didn't want to hear it. But he pushed anyway.

"Becky?"

"It just doesn't make sense, Don. The whole Jesse thing. I mean, why him? Why would someone, *anyone*, choose Jesse to torment over *our* son's disappearance? If anything, wouldn't they do these things to *us*? I've read enough articles to know that the parents are prime suspects in cases like ours. I just don't get it. I can't make sense out of it and I just wonder if…"

Don's heart rate quickened and the thumping in his chest felt like the beater of a bass drum against his ribcage. *Where is she going with this?*

"And you 'just wonder if' what?"

"Forget it, Don. I'm just…"

"Becky! Please!"

"All right! All right! What if Jesse *did* have something to do with it? What if he *did* take Danny? I mean, they couldn't have their own children and maybe it just got to be too hard for him to deal with. Danny trusted him like a father. Maybe he let Jesse bring him somewhere, maybe in the woods or to a house somewhere. He kept him there…as like a game or something, telling him he'd take him home as soon as the game was over. In the meantime, someone somehow knows the truth; they might've even seen Jesse take Danny and they're trying to tell us what happened without making themselves look guilty. I haven't figured out the details yet, but…"

Don shook his head, unsure whether he was losing his mind and hearing things or Becky had gone completely mad. Aside from the fact that Jesse had been his best friend since childhood, the man loved Danny as he would have his own son. For Christ's sake, he risked his own life driving in snowstorms, almost getting killed in an accident looking for Danny. What the hell could she be thinking?

"Becky, please." He took her hand. She pulled it away, her expression revealing full well she knew what was coming. He quickly decided to change course. "I agree," he said, letting the words sit between them for a few seconds. "It's strange. The whole thing is strange. The way Jesse's acted since the accident...the fact that a rock was thrown through *their* window...the breaking of all *their* planters...Danny's clothes in *their* garage." Leaning back, he tightened his lips, thinking carefully through his words before opening his mouth again. "It's obvious you've given this a lot of thought. And you know me well enough to realize I've done the same...over and over and over again." He looked directly into her eyes, once dark brown, now appearing faded by the dark circles beneath them. "But I have never, ever believed for one single second that Jesse or Melissa had *anything* to do with Danny's disappearance. Believe me, I've grasped at *everything*. There was even a time I thought these things happening to Jesse and Melissa were a set-up by Rivera and the cops. I thought maybe their lack of leads or the fact that the case was going nowhere forced them to devise a plan to deflect our attention. But to what end? It made no sense." He let out a sigh and shook his head. "Like I said, I was grasping."

He leaned forward, took her hand again and kissed it. "And I'm afraid that's what you're doing now – grasping. I swear to you that one day we'll get to the bottom of this and find out what the hell is going on. But if there's one thing I believe in my heart of hearts, Jesse and Melissa would give their lives for Danny. And if you try to put as much emotion aside as possible and think about it logically, you'll believe the same thing."

She used the dish towel to wipe the tears streaming down her cheeks. "I know what you're saying, Don. I really do. I just don't understand the *why*. None of it makes any sense."

"I know, Beck. I know. But until proven otherwise, we need to stand behind Jesse and Melissa, just like they've stood behind us all these months. I can't...I won't turn my back on the two people who have done everything humanly possible to help us find our boy. No matter what the 'evidence' might show. There's an explanation to all of this and we'll discover what it is. But please, imagine what *you'd* be feeling if the situation was reversed. Would you want them giving up on you?"

Becky glanced at the photos on the wall, then down to the floor. She shook her head slowly. Don could barely hear the word "No" escape her lips.

He knew what he was asking of her, and it was a lot. She'd finally recovered from her breakdown and although she was still depressed and had daily bouts with anxiety, he had been hopeful that her thoughts about things were becoming more logical. For her to suspect their best friends worried him. Was she heading for another breakdown? Had he presumed too soon that she was dealing with things reasonably and didn't need someone watching over her anymore?

Now more than ever he had to watch his words, and more importantly, her reaction to them.

"You know I get where you're coming from, right?"

She shook her head sheepishly.

"And I don't blame you one bit. We're *both* grasping. We have nothing else. I just don't want to *over* grasp and throw our best friends under the bus." He gently stroked her face with the back of his hand. "Other than each other, they're pretty much all we have left."

Becky forced a half-smile. "You're right." She took hold of his hand and held it to her chest. "I promise to try not to think like that again."

They both jumped, startled by loud knocking at the front door. Don rose from the sofa and looked out the bay window to see Jesse and Melissa, pale as ghosts, standing on their front step. He turned to Becky, the irony of the situation punching him hard in the gut.

"Speak of the devil," he said. "Looks like this might be the time to keep that promise you just made."

* * *

"They want to arrest him," Melissa said, rubbing the back of Jesse's head, which hung like a rag doll. The couple sat in the center of the sofa with Don and Becky in each of the armchairs on either side

Becky looked at Don, her expression displaying fear that her previous concern about her friends might be justified. He struggled to remain seated and thought about what he could say to try to calm them all, anything that would stop Becky from bringing up her theories. But he hadn't thought quick enough, and now Becky rose from her chair.

"For what?" Becky placed her hands on her hips, almost yelling. "What can they arrest you for?"

Don waited, uncertain where she was going with this.

Melissa shrugged her shoulders and sat back, apparently surprised at Becky's reaction. "I heard something about Danny's coat, positive DNA results, a whole bunch of crap. But we were sneaking out the police station door so we couldn't hang around to listen."

"Sneaking out?" Don asked, a concerned eye still watching Becky.

"Rivera helped us leave. He believes in Jesse's innocence and is trying to prove it before they actually arrest him. He thought it best that we call our attorney from the car and have him ready to go, just in case. Plus he said it was a good idea for us to come here so it'll give him a little more time to find proof of Jesse's innocence. I'm not sure how we'll ever be able to thank him. I'm just thankful that he believes in us and knows that Jesse would never do anything to hurt Danny."

Jesse covered his eyes with the palms of his hands and started to weep. This was the first sound he'd made since they'd arrived at the Madsen's.

"How could they think..." Jesse tried to speak through his sobs. "That I would do anything to hurt him? He made me laugh. He made me smile." Jesse sniffed and wiped his eyes. "He was one of the only things in this world that actually made me happy."

Don now turned to Becky. Her eyes welled up with tears, her sympathy increasing by the second.

Becky sat down next to Jesse and let him rest his head on her shoulder.

"Shhhh. It'll be okay, Jesse. We'll do everything we can to prove you had nothing to do with any of this. I promise. Even if they — "

"They could be here any minute to take him away," Melissa said, her voice trembling as much as her hands. "Our first step has to be to find out who the hell is doing this to us. The Rockland PD doesn't care about the truth. And other than Rivera, the FBI doesn't seem to give a shit about what the real story is. We need to hire a team of private investigators to figure out who is trying to frame Jesse for something he didn't do. Once we catch this lunatic, or lunatics, we'll at least have something to work with. Plus, it should also help us find out what happened to Danny."

The room fell silent, the four of them now looking at the floor. The elephant in the room had stomped its foot and was just too large to ignore or try to push out the door. Don held his head in his hands and closed his eyes. How are we going to move past this moment?

To his surprise, Becky made the first move.

"Have we ever met the lawyer who will be defending Jesse?" she asked.

"Chad Brennan? You might've met him at one of our get-togethers. I can't say for certain." Melissa started to rub the back of Jesse's head again. "What I can say for sure is that he's the top guy at the firm when it comes to defending innocent people. If they do try to arrest Jesse tonight, I have no doubt Chad will have him out by morning so we can start putting an end to this senseless nightmare."

Don walked to the dining room cabinet, took out four rocks glasses and set them down on the sofa table. He poured a bit of bourbon into each glass, lifted his own and waited for the others to raise theirs. Looking directly into Jesse's tear filled eyes, he crouched in front of him and smiled.

"There's a reason we've been best friends for over thirty years. You are one of the most loving, honest, caring and compassionate people I know. I believe that the truth will soon come out, you will be free of all these bullshit accusations and you'll be able to live your life again. This toast is to your freedom and for all of us to find a way back to a life worth living."

They all clinked glasses and sipped the liquor, allowing the huge gray elephant to slowly exit the room, taking its baggage along with it. They sat back in their chairs in silence, cautiously absorbing the subtle calm the bourbon created as it made its way through their veins.

Don was just about to reach for the bottle when the doorbell rang. Pounding on the door followed immediately, making everyone jump.

"We're here for Jesse Carlton," a male's voice yelled from the porch. "Please open the door."

Don looked at Jesse and offered the bottle of bourbon. "One more?" he asked.

Jesse shook his head as Melissa grabbed his shoulders and pulled him close. "It's going to be okay," she said through her sobs. "Chad and I will be there within the hour. Stay strong, honey. We're all here backing you up."

Don turned to Becky, who took a deep breath and clasped her hands together.

"You better believe we're backing you up. Now, the sooner we open the door, the sooner we can get you home."

Don stood, his legs shaky, his mind still in disbelief as to what was actually happening. But one thing was for certain, he and Becky were on the same page. And that wasn't only going to help Jesse and Melissa, but he was hopeful that it might just actually help keep their marriage alive.

14

After Rivera had finished a plate of buffet chow and Larsen and Perry had each finished two, they pushed the dishes aside and Rivera leaned in to let them know it was time to talk business. He didn't say anything about the DNA match or Jesse Carlton. He'd already seen, too many times, how easily these two could become distracted, and right now he needed their minds clear.

He said, "Think about the people you talked to and the things you saw that day you canvassed the neighborhood. Forget the folders. Forget your report. Forget the leads you *thought* you might have had. I need you to think from your gut for a minute." He paused, waiting for some kind of response, but there was nothing. "I want you to think back to the houses you visited and people you spoke with and remember if there was something that stood out. It doesn't have to be a breakthrough or someone's admission of guilt, just something that might have seemed a bit 'off' or captured your attention at the time."

They looked at one another. Larsen said, "There was this one woman on…I think it was Nutmeg Avenue?" He glanced at Perry for confirmation, and Perry nodded. Obviously, this was something memorable that didn't make it into their submitted summary to the department, exactly the kind of thing Rivera was looking for. "There was something about her that didn't sit right with me. I mean, she was probably around eighty, and old people act weird all the time, but I felt like she knew something she wasn't telling us. So, I kept at it, trying to see what she might be avoiding. But she gave us good answers that were consistent, so I didn't think about it much after that. Stuck with me, though."

"That's great, officer. Just the sort of memory I want to hear about. Perry, how about you? Do you remember anyone or anything out of the ordinary? Strange in some way? Don't worry about it seeming relevant or not. Just hit me with it."

Perry slowly shook his head, but in a way that suggested something possibly important.

Rivera uncrossed his arms and leaned on the table. "What is it?" he asked, keeping his tone free of duress. "What's on your mind?"

"Well," he replied, still avoiding eye contact, "we interviewed almost a hundred people. Some of them we talked to twice." He paused. Rivera kept quiet. "I think if there was something relevant, we would've picked up on it at that time. If we try to think of something now, it's like we're making it up."

Didn't he *just* tell this guy not to worry about whether it seems relevant or not? *For God's sake, how did these two* idiotas *get through the academy?* Rivera fumed, but held it inside the best he could.

Larsen and Perry were the only ones who could provide him with a lead that wasn't Jesse Carlton before Jesse was thrown in jail.

He said calmly, "I hear you. I do. But there have been many times when the obvious isn't obvious until you're not looking at it. The mind is a funny and complex thing. What didn't seem important while canvassing the neighborhood might pop into your head as a memory and just spark something." Although he really wanted to shake their heads until something useful fell out, he added in a self-deprecating manner, "It's happened to me a bunch of times—it happens to everybody."

"I could go for dessert," Larsen said. "They have—"

"*Officer*," he said sharply, then got ahold of himself and continued: "It doesn't even have to be a person who comes to mind. It could be a bicycle sitting on the side of the road…garbage bags on the curb too many days before garbage pickup…a broken fence leading to someone's backyard…a car or van with its windows blacked out…"

Perry interrupted. "There was this house on Lynch, I remember. As we walked toward it, we noticed there was a broken side window patched up with wood and plastic." He grabbed his smartphone from his carry belt and flicked the screen a couple of times. "I enter all my notes on here…yeah, here it is: 12 Lynch Lane. A Charles Hastings. We questioned the occupant and he said something about fixing a broken light bulb and falling against the window. It sounded a little suspicious, so after talking with Hastings, we checked out the side of the house to see if it looked legit. And it did."

"Did you check with his neighbors?"

"Yeah, well, there's another nutcase," Perry said. At Rivera's involuntary look of annoyance, he quickly added, "Sorry, I mean another senior citizen with memory issues. She said she heard something after the window broke, but Hastings said he yelled after he fell against the window, which is probably what she heard. He also stated that she was known for hearing and seeing things."

"So, you took this Hastings' word for it?"

"Actually no, *Agent*," Larsen put in, sounding a bit annoyed himself. "We went back to the woman's house and asked her some follow-ups."

"Barnes. Alethea Barnes," Perry read off his phone's screen, obviously proud of his note-taking skills.

"That's right, Mrs. Barnes. We went back to her house to ask for more details." Larsen shook his head. "Not only didn't she remember that we were at her house ten minutes before, she had no idea that her next-door neighbor's window was broken or how it might've happened."

"Damnit," Rivera grumbled. Something was rattling around in his brain; he needed a visual to help him get to it.

"Lynch…Lynch…*Lynch*… Perry, do me a favor and bring up 12 Lynch on Google Maps, lemme see the neighborhood."

The officer did as he was asked and turned the phone so Rivera could see it. "Okay, that's right in the middle of the neighborhood where that tip came in the night of the ice storm. The call from the woman who said she might have seen Danny." That was also the same evening Jesse drove his car into a ditch on the side of Forest Avenue. There was something here, something that would stand out immediately if he only knew just what he was looking for. "I'm going over there."

"But…" Perry said, glancing almost imperceptibly at the dessert section of the buffet.

"I'll let you know if I need you. You guys eat up. And hey, officers?" At their looks, he added sincerely, "Thank you."

* * *

Charles Hastings looked at what he had gotten accomplished and thought, *This has been a good day.*

Inside the corrugated tin shed in his backyard were three large gray plastic bins he'd picked up at Walmart earlier in the day. Within them he placed anything he had in connection with his unfortunate friend, Danny: the Patriots paraphernalia from his room, the extra toothbrush and other plus-one toiletries Danny had used, even some of the kids' food he'd picked up. He left the fish sticks and other things in the freezer that he himself liked and which could realistically be seen as food an adult would eat. But the chapter books, Disney movies, anything that might seem suspicious—and which Charles would have no need for until he found a *new* new best friend—went into the bins.

He was amazed at how much stuff was needed to take care of a kid. Three bins full, hundreds of dollars' worth, all garbage to be disposed of now. For the second time, he was glad Danny hadn't told him what pajamas he liked or other things Charles could get him to make him feel more at home. Less to go into the bins for the dump down in Norton. He was finally getting back to work and had to travel down that way to set up a home office for some hoity-toity entrepreneur. With all of this Danny tragedy behind him, he'd finally lit a fire under his own ass to get rid of this stuff. Not only did he want to get rid of the last traces of any connection to the kid, it also was depressing to have around. It was time, once again, for a fresh start.

The sun was on its way down and it was getting cold in the shed, which was fine, he was pretty much done with what he needed to do in there. He was ready for a well-earned shower and maybe a little *God of War* on the PlayStation. He needed to get a steamer for the couch and the twin bed, make sure all the i's were dotted and t's crossed. But after what he did at Jesse Carlton's house yesterday, there was really no rush anymore. He had time on his side and the real murderer was in the crosshairs now. He'd followed the police frequency yesterday and knew the cops had basically crapped themselves when they found the bloody coat and sneakers.

Yesterday had been a good day, too, now that he thought about it.

He wiped his hands on his sweatpants and took out his phone as he headed inside, starting a message to see if his usual *God of War* teammate "G8rH8r" was ready to kick some Valkyrie ass—

A strange twinge twisted within his gut when he looked up and noticed Danny's backpack hanging from a rusty hook on the opposite side of the shed. Had he purposely forgotten to place it inside the bins? Did he subconsciously want to hold on to one last tangible piece of the boy who had once meant so much to him? At this point it didn't really matter. Consciously or subconsciously, real emotion or bullshit remorse, he had to get rid of any sign of Danny. The rest of his life depended on it.

Charles pulled the backpack from the hook and held it close to his chest. He could almost hear Danny's voice echo inside his head. *"If this is where I'm supposed to be, fine! If this is where my mom and dad want me, fine! Just leave me alone."* Those were the last words he'd heard Danny utter, the final communication they'd had before the boy made his escape and had pretty much gotten himself killed. Charles used his forefinger to trace the stitching of Danny's name on the backpack's shoulder strap, shaking his head and holding back what felt like tears; fighting a sense of sadness he hadn't felt since... since... he couldn't even remember when.

He stopped moving his finger when he heard the low grumble of a car engine in his driveway. Paying careful attention to his steps, he tiptoed to the shed's door, peeked around its edge and saw a late-model sedan sitting in the driveway. The approaching dusk made it hard to see the color of the car, but Charles felt icily sure it was blue or gray, the typical colors of unmarked police cars. He heard the car door open and shut. He couldn't see the driver's side from where he was standing, but no one got out of the passenger side and there was no one sitting in the seat.

Okay, one person, probably a police detective or maybe a fed. *But not necessarily, Charles. Keep it together. Lots of people drive cars like that.* It might have just been the insurance adjuster about the claim filed on the broken window.

From where he stood, he could hear the visitor ring the doorbell *and* knock on the door. The blood froze in his veins. A claims adjuster wouldn't do that. Only someone with urgent business did that; in fact, Charles remembered, that was how the two cops who had questioned him summoned him to the door that day.

His fingers grew cold around Danny's backpack that he still held in his hand. His feet didn't seem to be getting any blood at all, either. He had to remind himself to breathe. What was he going to do? What did the person, cop or not, want from Charles?

He wasn't sure how long he stood there—it couldn't have been more than twenty seconds, although time seemed to have completely stopped. He had to move, get inside, hide, anything but remain where he—

A man came from around the front of the house. He was in a dark gray suit, short hair, well kept, Hispanic. If this wasn't an FBI agent, then goddamn Tom Brady wasn't a Patriot. Charles forced himself to move, slinging Danny's backpack over his shoulder and almost tripping as he made his way to the toolbox, grabbed his .357 revolver and cocked the hammer, just in case.

The agent must've seen the light from the shed and cautiously walked through the yard toward Charles. Although the man was still about thirty feet away, Charles could see his eyes looking right into his own. But it wasn't until the agent's gaze fell onto the backpack hanging over Charles's shoulder that he swiftly pulled the gun from his holster and pointed it directly at his chest.

"FBI!" the agent barked. "Lower your weapon!"

As if he were watching himself from the outside, he glanced at the revolver in his hand and he was suddenly enveloped by numbness. The voice in his head, speaking in almost a divine-like tone, informed him of his two final options: drop the gun on the table, fall to his knees and spend the rest of his life getting beaten and raped in prison; or lift his arm, point the gun at the man who was now only twenty feet away and pray that after the bullets had entered his body and taken his life, there'd be someone waiting on the other side to forgive him his trespasses. The voice grew louder as his choice became clearer. He lifted his arm and pointed the gun at the man who continued to stare into his eyes.

Two bright flashes came from the muzzle of the agent's gun.

The first bullet hit the right side of his chest with such force, he almost spun completely around. Until the second shot blasted through his ribcage and into his heart, jerking him in the other direction. Charles was surprised that he wasn't feeling pain. None whatsoever. The impact of the bullets was so powerful it was as though they'd numbed his senses. All sound had disappeared and his eyes saw nothing but pinpoints of white floating within a vast blackness.

He wondered if this is how Mark felt when he smashed the skillet into his jaw; or what Stevie from Framingham endured when he threw him from the cliffs of the Old Granite Quarry in Becket. He gurgled and hacked up warm blood while imagining this is what Danny must have suffered when slammed by the car and tossed into the woods. No feeling. No pain. Only thoughts, strange visions and an odd sense of regret.

From the blackness before him Daddy appeared, grinning at the pain his punches had inflicted. Charles saw his own reflection in the man's eyes, a little boy staring back at him, his mouth unmoving, his face pleading for affection. But Charles couldn't move. He couldn't reach out to hold the boy, to comfort him, to say his final goodbye.

With a slight whimper and then a sickening grunt, Charles staggered backward against the sidewall of the shed, his life over before he even hit the ground.

* * *

Oh, no. Oh, Christ in heaven, NO.

Rivera rushed back to the car and got on the local police radio, telling the dispatcher he had a man down and needed emergency services there immediately. He took a few seconds to gather his thoughts before requesting Washington and Daniels to the scene and that Boston FBI be alerted to their agent having discharged his weapon and shooting a civilian. He tossed the Glock 23 and his car keys into the vehicle, then locked the door and slammed it shut.

He ran to Hastings. Even though the man's eyes were open but flat and unfocused, Rivera felt for a heartbeat and checked for breath, for any sign of life. There was none. He could clearly see that one of the .40 caliber bullets had passed right through the dead man's heart.

"Jesus Christ," Rivera muttered to himself, "why the hell would he do that?"

The .357 was still in Hastings' hand, his fist still wrapped around the grip, his finger pressed against the trigger. And there was

Danny's backpack hanging off Hastings' shoulder; once holding the personal belongings of an innocent ten-year-old, now an empty sack lying on the chest of a psychopathic kidnapper. Sure, the killing was justified, but its impact was only beginning to reach its way inside Rivera's psyche.

He could hear the sirens in the distance. They'd probably arrive within three minutes and then he would be placed on administrative leave while the local police and his bosses sorted out exactly what had happened.

That made Rivera remember why he was there in the first place. The occupant of 12 Lynch Lane had acted strange enough for his behavior to stick in the minds of the questioning officers. Rivera had come to follow up with the man, and after knocking on the door and not getting a response, he walked around the side of the house...

Why did he come around the side? Why didn't he just leave when there was no answer? There was something inside him, something he couldn't ignore with Jesse Carlton about to be hauled in for kidnapping and murdering his best friends' son, that forced him to check out the backyard.

He looked up, at the tin shack almost hidden behind unruly bushes. Hastings was dirty, another gut feeling; he must have been doing something in the shed.

The sirens were getting louder. He had maybe two minutes until the ambulances and police got here. It was now or never.

Rivera stood, moved as quickly as he could to the shed and pulled the dangling cord for the light. When it came on, weak as tea, three brand-new plastic bins like those used for storing Christmas decorations stood out in the filth and gloom like a shiny gold watch in a drawer full of tenpenny nails. One stack of two and one by itself. If there was anything to be seen here, it was inside those bins.

He went to the single container and popped up the corner of the plastic lid.

Inside were a boy's blue corduroys and a backpack that had the name "Danny" stitched in the shoulder strap. *Holy shit, this is his stuff.* There was more in there, a camp shovel and some other items that at the moment seemed random but would probably make sense within a matter of hours. He ran a finger along the shovel. No blood; it wasn't even dirty. In fact, it looked brand-new.

Son of a bitch. This was the guy. This was the kidnapper, maybe even the murderer, if Danny was really dead—

His gaze snapped up toward the house: *Danny could be in there.*

Rivera shot to his feet and yelled "Danny? *Danny? Danny!*" as he rushed to the back door, ready to throw his shoulder into the peeling and water-damaged wood. But when he tried the knob, the door easily swung open and he raced inside. *"Danny! It's okay, it's the police!"*

Silence. Rivera knew he was being reckless, barging into the house without backup or his sidearm. But right now nothing mattered more than finding Danny alive and bringing him home to his parents. His heartbeat quickened and he felt a bead of sweat crawl down his back.

He took the largest knife from the kitchen block and held it exactly as he would a firearm, down low but ready to raise in an instant. "Danny? Where are you, son? Yell to me! Bang on something! Make a noise so I can find you! I'm going to take you home to Mom and Dad! *Danny!*"

Nothing.

He rapidly but carefully moved from the kitchen into the living room. No doubt Hastings was a slob, with dishes piled in the sink and clothes strewn around, but there was nothing he could see that screamed *kidnapper* or *pedophile*. Of course, those kinds of items were probably already stuffed into the bins inside the shed. If he had waited even one more day to ask the two uniforms about their interviews...

He shook the thought out of his head and proceeded into the hallway.

"Danny?" he called, quietly at first but then more loudly as he moved forward. He didn't want to scare the kid, but he wanted Danny to hear him calling just in case he was tied up somewhere.

He pushed open the first bedroom door with his foot and called for Danny again. He entered the room and saw the boarded-up window, the twin bed and a total lack of any decoration. No posters, no toys, not even sheets on the mattress. It looked like nothing more than a ratty motel room.

This is where Danny was held. He knocked out the window and made a run for it—that's when the witness called to say she saw him going for the conservation land.

The sequence of events was still very fuzzy but clear enough for Rivera to convince himself that Danny was no longer inside the house. The boy must have made his way to the conservation land and then…Rivera rubbed his head…and then. *Shit.*

Something happened before he could get to safety, and whatever it was caused the boy to bleed into the top of his fleece coat, so a head injury, most likely. Did Hastings catch up with Danny and bludgeon him with something, like a rock or a camp shovel? The shovel in the bin didn't have a dent in it, but it didn't have to have been that same shovel. Whatever killed Danny, Rivera felt nauseated with the certainty that the boy was dead and his body was somewhere in the middle of over 150 acres of forest. If the body was buried— which could be the reason that shovel was in the bin—it could mean weeks before they found him. That meant more torment for his parents, and realistically, more torment for all of them.

He could now hear the sirens from inside the house. He had about thirty seconds, forty-five at the most before the emergency vehicles showed up and he would have to step back from the entire crime scene until Boston cleared him to return.

He hurried out of the bedroom, still calling for the boy on the off chance he might be there and still alive. *"Danny!* Come on…*Danny!"* He swept the dingy bathroom—no kid's shampoo or toothpaste there—and then the master bedroom. An unmade bed, clothes on the floor, but no sign that Danny was there or had ever been. Hastings had done a hell of a job getting every trace into those goddamn bins.

The closest sirens stopped, but more were in the distance. Rivera looked through the sheer curtains and saw an ambulance and two squad cars. He knew they wouldn't just run into the situation, but instead wait for the FBI agent already on the scene to come to them. That gave him maybe another sixty seconds or so. He used it to hurry into the basement, where, again, he found nothing.

Disheartened, he climbed up the basement stairs, put the knife back into the block in the kitchen and walked to the front door. He flipped the porchlight switch on and off three times, then flipped it on again to alert the local cops, who were standing behind their open car doors with their weapons out, that someone would be exiting the house.

He took out his ID, very slowly opened the door and stepped over the threshold with his hands raised and clearly visible. He called out "Agent Antonio Rivera, FBI! I am moving out onto the porch!" and took a few steps outside. The cops relaxed their stances, one coming out from behind his squad car's door with his weapon trained on Rivera. When he got close enough to see the ID, he lowered his weapon and backwaved to let the others know all was okay.

"Agent Rivera," the officer reaffirmed. "Is the situation contained?"

"Yes. There's a man down in the backyard shed. He's dead. My weapon and keys are in my car." He said, pointing to his vehicle.

"All right, Agent, thank you." He turned and told the officers, "Stand down. The scene is secure. EMTs, move in."

The medical personnel followed his instructions on where to find the injured subject—Hastings was dead, of course, but that wasn't his official determination to make. It was coming on full dark now and Rivera could see the flashing lights of more first responders still a few blocks away. The forensics team, more uniforms and Detectives Washington and Daniels were probably among them. The Bureau team would no doubt be there within two hours to debrief him and assist the Rockland PD with their investigation. It was protocol for him to wait for the team at the scene of the shooting, so he took a seat on the porch and asked the officer, "Were the detectives notified, Daniels and Washington?"

"Let me check, sir." He used his shoulder mic to call into dispatch and they squawked back that the detectives were in the middle of an arrest but they would proceed to Lynch Lane as soon as their suspect was booked.

The color drained from Rivera's face. That had to be the arrest of Jesse Carlton; he wasn't going to be hard to find, which was the whole point of having him take care of his business at the Madsens'. He wouldn't seem to be on the run—which was good, because he wasn't. Now the Rockland cops had located him and were bringing him in. They had no way of knowing the case had just been solved.

"Officer, how long would it take to get to 120 Roseto Street in Rockland from here? With the emergency vehicle light kit going?"

The uniform thought for a few seconds. "Rockland's about fifteen minutes from here, twenty the most. Do you need assistance, Agent?"

Rivera was always gratified when local police were willing to help their federal colleagues. Oftentimes, it was because they hoped to one day be in the FBI themselves, just like he himself had when he was in uniform. "Can you leave the scene with me? I need to be back in ninety minutes at most."

As Rivera said this, three more Rockland PD SUVs pulled up, lights flashing. "That's gonna be my captain," the officer said with a smile. "Lemme ask her."

He made quick work of approaching the cop in charge, asking her and getting a nod. As he returned to where Rivera now stood, the captain shouted, "I need you back here ASAP, Agent Rivera. You know how this goes!"

Indeed, he did. He gave her a thumbs-up and a nod of appreciation.

The helpful uniform gestured toward his squad car. "I'll get you there and back within ninety minutes, sir. Let's move out."

Rivera stood and followed the officer to his car, not used to taking orders from lower level personnel. At this point he didn't care. He needed all the help he could get.

* * *

Jesse began to panic as the sirens in the distance grew louder with each passing second. He stood and looked through the bay window at the street, where two police SUVs sped into view and came to quick stops that formed a V in front of Don and Becky's house. A third vehicle, this one a Rockland PD sedan, pulled up at the curb a moment later.

Just as Agent Rivera had said, the police had quickly found him, but not too quickly. He'd had enough time to inform his friends that it really was Danny's blood on the coat and that he was going to be arrested and charged with kidnapping and murdering their son. There were tears, so many tears, but Don and Becky let him know they didn't believe he was responsible and someone was framing him for this horrible crime.

As they all held one another and cried, a thought flashed through Jesse's mind: *I'm innocent. Everyone knows I'm innocent.*

Then why don't I feel innocent, for Christ's sake?

There was also enough time for Melissa to get hold of the best criminal lawyer in her firm and have him wait for them down at the station. If bail was set, the money could be raised to keep him free until trial. And there would be a trial if the charges, despite all odds, were made to stick. No one brought up the possibility of him pleading guilty, and for that he was supremely grateful.

He was ready. When the two detectives, the black lady and the white man he'd seen making statements on the news, approached the door with four officers in bulletproof vests who had their pistols out and arms extended, Jesse yelled, "I'm unarmed! The door is unlocked! I'm kneeling on the floor with my hands behind my head!" He assumed the position he described and sensed palpable relief on the faces of the uniformed officers when they walked through the door.

"Thank you for your cooperation, Mr. Carlton," Detective Washington said. "You are under arrest for the abduction and murder of Daniel Donald Madsen." She read him his Miranda rights as Detective Daniels brought his hands down behind his back and fastened cold handcuffs around his wrists. Then Daniels and the officers stood him up and firmly guided him out of the house to one of the SUVs.

He was helped into the back seat by an officer, who shut the door and left him alone in the vehicle. Two of the cops stayed nearby and the two detectives talked to Melissa and the Madsens. His heart broke watching Melissa sob, her gaze not moving from the vehicle in which he sat. He knew the tint on the windows prevented her from seeing him, but he also knew she wanted him to feel as though she were with him. He swallowed hard, the lump in his throat swelling as he stared back at her. The nightmare continued, a nightmare filled with immeasurable pain and sadness, a nightmare from which deep down inside he knew he'd never be able to escape.

He watched the two uniformed officers who waited next to the vehicle talk to one another, hearing only mumbles through the thick glass window. Why weren't they bringing him down to the station yet? What were they waiting for?

Jesse looked around the car, trying to get a sense of his surroundings. There was a metal grate between him and the front seats. There were no interior door handles, of course, and he was sure the windows were made of seriously reinforced glass. This was his first time inside a police vehicle...although, he thought with a spike of anxiety, it would almost certainly not be his last now that he was in the custody of the Commonwealth of Massachusetts.

His mind raced to pictures of courtrooms, prison, even the table where they performed lethal injection. The death penalty wasn't used often in liberal Massachusetts, but Jesse believed they would make an exception for the kidnapper and murderer of a ten-year-old boy.

The fearful thoughts that entered his mind made sense. What didn't make sense was the odd sense of calm he was feeling for the first time in months. For the first time, in fact, since the night of his accident.

What made even less sense was what he felt when, out of what seemed like nowhere, Agent Rivera appeared next to the SUV door and opened it while telling the Rockland detectives, Melissa and the Madsens that the kidnapper had been shot dead. That Jesse was not the abductor and the Chief would be calling them any minute to instruct them to let him go.

No. It made no sense, not at all, that the news hit him first with a wave of sorrow…and then a surge of anger like he'd never felt before.

* * *

They both lay in bed that night, each staring at the ceiling in their own orbit of thought. Melissa, getting ready to take off her rings, twirled them around her fingers in an effort to allay some of her overwhelming anxiety.

She tried to put the events of the day somewhere behind her, at least in another part of her mind where they wouldn't keep her up all night. But it was difficult, especially with her inability to understand Jesse's baffling anger. She, too, was angry at this Charles Hastings, but Jesse's anger didn't seem to be directed at the man who had kidnapped Danny. No, it seemed to directed somewhere else. Where, though, she couldn't put her finger on.

Was he angry at the police? Rivera? She was sympathetic to this, too—could they have found Danny if they pounced on Hastings earlier? Maybe, but since the public, even Don and Becky, didn't know anything about the trail that finally led to the sick bastard, anger at law enforcement seemed premature. They did finally identify—and then *kill*—the man responsible for Danny's disappearance. And, according to the late night news, they linked this same man to other abductions and murders of small boys in the eastern part of the state.

Melissa continued to twist the rings on her fingers and rack her brain. Emotion wasn't rational thought, of course, but weren't sorrow and regret more appropriate feelings right now? Any anger she might have felt at the FBI or Rivera personally completely evaporated at the thought of what Rivera had done to make sure her husband didn't have to spend a minute behind bars for a crime he had nothing to do with. Why didn't Jesse feel the same way?

She wanted to end the night on a halfway decent note, so she turned on her side and gently touched Jesse's cheek with her hand. It was dark, but she could see a glint of moonlight reflecting off his eyes. "I know today has been absolutely crazy. No one should have to go through what you went through. But let's try, as hard as it might be, to be thankful that you didn't end up in jail and the maniac who took Danny and invaded our home is dead and gone." Jesse didn't say a word. "I know...I know...if only they'd caught him sooner, maybe..."

"It wouldn't have made any difference," Jesse interrupted. "Danny died weeks ago, I just know it."

"You don't know that, Jesse. You can't. The only person who could possibly know that was shot and killed today. There is still hope, Jesse. Until they find his body, there will always be hope that Danny is alive."

Jesse made a scoffing sound, one she'd heard many times over the years when he felt she just wasn't "getting it." In the dim light of the bedroom she watched his eyes darting around the ceiling in agitation. "I promise you, honey—I swear to you— whoever is responsible for Danny's death is going to pay with his life."

That set off her internal alarm. She sat up, switched on the light and then turned back to make him sit up and look at her. "What are you talking about? Charles Hastings is *dead*. Nothing on the news said anything about accomplices. He was just a socially isolated psychopath, a goddamn loner, a child molesting *son of a bitch*. The person responsible is in the Plymouth County morgue right now. They'll probably have to cremate him and dump his ashes in a pit because no one is going to care enough to claim them. Don't you see that, Jesse?"

Reluctantly, and she was sure it was just to shut her up, he said, "Yes."

She turned off the light and lay back down. She thought she heard Jesse mutter something as his head fell back onto his pillow. "Hmm?"

"Nothing," he said, but she watched his eyes again, still slightly lit by the moonlight beaming through the window. They no longer darted around. They were now fixed on one specific point on the ceiling. Then he said, very quietly but unmistakably, "He'll pay."

Melissa turned on her side and placed her rings on the bedside table. There was no doubt she'd have to get Dr. Bradley on the phone first thing in the morning.

15

It was almost 2:00 a.m. before Agent Rivera's head finally hit the motel room pillow.

The evening had been spent making sure the Rockland police had all the information they needed to close the case files. The credit would be shared between Rockland PD and the FBI for ending the heinous career of a person who was behind, as they knew at this point, at least three child abductions. This became obvious from evidence carted from Hastings's property following the incident. Not only were items belonging to Danny Madsen in the tubs located in the shed, but also those of two other missing boys from the area.

Rivera was grateful to God that he went to visit Charles Hastings immediately after talking with Officers Perry and Larsen. If he hadn't, these crimes would never have been solved, and Hastings would have been free to destroy even more lives.

By 10:00 p.m. the Rockland PD had all the information they needed, and Rivera was about to leave when two fellow FBI agents from the Boston office walked into the conference room to start their debriefing. He knew the two women well—Olson and

Fitzgerald—and had worked with them on other cases over the past couple of years before each moved to the Office of Professional Responsibility, the Bureau's equivalent of Internal Affairs.

This was the first time Rivera had ever discharged his weapon in the field. He and every agent were trained *ad nauseum* on the proper use of firearms in the line of duty, and each year every agent had to complete a certain number of hours on the firing range. But firing a shot in real life was something else entirely, no matter how "ready" a law enforcement professional might consider himself. When he got back to Boston, during his period of administrative leave, he would most likely receive counseling regarding his emotional state after using his gun to take down a suspect. Actually, he looked forward to it in a way; he didn't want himself, Maria or Tonio Junior to suffer from any unaddressed PTSD.

And now, as Rivera lay in his motel bed watching shadows cast from peregrine truck headlights dance across the ceiling, he played the debriefing over and over in his head; he hoped he hadn't left out any significant details. Olson and Fitzgerald had him review the events leading up to the shooting at least three different ways. Each time, they had him begin from when he got the potential lead from the Rockland cops and work his way up to the moment the OPR agents responsible for investigating possible law enforcement misconduct "took custody" of him from the locals. His truthful narrative was completely consistent with each telling, even though they asked him a new set of questions each time, focusing on different aspects of the story.

Considering the fact that, for the previous seven years, every shooting by an FBI agent had been deemed a proper use of deadly force, Rivera wasn't concerned his actions would be found lacking in some respect. However, in exactly the same way it made him shudder to think of what would have happened if he had gone to 12 Lynch Lane after Hastings removed the three huge containers of evidence, his mind also made his blood turn cold when he thought, *What if Hastings* hadn't *been the kidnapper?*

Legally, the result would no doubt have been the same: with the appearance of the large black cell phone case being pointed toward him in the dim light of dusk, he was sure his lethal engagement would have been seen as justified, if unfortunate. But it would have haunted him for the rest of his career, if not his life.

As it turned out, Charles Hastings was a sick *bastardo* and Rivera was being deemed a hero. But it just as easily could have been that he became a pariah.

He had gotten lucky.

And so had Jesse Carlton. The closeness of his relationship, not only with Danny's parents but with Danny himself, plus the discovery of the boy's bloody belongings, would have sent Jesse to the Federal Medical Center Devens for sex offender treatment and he probably would've never again seen the light of day. After Devens,

God only knew where the innocent man would have been locked away to rot.

But it didn't happen, Rivera reminded himself. *Jesse Carlton is fine.*

However, Jesse wasn't "fine," was he? When Detective Washington had the uniforms release him, even after she apologized to him for what he'd been through, Jesse looked more haunted than when Rivera had initially told him he was going to be arrested.

In fact, the man looked more stunned at being released than he did sitting in the police SUV waiting to go to jail. Rivera couldn't blame him—this had all happened in the course of just a few hours—but it bothered him that such an obviously good man was suffering so damned much for events he had nothing to do with.

He understood that Melissa was getting him quality psychiatric help, though, and Jesse was lucky to have her. Maria would do precisely the same for him if he weren't already required by the Bureau to see a team of counselors. They were *both* very fortunate men.

His mind was shot, and his eyes burned, forcing him to let them close so he could try to catch a few hours' sleep before getting in his car and driving home to his family. Finally, he was able to get some well-deserved rest and enjoy a bit of mental and physical relaxation.

Until just a few hours later when he heard the incessant knocking on his motel room door.

* * *

Melissa Carlton awoke with the springtime sun streaming through the window. Her first thought upon opening her eyes was that she would call Dr. Bradley at 9:00. But that was hours away. She got out of bed carefully, so as not to wake Jesse, hoping that sleep would help erase at least a tiny bit of what he'd been through yesterday.

She wasn't quite careful enough, though, since Jesse shifted and mumbled groggily, "We're getting up already?"

"Not *we*, sweetie. You stay right here. I need a run to burn off some tension."

"I only run when chased," he said with a little smile and his eyes still closed, the setup for one of their classic little jokes.

She finished it: "And you're rarely chaste."

By the time she got her face washed and her running gear on, she could see that he no longer stirred under the blanket. *Yes, sleep baby,* she thought with affection. *Let's pretend it was all just a bad dream.*

She left the house as quietly as possible, gingerly shutting the front door so as not to wake Jesse again. Then she hit the pavement hard, pounding the stress out of her body and taking great lungfuls of the clean spring air. She consciously chose to run in the opposite direction from the Madsens' house, trying hard not to insert herself into their need to grieve privately, no matter how badly she wanted to hug the both of them and never let go.

The run used up all of the stress in her body over the forty-five minutes it took to complete her wide loop through the residential neighborhood; strenuous exercise was exactly what she wanted and needed. The streets were completely empty at six in the morning, although she saw one or two friends jogging down near the park. She waved at them and they waved back. It all felt so much closer to *normal* than it had been for months. Like the removal of Charles Allen Hastings from the world had restored so much of what had been lost over the past several months. Except when it came to Danny, of course.

This was her "new" *normal,* a life of living each day with the underlying feeling that something was missing with each breath; knowing on the surface of every thought and action that the giggle that used to fill her with joy, the giant smile that so often gave her courage, or the gentle touch that allowed her to experience the distant delight of motherhood, would forever be missing from the world.

If these were the emotions she had to deal with, she couldn't even begin to imagine what Becky and Don were going through. What happened to Danny would haunt them all for the rest of their lives. As she rounded the corner onto Roseto Street, she came to the heartbreaking but true fact that their lives would never be the same.

When she got back to her street, she stopped on the sidewalk in front of the house, leaning forward with her hands on her thighs as she caught her breath before going inside for a shower. She'd probably make a giant breakfast that would completely negate the slimming effects of her long run, but that didn't matter one bit. What mattered was...

Out of the corner of her eye, she saw that the garage door was slightly open, only a foot or so. She'd driven herself and Jesse home last night after the whole ordeal and specifically remembered waiting for the door to close fully before entering the house. Or did she? Was it yesterday she remembered waiting for the door to close or was it two days ago? Was she so worried about Jesse that she'd unintentionally left it to chance? But that wasn't like her. Every so often something would get in the way of the door sensors, like a bucket or even a crumpled-up leaf, which is why she always paid such close attention to the door. She'd be lying to herself, however, if the fresh memory of Hastings planting Danny's bloody clothes didn't flash into her mind, and she approached the garage with trepidation almost approaching fear.

The door was set to open if pressure was applied to the bottom, so she gave it a little lift, and it started opening the rest of the way automatically. The grinding sound wasn't any louder than usual, but it seemed louder in her mind, her heart now beating fast and not just from the exercise.

When the garage door lifted higher than the back of the car, her mouth dropped open at what she saw, and it felt as though every bit of blood was being flushed from her arms and legs. She couldn't even find the breath to scream.

It was Minx, her beautiful cat. He was dead —but not just dead. He'd been horribly mutilated and displayed like a victim of medieval torture.

The cat's carcass was stretched impossibly far across the trunk of the car, his stomach slashed open and innards allowed to spill out onto the metal. Written across the back window in his blood was that one familiar word, scribbled in the same handwriting as before:

MURDERER.

Melissa's system revolted, and she doubled over and retched. There was no food in her stomach; only bile streamed from her mouth. But it didn't matter; she heaved and heaved until her stomach muscles could do no more. Then she saw the concrete driveway rush up toward her and all went dark.

***

When she opened her eyes again, paramedics stood over her and darted a penlight across her eyes. "Mrs. Carlton? Do you know where you are?"

They sat her up carefully and she blinked some of the tears from her eyes and looked around. There was an ambulance and a police car. The neighbors from across the street stood a few feet away, still in their bathrobes. *What happened?* She knew what happened, though; she had passed out after seeing—

"Jesus Christ! Minx! Where's Jesse? Where's my husband?"

"I'm right here, babe. Jenny and Bill saw you lying here and called 911. You're okay, you're going to be okay."

She looked at one of the paramedics. "No pain?" he asked. "No dizziness? I mean, are you feeling any excessive dizziness?"

She shook her head, and that seemed to satisfy the two paramedics. She started crying, however, as Jesse helped her up. "Did you see what they did to Minx?"

"I saw, honey. We'll talk about it, okay? But let's get you inside first. The police are here, and they want to hear what happened." He offered a quick smile to the paramedics, thanked Jenny and Bill and walked her toward the house. The garage door was mercifully closed now. She wondered if Minx was still inside and who would take care of getting his remains off the car. She couldn't do it, and she doubted Jesse could, either. He loved that cat almost as much as she did.

He sat her down in the dining room and made her some hot tea. She sipped it gratefully and wiped her eyes with a tissue a couple of times. Then she said to the officers, "Are Detectives Daniels and Washington on their way? And Agent Rivera from the FBI? Has he been notified?"

The cops looked confused. Jesse said to them, "The detectives and Agent Rivera were the investigators on the Danny Madsen case."

"Oh," one of the officers said, clearly not seeing the relevance of a kidnapping to a harassment and animal cruelty incident. "Um... no, Mrs. Carlton. For right now, we're on this case." He flipped open his small notepad and clicked his pen. "When we arrived here this morning, you were pretty much unconscious. We rang the bell and kept knocking on the door until we woke up your husband, who couldn't even remember why you weren't in bed with him."

"I was out like a light and in the middle of a dream that..." Jesse started.

"It's okay, Mr. Carlton. I totally get it. I've been able to sleep once or twice in my life as well." He faked a smile, turned to Melissa and continued. "Since your husband was asleep and has no idea what occurred, I have to ask what you did and what you saw this morning.

I'm very sorry to make you go through it again, but we need your insight into anything you can think of, anything you remember leading up to your discovery of the crime."

She appreciated that they were calling it a "crime" and not just "vandalism." She had nothing to tell them other than that she went for a forty-five-minute run through the neighborhood and nothing appeared out of the ordinary until she saw that the garage door was slightly open. Considering that Hastings had breezed right into the garage when he planted that evidence, she told them, the fact that he had gotten in again was less than surprising.

The officers looked at each other and at Jesse, plainly wanting to say something. Finally, Jesse said gently, "Babe, Hastings was dead by the time we got home last night, remember? This couldn't have been him."

"But then..." she muttered weakly, "...how... ?" Blackness overwhelmed her again, and when she regained consciousness this time, the police were gone, she was in bed, and Jesse was applying a cool cloth to her forehead.

The bad dream, the waking nightmare, wasn't over. Visions of Minx and unanswerable questions spun inside her head like an out-of-control whirligig. Logic was missing from every direction and a sense that her world was being ripped apart by the seams she'd so carefully stitched made her worry about her own sanity. She leaned into her husband's chest and cried, after a moment or two feeling the heaving of his chest as he cried with her.

* * *

Rivera grabbed the sweatpants hanging over the back of the desk chair and slipped them on, still wobbly from getting awoken so suddenly. He rubbed his eyes as he searched for a shirt. Luckily, he had thrown the dress shirt he'd worn last night onto the bed, where it hadn't moved during his sleep   four hours that felt more like a short nap than a true slumber.

The knocking continued.

"I'm coming...Jesus... Gimme a second..." he yelled, becoming more irritated with every rap on the door. When he finally opened it, he stepped back, shocked by the brilliance of the sun as well as the person who stood before him.

A man looking no older than thirty and standing what had to be, at most, five and a half feet tall, held a Starbucks coffee in one hand, a laptop in the other and a satchel over his right shoulder. He extended the arm with the coffee toward Rivera, big brown eyes as bright as Rivera's would've been if he'd just been able to get a decent night's sleep.

"This is for you," the young man said, lifting the coffee upward as though Rivera couldn't see it from such heights.

Rivera grabbed the cup, pulled the lid's tab open and took a sip. *Ahhh.*

"Who the hell are you?" he asked, still squinting.

"Agent Jason Morris, Computer Analysis and Response Team." He moved closer to Rivera. "Shot down here from Boston after analyzing a shitload of data uploaded to our team last night. I needed to speak with you right away about two things."

Morris must've been part of the Bureau's forensic data analysis group, and since Rivera wasn't technically on the job, he quickly determined that if Morris was here to see him, it must mean they found something on Charles Hastings's computer. If he had to guess, it was either child porn or something linking the dead man to those other abductions. Of course, he would assist CART however they needed, as long as it was permitted by his leave status.

"Agent, I intend to get in my car and go to my home in Boston where my family is expecting to spend seven days in a row with me. You *do* know I'm on administrative leave, don't you?"

"Um, not anymore. Your chief is working to get you active again as we speak."

Goddammit. Rivera stepped aside to let the man into the room. This had to be something truly awful if it couldn't wait a week or be handled by one of the hundreds of Boston agents who *didn't* just shoot someone to death. "What the hell was on his computer?"

Morris threw his satchel on the floor, sat down at the desk and lifted the lid to his laptop.

"Not computer, Agent Rivera. *Computers*," Morris said, "Definitely some disturbing stuff, but other agents are handling that. No, I'm seeing you about information we discovered on his cell phone. The one he was holding when you, um, *encountered* him."

Rivera had seen pictures taken on cell phone cameras of abductions, rapes, torture, even murder, images that frequently still haunted his dreams. He didn't want to see photos or video of Danny Madsen being abused or possibly worse. However, if there were something he could do to help them find the boy, or at least discover what had been done with his body so his parents could have a memorial service of some kind, he'd do it. "I don't know if I'm cleared just yet—"

His own cell phone buzzed from atop the television. He snatched it angrily and saw his supervisor's name. He had a hunch it was the emergency approval for his return to office work at the least; his gun probably wouldn't be returned until the week was out. After a one-and-a-half-minute conversation with the boss, it was apparent his hunch was right.

"Okay, Morris," he said with a sigh, "I guess I'm back." His seven-day leave of bliss had just been cut to a day and a half. He'd have to drive up to Boston and check in with HQ before spending the night and Sunday with Maria and Tonio. Like him, they were not going to be happy with the news. "Shit. Now tell me about the cell phone. What have you got?"

Morris clicked open screen after screen on his laptop, so quickly Rivera almost lost his balance. After a few more seconds, he landed on one particular page and zoomed in. "A call log showing two calls, one to a pizza place and one to the county DMV."

"Two calls in how long?"

"Just two calls, period. Not a real socialite, I gather. The pizza contact was from last week, but the DMV one is from several *months* ago. We're assuming he used burner phones for his tip to 911 or for other incriminating activities in the meantime. It would seem that he considered these two calls unremarkable, but the DMV contact raised a yellow flag."

"Very cautious of you. Can you tell me what the goddamn issue is here, already?"

"Sorry, Agent. Hastings did not have any registration renewals coming up, no tickets, no insurance issues, nothing we could find that would obviously necessitate a call to his local Department of Motor Vehicles."

"Interesting."

"Yes." Morris scrolled toward the bottom of the page and pointed to the screen. "Look at this...Hastings called the same DMV number three times in a row, and each of those calls lasted for about

2.5 seconds. On his fourth try calling the number, which, by the way, is a supervisor's office, *not* the DMV information line, we know he got through because look right here..." Morris glided his pointed finger to the right edge of the screen. "The conversation was a little over four minutes in length. We have the contact's name: Mark Kellison. I don't know if he's turned up in your investigation or anything, but it seemed worth mentioning."

"Good work, Agent. I'll get in touch with Kellison ASAP to see if he can shed any light on why Hastings called him. Do you have a..." Morris opened his satchel and grabbed hold of a few pieces of paper. He handed two of the sheets to Rivera. They held a printout of the phone records along with Kellison's contact information.

"Wow, you're good," Rivera said, taking the pages and patting Morris on the shoulder.

Thinking the meeting was over, he took his phone and started to call Maria when he noticed Morris looking up at him. There was something else on his mind. "Oh, right—you said there were *two* things?"

Morris practically bounced off the chair with enthusiasm. "Yes! I saved the best for last."

Rivera knew that throwing Morris against the wall and telling him he wasn't in a freakin' movie was probably not the best course of action if he ever wanted to get the information out of him. Instead, he just said, "Yeah?"

"First, let me explain how we were able to access his phone! We don't know why, but apparently, Mr. Hastings didn't have an access code enabled on—"

"Morris!"

The CART agent shrunk back. "Sorry! We found a saved map on the phone. It leads from 12 Lynch Lane to an apparently random terminus within the conservation land inside Plymouth County."

Rivera felt his frustration with Morris instantly melt away. This could only mean one thing: this was Hastings's trail to where Danny Madsen was buried.

"Excellent work, Agent. I'm going to need..."

Before he finished his sentence, Morris handed him a printout with not only the coordinates he was about to request, but also with a map of the conservation land and a red location icon marking the exact location.

Rivera's heart sank. Danny Madsen's life had ended in the middle of nowhere, and there was nothing left to show for it but a tiny red marker.

16

"Thanks for seeing Jesse on such short notice—and so early on a Monday morning," Melissa said as she shook Dr. Bradley's hand.

At first he thought her runny nose and slight face puffiness were due to the fact that it was only seven thirty in the morning, until he saw the wadded-up tissue in her other hand. She'd been crying, and from the redness of the rims around her eyes, it had been going on for more than a few hours.

"Are you okay, Melissa?" he asked. He turned to Jesse, who merely shook his head.

"I'm fine. It was just a very rough weekend."

Bradley could sense there was something else going on, something she didn't want to talk about.

"Are you sure? You know, I can have the both of you…"

"No, doctor, please," she cut him off, her agitation very apparent. "This is about Jesse. We need to get him to be okay. We need to get him better." Her voice started to crack. "I need him to be who he used to be."

Dr. Bradley gently touched her arm. "Of course, Melissa. That's why I'm here," he said. "Please make yourself comfortable in the waiting room." He looked at Jesse. "Jesse, are you ready?"

Jesse nodded and gave his wife a wave like he was a deep-sea diver about to enter the water. They entered the room and Jesse seated himself in the chair across from where Dr. Bradley usually sat.

"Before we start," Jesse said, "I just want to tell you that I've been cleared of any charge regarding what happened with Danny. They got the guy on Friday—shot him and killed him, actually."

"Yes, I believe I saw that on the news. I'm sorry a man has died, but I'm glad the case can now be closed." Dr. Bradley opened his notepad and sat back. "May I ask why you wanted to say that first today?"

"Well, I was arrested. I don't know if Missy told you that. I was in the police car and everything, just waiting to be taken to jail. I didn't know if I'd be granted bail or not, if I'd ever be free again."

"That had to be frightening."

Jesse let out a chuckle. "Yeah, it was scary as hell."

"But they did let you go, obviously."

"They did. But I…and this is why I was good with coming here first thing this morning to see you…I think I felt worse when they told me they got the guy who did it. Be in touch with my feelings, right? Isn't that what you've been trying to get me to do?"

Dr. Bradley smiled and said, "Yes. For sure. That's *one* of the things we're doing together."

"Well, my feelings were anger and…I don't know, sort of disappointment."

That's interesting. "What do you think you could have been disappointed about? I'm pretty sure nobody wants to go to prison," Dr. Bradley said, but he immediately recalled there was a reason some people *did* want to be locked away. He scratched a note on his pad: *Protect others from himself?*

"I don't know. Anger was ninety-nine percent of it, though. There was just a shade of disappointment, if it even was that."

"Your wife told me that you wanted to make the person responsible pay for Danny's death. I hope you'll excuse me for working with the tragic assumption, for our purposes, that your godson has indeed left us." At Jesse's nod, he continued, "Maybe this disappointment has to do with you not being the person who pulled the trigger? I'm not implying you would actually kill anyone, of course, but could this desire be behind that emotion, at least in part?"

Jesse looked surprised at this, like a light bulb went on inside his head. "Huh. Yes, maybe. But don't get the impression that I wouldn't have killed the son of a bitch in a second if I had the chance. I appreciate your good opinion of me, but even prison would have been worth killing the person who killed Danny."

"I understand," Dr. Bradley said, leaving some silence for Jesse to continue talking about this. After a moment, however, he could see that Jesse was done. "It's my responsibility to ask you right now if you have any homicidal or suicidal plans."

Jesse replied, "No, he's dead already, thank God. I may be disappointed that I didn't get to do it, but it's also a relief that this amazing FBI agent was the one who did it. He made sure I stayed out of jail and took the guy down to boot. All in all, it's a positive thing."

"Excellent. Do you want to talk about the anger now?"

"Sure, of course. I hope Charles Allen Hastings is rotting in hell for eternity. How's that for anger?" he said, and laughed. "No, now that it seems like it's over, to use your language, I guess I'm allowing myself to feel my hatred toward the man who did this, just all-out furious anger. I'm angry at him, at myself, at the whole freaking universe, to be honest."

"Why at yourself?"

Jesse seemed shocked at the question, like it was the most obvious thing in the world. "*Because I let it happen.* What if I had offered to pick him up at school that day instead of having him take the bus? Everything like that. It could have been avoided, all of it, if I had just done my part."

"Did you usually pick Danny up from school? You have a full-time job during the day."

"No, not usually. But every now and then I would. Like if he had to stay late or something and Don or Becky weren't able to get him. I go in and out of the office a few times a day anyway so I could've been there for him. I could've—"

"This sounds to me like your guilt coming out again, Jesse. It's very common for caretakers to feel like they could have done something to save the day, but this is only because you're experiencing all this in hindsight. If I can give an example, I knew someone who was wracked with guilt for years because he drove his wife to Logan on 9/11, took her to get on Flight 11. There was that same anger at himself, a terrible guilt he should somehow have known to turn the car around and not let her get on that plane."

Very slowly, Jesse nodded in understanding. Then, in a low voice, he said, "What do you tell them? How do you get rid of that feeling?"

Dr. Bradley knew he had a moment here, just a moment, to help put Jesse Carlton back on the track to the life he'd had before this whole tragedy began. "For ethical reasons, I can't say more about this than what I'm about to tell you, do you understand?"

Jesse nodded.

"That person is me."

"Holy shit," Jesse said flatly. "I'm so sorry."

"Although I do appreciate your compassion, the point of telling you this is that I understand the anger and the guilt of wishing you had done something differently. That's all I'm going to say about it, but I *understand*. Your feelings are painful, terrible, but we can work you through them."

"Thanks for sharing that with me," Jesse said with sincerity. "So really, there's nothing wrong with my feelings."

"Of course there's nothing wrong with them! There's nothing wrong with any feelings—what matters is how you deal with them. Even then, there's no right or wrong, just more helpful or less helpful."

Jesse took a moment to reflect on these words. Dr. Bradley knew that these ideas were easily comprehensible intellectually, yet emotional understanding would come only with time. There really was no way to get rid of these feelings; the only way out was through. He didn't say this to Jesse right then, but he would share it during future sessions. As he knew from his own therapy following 9/11, it was only the gradual discernment of his emotions and reactions that helped him. "Getting it" intellectually without feeling it emotionally would only leave him traveling in circles of self-recrimination. Time would help heal, but until then...

"All right. Maybe next you'd like to—"

"It isn't over, though."

"No, of course not. That's what I'm saying, Jesse. It will be quite a while until 'it's over,' no matter if they find your godson alive or...not alive this very day. I hope you'll work with me on the road to—"

"No, Dr. Bradley, I mean it's literally not over. I thought, the police thought, *everybody* thought that the same person was behind Danny's disappearance and the vandalism at our house. But our cat, Minx, was killed on Saturday with the *MURDERER* message left right next to him. This was *after* Charles Hastings was shot dead."

What? "That's...my god, that's awful."

"We loved that cat."

"Of course you did. So it couldn't have been this Hastings person." This was quite a development, and Dr. Bradley had a little trouble pivoting to this new reality. "I understand your anger in a new light now. Obviously, you're distressed and heartbroken about Minx, but can you share your feelings about the incident aside from that?"

"Somebody, some asshole, is still calling me a murderer. I would say I feel pretty damn negative about that."

He wrote on his pad: *Persecution?* "Why do you think *you're* the one being accused and not Melissa?"

Jesse looked shocked. After a few seconds, he said, "Huh, that's…I never thought of that before. I mean, I just assumed. Melissa wouldn't have anything to do with this whole mess."

"Doesn't she have just as much 'to do with it' as you?"

"I guess so, now that you say that."

"Can you tell me why you believe the messages are meant only for you, or at least are only *about* you? The window that was broken is on the house belonging to both of you. The pots that were smashed were meant for her garden, right? And your poor cat was beloved by both of you, I would think."

"But…Melissa isn't a murderer."

Dr. Bradley leaned forward for emphasis and said, "Jesse, neither are you."

"I feel sick."

"Do you need to use—"

"I have to go," Jesse said, sounding almost panicked as he began to get up from his seat. "I'll set up another appointment, okay? Our time's almost up anyway, isn't it?"

It wasn't, but Dr. Bradley chose to ignore the inaccuracy. "This could be important, Jesse. I hope you'll stay and talk about it, but of course you're free to leave at any time you choose. Please just take a deep breath, hold it for a few seconds and then let it out slowly," he said. Jesse settled back into his chair and inhaled with his eyes closed. After a minute or so of breathing like this, Dr. Bradley said, "Talk to me, if you can. What do you think upset you just now?"

"They're not after Missy. They're after me, it *has* to be me."

"Who do you think is 'after you,' Jesse?"

"I don't know. Obviously, I don't know."

"I know you don't. So let's try something. Very calmly, make a guess—any guess—as to who it could be that's tormenting you and your wife. There's no right or wrong guess for our purposes here, Jesse. Any stab you make at it, like everything else we talk about here, won't be shared with another soul. You're not slandering or accusing anyone, no matter what you say to me. Let your subconscious flow." He gave him a few seconds to stop thinking and start guessing. "All right, now: who could possibly be doing this to you and Missy?" He hoped that using the name Jesse used for her would help facilitate his brainstorming.

"Agent Rivera," Jesse said. "But that's ridiculous."

"No, it's not. There are no ridiculous guesses in this room. We're not trying to solve these crimes in here, Jesse. We're just trying to get things out of your brain so you stop chewing on them uselessly, like a dog with a dry bone."

"Okay," Jesse said with slight amusement. "I guess it could be Missy. I mean, it couldn't be her, and even if it could, when would she have had the time to—"

"That doesn't matter. You said her name because she's a person in the situation. You're not trying to be a detective, so you're not actually pointing the finger at anyone. Who else? Let's get to five names." He could see that Jesse was relaxing into the exercise, which was very good, indeed. The man needed a break from his own guilty, circuitous thoughts.

"Me," Jesse said.

Dr. Bradley smiled widely. "Yeah? Are you testing my assertion that there are no dumb guesses?"

Jesse laughed and asked, "What did Sherlock Holmes say? 'Once you get rid of the impossible, what's left is the truth'?"

"Something like that. But he *was* a detective, wasn't he? I mean, fictional, but again, your role here isn't to be a detective. I said guess anybody, and you did. Who else?"

"You."

The therapist's mouth twitched as he tried to keep from saying that guess was out of bounds. Besides, he knew it wasn't an accusation—it was a test whether he meant "anybody" or not. He did, so he just said, "All right. One more."

Jesse's smile fell away. "I can only think of one other person, and I feel sick again even thinking it. I mean, I *don't* think it."

"You also don't really think it was the FBI agent, your wife, yourself or me. At least, I hope not."

"No, Jesus, of course not. All right: Don Madsen. Danny's father."

He made sure it didn't show on his face, but Dr. Bradley swore to himself that he'd never again try this technique with someone in Jesse's tenuous frame of mind. He did hope that it would help with his patient's persecution complex. Or was it a complex? Someone *was* doing all these horrible things to the Carltons. He wanted to ask if he really thought Don Madsen was even a remote possibility, but that wasn't the point of the exercise, as he kept reminding Jesse. Besides, if Danny's father thought Jesse was behind Danny's death, he would probably just shoot him dead, not bother with accusations scrawled in the dirt. "Jesse, I'm sorry if this took you to a bad place."

"No, it's actually okay," he said. "Every person I just said, it makes no sense. Maybe I was secretly thinking it was somebody I know. Now I see that's stupid as hell."

"Let's not say 'stupid.' But yes, your candidates do seem unlikely to me, not that I'm a detective, either," he said with a smile, which, thank goodness, his patient shared. "Have you considered the possibility that it might just be someone who wants to disrupt the lives of people they know from television? I saw you and your wife on the news with your names on the bottom of the screen not long after Danny disappeared. There are people who like to scare or intimidate people they consider famous or celebrities."

There went the light bulb over his patient's head again. "Holy crap. That does make sense, Dr. Holmes." They both laughed at that. "Although I wouldn't really consider us celebrities. Just heartbroken godparents who were on camera one night."

Dr. Bradley smiled and closed his notepad. "I think we're good for today. Before you go, though, I'd like to give you an assignment to do before next time."

"Sure, what?"

"I want you to devote half an hour every day to thinking of absolutely nothing. Not work, not your wife, and not the things that have happened over the past few months. Sit in a quiet room with your eyes closed and focus on your breath. Basically, meditation. You'll find that things arise in your mind unbidden, maybe things you've never really thought about before. When that happens, don't get mad at yourself—just go back to focusing on your breath and allowing your mind to clear."

Jesse looked skeptical, to say the least. "I will, but I have to ask: what is that supposed to accomplish?"

"Nothing, Jesse," Dr. Bradley said. "That's the whole point. Stop trying to do anything or figure anything out. The man who took Danny from all of you is gone now. You can stop searching for him. Half an hour each day. All right?"

"All right," Jesse said. But he didn't look all right with stopping anything, not at all.

* * *

Before Rivera was sent to find what everyone was certain was Danny Madsen's grave, the Bureau gave him back his Glock 23. It sat in its shoulder holster as he took the hour-long commute through mid-Monday Greater Boston traffic to Rockland police headquarters, and for the first time since he was a rookie, he was keenly aware of its presence against the left side of his chest. There had been a lot of media attention over the shooting, but no public outcry, even in blue Massachusetts. It seemed that killing a child abductor, probable murderer and likely molester——was seen as less than a bad thing. Thus, instead of a week of administrative leave, Rivera was packing again in less than seventy-two hours.

Still, it would take him some time before his firearm didn't feel like an outsized presence on his body. He hoped that finding the boy's body and returning it to his parents would make him feel like an FBI agent again, not just someone who faced no consequences for shooting a criminal to death.

He had alerted the Chief of Police in Rockland that he was on his way with fresh information. He had to assume the Chief told his two detectives on the case that something was up and that something may very well be the location of Danny Madsen. Rivera hoped Washington and Daniels wouldn't be peevish that he hadn't sent them the map, but the FBI enjoyed credit for its work as much as a suburban police department did for its own. There would be more media frenzy over the finale of the tragic story and Rivera's bosses wanted the Bureau represented by the agent who cracked the case.

As he turned off I-93 onto Highway 3, it occurred to him that he had in his notebook the name and phone number of the person Hastings had called soon after the abduction and just before the first episode of vandalism at the Carlton place. Maybe he could use his drive time by interviewing this Mark Kellison on the way. He didn't necessarily have to be the one to talk to the DMV employee at all, but he had to admit he was curious as hell what Hastings had been up to before he began his reign of terror against the Carltons.

Rivera first called his boss to ask him to contact the DMV and provide his bona fides to Kellison's supervisor, who hopefully would then clear his subordinate to speak with the FBI. Kellison could legally refuse to answer questions over the phone, but it was worth a try if it meant Rivera could dedicate his time in Rockland to dealing with whatever they might find in the woods.

Once he got the go-ahead, he entered the number verbally into his phone so he could hear Kellison through his car speakers. A man came on the line: "Mark Kellison."

"Good morning, Mr. Kellison, this is Special Agent Antonio Rivera with the Boston office of the FBI. I just wanted to ask you a couple of questions about any contact you may have had with Charles Allen Hastings, okay?"

There was a pause, then the man said, "Okay. But there's not much to tell."

"No, sure, I understand," Rivera said placidly, having heard that sentence many times over the years, usually when there was more than plenty to tell. "I want to let you know before I ask anything that you are not a target of this investigation. Now, I'm sure you have seen on the news that Charles Hastings was shot and killed Friday night."

"Yes," Kellison said with a slight hitch in his voice. "Look, you must already know that Charles called me a couple of months ago, right? Or you wouldn't be contacting me. What, did you find my number on his phone?"

Rivera ignored the question. "What did he contact you about? I'm making the assumption that you're not close friends with him since this number appeared on his phone only once."

"We used to be friends. The last time I saw him before he called was when he hit me in the face with a cast-iron frying pan, so yeah, we're not friends anymore. Or weren't, when he was still alive. You know what I mean."

"Yes, of course. So, what did he want?"

There was a long pause. Rivera could hear the background noise of the man's office, so he knew Kellison was still on the line. "I...listen, if I tell you, I could lose my job."

Don't make me do this, Rivera thought, but the guy was making him do it: "If you don't tell me, I will put you in jail until you do. Try to keep your job then." If Kellison said the words *Fifth Amendment*, he was going to scream.

But Kellison didn't. "All right, sir, okay. He wanted me to give him the name and address of the owner of a car with a certain license plate number."

Rivera almost slapped his palm against his forehead. *Of course! That's what it was. What the hell else could it be, contacting a source at the DMV?* "Do you remember the plate number?"

"Yeah, I remember. It's a pretty easy plate number to remember. It was L-C-K-Y-1-2-3, like 'lucky' without the 'u.'"

"Thank you, Mr. Kellison, that is very helpful. You provided him with the requested information, I assume?"

Another pause. "Yeah."

"I have to ask: why would you help someone who hit you with an iron skillet?"

"He gave me five hundred dollars."

You asshole. "I see. Okay, I very much appreciate your cooperation, sir. I don't know for sure if Rockland police, Plymouth County authorities and federal law enforcement officers will be charging you with conspiracy to receive bribery, unlawful disclosure of personal information and unlawful use of a computer...but I certainly hope so. Have a good day, Mr. Kellison."

Rivera cut the connection before the man could say anything else. Thanks to this piece of garbage, Hastings had been able to make Jesse and Melissa Carlton's lives a living hell. The information about the DMV contact was going to be in his final report on the Madsen case anyway, but now he was glad he'd made the call himself.

The jerk should've taken the Fifth.

* * *

Within an hour of Rivera's arrival in Rockland, the two detectives, half a dozen uniformed officers and a county parks crew set out with shovels and other equipment. They tramped through what felt like miles of thickets until the secure FBI cell loaded with the map data announced that they had reached their destination. Alongside them were a man and a woman from the medical examiner's office with stretcher and body bag at the ready and a two-man RPD forensics team, all standing with arms crossed and expressionless faces devoid of color.

Despite months of snow, rain and animal activity, a five-foot-long disturbance in the soil was immediately apparent to Rivera and then to the rest of the party. "Goddammit," he muttered under his breath, and he could feel every one of them let out similar utterances of sadness and resignation.

"This is it, everyone," Washington announced to the group. "This must be it." She nodded to the forensics crew to get started and they took dozens of photographs of the gravesite and the surrounding area. Then she gestured for the grounds unit to begin.

This wasn't the first shallow grave Rivera had ever seen and he was sure it wouldn't be the last. But hearing the shovels hit something that wasn't dirt after one minute of digging made him sick this time in a way he hadn't experienced before. A small, bare leg and foot were revealed under the soil, and the intense silence made it clear that every one of them knew this was the body of Danny Madsen. He turned away, tears forming in his eyes, professionalism be damned.

The forensics halted the digging crew for more photographs and then the careful exhumation of the missing boy continued. This starting and stopping went on for about half an hour until the badly decomposed corpse was fully visible. In that moment, he was so glad that he'd been the one who ended the life of Hastings. He knew it wasn't entirely healthy to close his eyes and savor the moment when he put two bullets in the chest of another human being, but he didn't care. He'd work it out with the FBI counselors if he had to, but right then he couldn't have been more satisfied with himself to have shot Hastings dead. All of those responsible for anything to do with this tragedy were getting what they deserved this morning.

He stood back and let the other professionals do their jobs. He was already dreading having to tell the Madsens that their son was not only dead, but had been disposed of and left to rot in a hole in the ground like a dead family dog in the backyard. Washington and Daniels would no doubt be there as well, sympathetic but only professional. They didn't know these families like Rivera did. For him, maybe because of what happened with Benji or perhaps just because he knew the kind of people the Madsens and Carltons were, this had become personal.

He had Morris upload the map information from Hastings's phone onto his own so that he could try to get his bearings and a feel for his exact location in the untamed Terence Ford Conservation Land. Why had Hastings taken the body so deep into the woods? Sure, he didn't want the body to be found, but then why didn't he take Danny closer to the middle of the brush? The grave was farther from his home than from the other side, Forest Avenue, from where it was much more likely that people searching for the boy, or anyone who might have accidentally come across the grave-like disturbance in the dirt, would have approached.

Endless possibilities flew through his mind. Maybe Hastings drove on Forest Avenue with the body and simply picked a random location to bury it. But that seemed like a good way to get caught, especially if the burial happened as close to Danny's disappearance as the decomposition status of the corpse would seem to indicate. And given Charles Hastings had gotten away with three previous abductions and murders, this didn't seem to be the type of mistake he'd make.

After a moment of analyzing the map, Rivera thought back to that stormy night Jesse's car skidded into a ditch. He'd gotten Melissa's call, which he had taken as something potentially significant, and made his way to the site to check on her husband. He hadn't thought it had anything to do with the disappearance at that point. In fact, it wasn't until this very moment, when he realized the grave was closer to the ditch than to Hastings's house, that he started to feel there was somehow a connection.

Rivera had been a criminal investigator long enough to pay attention when these sorts of connections appeared. He didn't have to know exactly how—it was an "itch" from his core that alerted him to automatically follow his instincts. And his instincts were telling him that Hastings saw the accident while taking Danny's body into the woods.

Holy hell. Hastings must have been parked by the side of Forest Avenue when he saw Jesse pass by and then skid off the road. He probably panicked for a minute or two, and then saw his golden opportunity: he'd pin the crime on the driver who happened to be in the wrong place at the wrong time.

But something didn't make sense. Why wouldn't Hastings just leave the body on the road or even put it next to Jesse's car? Was he afraid that Jesse might be conscious and able to identify him? Or that emergency vehicles might be on their way and could possibly see him with the body? Fear of being caught probably took precedence, and he must have hauled ass with the boy into the woods, far enough not to be discovered but close enough to implicate Jesse further if the body should ever be found.

All of this went through Rivera's mind faster than the warm breeze that stirred him from his thoughts. Once he had worked this out, the whole scene looked different, and for a quick moment, he thought about the lucky breaks he'd encountered throughout this case. But was it luck or was it years of training, hundreds of cases and his inability to let go of things that forced him to "scratch the itch" until it stopped annoying him?

That little itch told him to talk with the two cops to discover if anything unusual occurred on their neighborhood canvassing. It was the same itch that pushed him to go speak to Hastings that very night, creating even more luck by getting to him before he had a chance to dispose of all the evidence. Was it the itch or was it luck that allowed the *bastardo's* cell phone to be unlocked so they could so easily find the boy's grave? And now he'd followed up on that luck by figuring out why and how Hastings chose Jesse to use as a scapegoat for his crimes.

Was it the itch or was it luck? Since he hadn't found Danny until it was too late, he had to give all credit to the itch. If it were luck, he'd be heading to the Madsen house with a smiling boy close by his side, instead of alone with grievous photos and muddy shoes.

* * *

As had been the case with every missing child confirmed dead in his investigative career as a Boston police detective and FBI agent, the news of the gruesome discovery left Danny's parents both devastated and relieved. There could now be closure. No more violence would be coming, not physically or mentally, to Jesse and Melissa Carlton or to Don and Becky Madsen. There were some loose ends to tie up, but the ordeal was over. The Madsens could bury their son with the dignity he deserved.

By noon, he was able to go down the block to the Carlton house and update them on what he hoped would bring them closure as well and allow Jesse to move forward on the road to recovery. As he pulled up to the curb, however, what he saw was disturbing: Jesse sat on the porch in a dirty t-shirt and sweatpants, unshaven, bleary-eyed and with what Rivera immediately recognized as a seven-shot Smith & Wesson 686-plus revolver.

This was not good.

"Hey, Jesse," he said in a calculatedly casual manner, "shouldn't you be at work or something?"

Jesse grunted and fingered the gun. "Not today. Probably not tomorrow either."

There was something going on that appeared as though it would be better helped by a psychiatrist than an FBI agent. He nodded toward the gun. "Whatcha got there?"

Jesse jumped a little, like he hadn't noticed Rivera pull up to the house, get out of the car and walk up the driveway, but thankfully, the gun stayed in his lap. Jesse's sallow expression and the redness of his eyes were apparent as soon as Rivera was close enough to see them.

"They killed our goddamn cat," Jesse said, his voice sounding as rough as his appearance. "First they killed our boy and then they killed Minx. They wrote *MURDERER* on our car with his goddamn blood."

What the hell? Rivera thought with renewed alarm, but only nodded with overstated empathy so Jesse could see it even through his bleary vision. "When did this happen, Jesse?"

"The day after you shot Hastings. Saturday."

It must be a copycat, Rivera concluded, but since none of the vandalism and harassment had been included in the Madsen case file and the media hadn't reported anything about it, the perp had to be within the police department. If there even was a perp other than Hastings. Could Hastings have done it in the hours before Rivera encountered him, trying to frame this poor soul to the very end? He didn't want to get into the time frame with Jesse, not when the man looked about to collapse. Instead, he chose to assume that this couldn't have been Charles Hastings.

"I was in Boston after the Hastings incident, off the case— off *any* case, really. But that barely lasted a day. Now I'm back and I wasn't made aware of anything with, um, Minx." He had rushed from the Rockland police station to the conservation land with Washington, Daniels and the rest of the team, not really giving the detectives the opportunity to bring him up to speed on further developments. Actually, he realized, they probably wouldn't be involved, either, now that the case had been solved. A local department's main detectives wouldn't be consulted on something this small, even as awful as the killing of the Carlton's cat. But it did make Jesse sitting on his porch with a loaded weapon seem a bit, a very tiny bit, more logical.

Now to get it from him.

"That's a heck of a gun there. I've never actually held a 686. Always wanted to, though."

Jesse looked at him for the first time and said, "You wanna hold it?" He lifted the gun with the barrel pointed at Rivera. "It's heavy as hell."

Rivera quieted the chill that arose from having a powerful weapon aimed directly at him, moving out of the line of fire and coming up on the porch obliquely. Jesse didn't move the gun to keep it on him, showing that in his exhausted state he was just holding it out for him to take.

Rivera gingerly took the gun, putting the safety on at once and popping out the cylinder so it couldn't accidentally—or purposely, for that matter—be fired. "This is a beauty. I can see why you like to hold it. It has great heft."

"Right?" Jesse said without a smile in his voice. "Bastards try to come again, I'm gonna do what you did with Hastings. Bullet right through the heart. Done."

Where's Melissa? Rivera wondered. *She can't be allowing this.* "Is your wife around? I have some news."

"She's around somewhere in there." Jesse scratched the arm of the wooden rocking chair with his index finger, picking at fragments of splintered wood. "We had a big fight."

"Yeah, I bet you did. About you sitting out here all night with a loaded gun in your lap, I'm guessing." He waited for a response to that educated guess, but when none came, he added as casually as possible, "So…you've been sitting out here all night with a loaded gun in your lap, waiting to kill someone?"

Jesse's expression turned quizzical. "You don't think they deserve to die? Agent, *they killed Minx and left me a message in her blood.* They'll stop at nothing now that everyone thinks Hastings was responsible."

"Um…Jesse, listen…I know you're terribly stressed and worried, but Hastings *was* responsible. Every bit of evidence shows unmistakably that he kidnapped and killed Danny. In fact—"

"Agent Rivera!" Melissa interrupted as she opened the front door. She sounded truly relieved that he was there. "I didn't know if we'd ever see you again! Can you please tell Jesse that Charles Hastings can't hurt us anymore?" She spoke as though her husband wasn't sitting right in front of her.

"We were just discussing that, actually. Please sit, Melissa. I have news that will explain everything." Well, not *everything*, he supposed, if someone killed their cat after Hastings was taken out of the equation, but at this point his theory about Hastings's and Jesse's connection still held firm. "We found Danny's body this morning. Hastings buried him in a shallow grave in the conservation land. We've recovered the body and told Don and Becky. It's all over now."

"It's not over," Jesse muttered. His eyes went to the revolver in Rivera's hand.

Rivera ignored him and addressed Melissa. "I haven't filed the final report yet, obviously, but I can tell you unofficially now, I'm sure I figured out how and why Hastings chose *you* to frame and torment and basically try to drive you crazy." *Maybe "try" isn't the right word,* he thought, *'cause you look like you might already be there.* He shook that off and continued, telling them both everything he had figured out that morning: how the proximity of the grave didn't make much sense unless he had brought the body from Forest Avenue. How Hastings's car must have been there when Jesse had the accident, maybe even caused the crash on the icy road. How he must have seen the LCKY123 license plate, then used his DMV contact to get Jesse's name and address. It all fit together.

"Holy shit," Melissa said, and Rivera could tell she wasn't accustomed to profanity.

Jesse didn't even look up, but said, "There were no other cars on the road that night. None that were driving and especially none that were parked. Nothing. No one."

Rivera sighed. "With all due respect, Jesse, you haven't been able to remember anything about that night after your call with Melissa. Now you remember the road was empty? I'm not sure I can take that memory as fact."

"Take it however you want," Jesse mumbled.

"There are still some details I need to investigate, of course," Rivera said, attempting to disregard Jesse's growing distaste for him.

"But everything I've told you does seem to explain all the facts. I can tell you with confidence that it really is all over."

He found himself checking Jesse's face for any sign that he might be listening to and believing what he was saying. Melissa was doing the same, a tear streaming down her face as she said, "Jesse, honey? Do you hear that? It's over."

His expression never changed. "It's not over," he said again.

Jesucristo, Rivera thought and shook his head in genuine sadness. "Mrs. Carlton, I'm leaving now. I'm going back to Boston the instant I debrief the local police. In my official capacity, let me tell you that this concludes my investigative involvement with the Danny Madsen case. You need to get your husband help at the earliest opportunity, even if it means bringing him to the psychiatric center at South Shore Hospital for observation."

Melissa nodded, openly sobbing now. He handed her the Smith & Wesson, which she took with the unspoken understanding that it needed to be kept away from Jesse. The confusion and sorrow written all over her face almost made Rivera want to stop in his tracks and offer her a hug. Almost.

"Agent," she said, wiping her tears on her sleeve. "Minx was definitely killed after Charles Hastings died."

Not you, too. "I'm sorry, Melissa. I can't help with that. You need to deal with the local police regarding your cat. I'm going home now. I'm going back to Boston." It was painful for him to just walk away like this, after everything they'd been through. "Unofficially, and from me as a person and fellow human being, I hope God will bless you and keep you both. I wish I could do more. But I can't. I just can't."

He walked down the front steps and used every ounce of energy he had not to turn back around.

17

God bless us and keep us both?

The words echoed inside Jesse's head after Rivera left. God hadn't done anything to bless them or anyone else involved in this nightmare. Not him, not Melissa, not Don or Becky, and certainly not Danny. No. God—if there was one—had left them to their own fates and put the "God won't give you more than you can handle" bullshit to the test.

Jesse could feel the exhaustion creeping into the depth of his bones. He knew Rivera had seen it and that Melissa was all too well aware of it. But what was he supposed to do? The person or people trying to torment him were still out there, whether they had anything to do with Danny's murder or not. He could barely form words, let alone argue the facts with an overconfident FBI agent, but he'd wanted to scream at Rivera to listen to what Melissa told him: their precious cat was killed *after* they drove back from Don and Becky's. Hastings couldn't have done it. There was another or others involved. Why couldn't Rivera see that?

Melissa did it. Rivera did it. Don and Becky did it. He'd accused them all in front of Dr. Bradley. He'd even accused *himself.*

God, he really *was* losing it. Maybe going to a psychiatric hospital for a while was, in fact, a good idea. His thoughts and emotions had been scrambled since the night of the accident and Bradley wasn't helping him as quickly as he needed. A mental ward might be the only place for him to once and for all get his shit together. It was as if reality had split down the middle that fateful evening and he was finding it impossible to make his way back over the giant fissure.

He looked around for Melissa. Maybe she could help him make the decision. After Rivera had left, she'd gone into the house to hide the gun. Yeah, that was a joke. After fifteen years he knew exactly where she hid things from him — candy when they'd attempt, unsuccessfully, to do the low-carb thing, small Christmas presents, and now the gun. Always the same place at the back of the kitchen cabinet, behind the baking supplies.

She didn't just think he was crazy; she thought he was *stupid* now, too.

But he wasn't crazy. His garage door was hacked by Hastings who planted Danny's stuff and by the bastards who killed Minx. Was that merely a coincidence or were they somehow working together? Collusion was the only possible explanation. Although the *why* still didn't make sense. Rivera came up with some bullshit scenario, and now everyone was okay with just moving on with a false sense of "closure". Really? Until when? *Until it happens again and they try to kill one of us?*

Not gonna happen.

He looked at his watch, barely able to see the digits through his bleary eyes. It was 12:30 and he had an appointment with Dr. Bradley at 3:00. Melissa would tell him to take a nap before the session, but other than Dr. Bradley, Jesse was through listening to anyone about anything anymore. Only his psychiatrist could possibly help figure out how and why the people, whoever they were, were trying to break down his mind, piece by piece.

Or was he imagining all of this? Was Minx really killed after Hastings was shot? Did he have the timing right? He couldn't even think clearly enough to make sense of time. At this moment, only two things stood out with pure clarity: He couldn't kill the devil who had stolen Danny from his life, and that was a regret Jesse would suffer with forever. But as soon as he got his act together and found the person or people torturing him and his wife, he would kill them. He knew exactly where the gun was and there was no doubt in his mind that he was going to use it.

* * *

It was a little after 2:00 when Rivera finished debriefing the detectives and Chief at the Rockland PD station. They were impressed with how he figured out the connection between Charles Hastings and the Carltons, his motive for the vandalism and planting the coat and shoes in their garage. Rivera didn't bring up the dead cat since he was certain that in all of the trauma of Jesse's arrest and

Hastings's death, he and Melissa just couldn't piece together the timing correctly. If it turned out to be some asshole copycat with access to records at the station—anyone from an officer to an intern to a file clerk—the local cops could handle it, anyway. The case was closed and he could finally return to Boston without delay.

After thanking everyone and saying his goodbyes, he walked to his car in the parking lot, took a deep breath and started the engine. It was finally time to get the hell out of Rockland, Massachusetts.

* * *

About halfway through their session, Jesse took a breath after telling Dr. Bradley everything his tired brain could recall about what had happened since he saw him just yesterday: the discovery of Danny's grave and body, Agent Rivera's explanation of how Charles Hastings chose him to torture and frame. He even shared that he'd sat out all night with a gun in his lap, waiting for the sons of bitches to try and strike again.

Jesse could see the intense concern on Dr. Bradley's face. "Jesse, I have to tell you that I'm *very* worried about you right now. You have had no rest in the past…what, thirty hours, at least?"

"That sounds about right, yeah."

"Do you feel tired at the moment?"

Jesse thought for a second and let out a scoff of surprise. "No, to tell you the truth. I feel really *alive*, really wired. A lot better than I felt before I got here."

As soon as he answered, it was obvious Dr. Bradley didn't think this was a good thing.

"Did you know that people who are *in extremis* with a loss of sleep are eight times more likely to suffer a psychotic episode, even one that involves violence?"

"English, please, Roger. English."

Dr. Bradley let his notepad fall onto his lap. "The more tired you are, the less 'well' your mind functions. This lack of sleep and irregular brain activity could lead to violent acts, especially when your thoughts are already revolving around violence."

"Okay. No, I didn't know that," Jesse said flatly.

Bradley waited for more. When Jesse had nothing else to respond with—what else was he supposed to say?—the doctor said, "You pointed out that both the FBI agent and your wife mentioned possible inpatient status at a behavioral health facility?"

"Yes, they did. Do you agree?" Jesse made sure to look directly into Dr. Bradley's eyes.

"I'm not necessarily saying that, Jesse," he said, although Jesse could see in his eyes that this idea was precisely what he was trying to get his patient to consider, "but now that you've shared your experiences and the way they made you feel, can I suggest something in the time we have left today?"

Jesse gave a shrug that said *Sure, why not.*

"I'd like you to just sit there with your eyes closed and feel your breath. I'll do it, too, and I promise not to peek."

Jesse smiled but didn't laugh. There had been no laughing today. "Am I paying you to sit and do nothing?"

From Dr. Bradley's reaction, it was apparent he was expecting a response like that. "I'm not going to bill for this session. I want you to get better, Jesse. This one's on me."

"Whoa. All right, you've convinced me."

"Excellent." Dr. Bradley lowered the lights in the office and set his time for twenty minutes. "And don't worry if you fall asleep. A good rest might have just as much positive effect as meditation."

He must think I'm stupid, too. He just wants me to sleep.

Jesse would play along with Dr. Bradley; after all, he wasn't being charged for it, and it did feel really good to close his eyes. He hoped he wouldn't start nodding off, but if he did, he'd take that as a sign that his body didn't give a care about whatever came next. He'd listen to his flesh and bones, and if the message was to sleep, he'd sleep. If it was to sit outside again all night waiting for those assholes to return so he could kill them, he would. He'd even go to the nuthouse for a while if that's what his body told him. It seemed that his own mind no longer had any say in the matter.

For now, however, he'd enjoy the supervised silence and non-thinking time Roger was making available to him. He let his mind empty and welcomed whatever insights might float in. Nothing had happened when he tried it at home over the past two days, and nothing, he knew, was what would happen now. Still, maybe being here with someone he really trusted would help make it work better for him.

He went deep into darkness and stillness, allowing

(driving in darkness)

random images to flicker in his mind, which supposedly always happened during "meditation," if that's even what this could be

(ice)

called. He remembered driving along Forest Avenue

(skidding)

the night of the accident, although he had no idea why that would pop up right now. He'd thought

(Danny's face)

about that night a thousand times

(brightness)

since…wait, did he just see Danny on the road, his face all lit up? Jesus, would the guilt never let him be?

He regained his calm and settled back into darkness and

(Danny's scream)

"No," he said out loud, his eyes popping open.

Dr. Bradley opened his eyes as well. "Everything okay?"

"Yeah, sorry," he said, although everything was *not* okay. He closed his eyes again and resettled himself in the chair. He relaxed and let himself

(skidding

screaming

Danny flying off into the darkness)

Jesse opened his eyes again, his heart about to beat out of his chest. He didn't make a sound, however, so Dr. Bradley, true to his word, kept meditating. Jesse closed his eyes. Why was his brain doing this to him? He remembered Dr. Bradley once talking about a "psychotic break"; was that what was happening?

It couldn't be; he knew exactly where he was, what day and time it was and what he was doing here. Also, he was overcome by a distant but approaching feeling of clarity, something he hadn't experienced in months.

Since that night.

He squeezed his eyes shut and shoved everything out of his mind. He could feel the agitation in his body and forced it to relax. He felt each inhale and exhale as his breathing slowed. Maybe he would fall asleep; that was sounding more and more like mercy. But after another few seconds, he knew that wasn't going to happen.

(dark road

   ice

      skidding

         Danny's face flooded with light

            screaming

           Danny flying off into the darkness)

"Oh my God! No! Oh Jesus! No!" he yelled and jumped to his feet.

Dr. Bradley jolted forward, his notepad falling on the floor. "Jesse, what is it? What's going on?"

"That night…the car…skidded on the ice…I…" Jesse's voice was cracking. *"I slammed into…oh my God…he went flying into the woods!"*

"Okay, Jesse." Dr. Bradley started to rise from his chair. "I need you to—"

"I killed Danny! Oh my God! Help me! I am *the murderer!"* Jesse cried out.

He slammed himself against the office door then stood back and threw it open like the flap of a cardboard box. Looking down the hallway, the office doors on either side appeared to be moving—drifting, floating in all directions like a drug-induced hallucination. He held onto the door jamb to steady himself and was about to vomit when a hand on his shoulder make him jolt backward.

Jesse heard a voice, but the words were incomprehensible. Nothing made sense; the floating doors, the noise behind him, the images of that night, Danny's face. He was being deceived by his own senses, drowning in the horror of his thoughts. An immense wave had crashed on top of him, and his insides were being pulled out with the tide and getting swallowed up by a bottomless ocean.

He wasn't sure which way to turn, so he ran straight to the end of the hallway and out the door that floated beneath the EXIT sign. As Jesse ran down the stairs, he heard nothing but his panting breath, a voice in the distance calling his name and the haunting echo of a little boy's scream.

* * *

When her cell phone rang, Melissa Carlton was sitting with Becky and Don Madsen, listening to the droning sound of a cadaver-like funeral director providing options for Danny's funeral.

She was still ill with the image of her godson's face that had been buried for months in the dank earth, but someone had to provide the official identification, and she wasn't about to let the Madsens live through that. It was still unmistakably Danny, the sweetest kid she'd ever known, the boy who lit up every room just by being in it.

When she had come out of the Medical Examiner's office, she tried to be strong for Becky and Don, but after she nodded to confirm it was their boy in the morgue, she could no longer hold back her sobs. The three of them stood holding each other in the cold hallway, crying and helping one another remain standing. She told them she needed to go to the ladies' room to wash away the tear stains, but it was really to allow them a moment alone together to share the terrible grief that only they could understand.

After a few minutes, she exited the bathroom where Becky and Don were waiting for her. They asked if she'd come to the funeral home with them to help make arrangements. They cried together some more and when they found the strength to leave the building, they got into Melissa's car and she drove them to the mortuary.

And now, in his monotone voice, forced kindness floated out of the funeral director's mouth like a counterfeit bill, falling on the floor of a room in which Melissa felt the heaviness of every other grief-stricken person who'd sat within its walls. The director was explaining the difference between a closed-casket viewing and a memorial service, lilies versus roses, when the incongruous music of her ringtone emanated from Melissa's phone. It was Dr. Bradley. She looked at the time of 2:48 on the touchscreen and ice ran through her veins: it wasn't time for Jesse's session to be over yet. There was something wrong.

She stepped out of the room and answered the call. "Dr. Bradley?"

"Mrs. Carlton, I'm sorry it took me a moment to find your number—your husband ran out of my office before we were finished. I tried to go after him, but he was gone before I could get outside the building."

"*What?*" Panic spread throughout her body. "For God's sake, what happened? Why would he leave early?"

"He didn't just leave early," Dr. Bradley said, and she could hear the distress in his voice. "He was screaming…that, um…"

"What was he screaming?!"

"He screamed 'I killed Danny.' Something snapped in his mind during our session. I think he might have suffered a psychotic break of sorts."

The lobby of the funeral home seemed to sway, but she kept her bearings. "Why would he say he killed Danny? What could've been going through his head that—"

"It appears as though memories from the night of the accident pushed through into his consciousness," Dr. Bradley said, surely trying to sound calm. But it wasn't working. The tremble in his voice increased Melissa's anxiety tenfold. "He mentioned skidding on the ice, slamming into Danny and the boy getting thrown into the woods."

Silence.

Melissa shook herself from her thoughts. "I—I need to call him. I need to call the police."

"I called both of them. Jesse didn't answer, and legally, I had to alert the authorities. I told them that in the state Jesse is in, he has the potential to harm himself and possibly others. Think of the places he might have gone. I gave the police your address, so they should be heading there right now. I'm hoping that's where he went."

Melissa closed her eyes and was incredibly grateful that Agent Rivera prompted her to hide the gun. Jesse would never find it in the back of the baking cabinet; since they moved into that house, he had never once found anything she hid there. "I'm going to call him *right this second*. Thank you, doctor."

"Wait, Melissa—" he started, but she cut the line and dialed her husband's cell.

It went to voicemail. Hearing his chipper voice on the recording made her feel sick to her stomach. He hadn't sounded like that in months and God only knew what he would sound like right now. At the beep, she yelled into the phone, "Jesse! Baby, call me! I spoke with Dr. Bradley! Everything's going to be okay. Just call me back, baby! When you get this, go home *go to the house!* You'll be safe, okay? You'll be safe…"

She hadn't even noticed she was sobbing again until she hung up. When she turned around, Becky and Don stood in the hall looking at her, one more confused than the other. The funeral director was there, too, but remained standing at the door to his office.

"It's Jesse! *No one knows where he is!*"

"We heard," Becky said. "Let's go."

As they hurried to the car, Melissa dialed a number on her phone. "I'm calling Agent Rivera," she said. "Maybe he can do something. Anything. I can't think of anyone else."

* * *

What a day, Rivera thought as he took the curve of Hingham onto Highway 3 for the trip back to Boston. Even just being a few miles out of town made him feel lighter somehow. From now until the end of time, Rockland would be a place of shadow, darkness and pain for him. When he wished the Carltons God's blessings, he meant it; they'd been without good fortune for much too long. Now maybe they could get on with their lives and he with his. It had only been a day, but he longed to see Maria and Tonio again already.

He started on the nearly 270-degree turn onto 3, never caring for the vertiginous effect of the sweeping curve. Then, about a half a yard ahead, he saw a deer jump up onto the road from out of what seemed like nowhere. Knowing there was going to be a collision of some kind, he stomped on his brakes and—

"Oh, no," he said aloud, as a white sedan, about two car lengths ahead, skidded and swerved to avoid the deer.

Although the car just missed hitting it head-on, the vehicle went into a spin, its rear panel swinging directly into the deer at high speed. The impact flung the animal ten feet into the air and what appeared to be fifty or so feet forward into the parking lot of a gas station located directly off the side of the road. The out-of-control sedan skid a few feet further on the asphalt and into a ditch near a small stretch of landscaped trees.

Rivera was stopped now, as were all the vehicles on the curve. He was about to call emergency services when he saw a squad car in his rear-view mirror. The officer threw on his lights and immediately passed them all on the narrow strip. Getting out beside the white sedan, he put up his hand to keep traffic from resuming until he could assess the situation. Rivera was only a few feet away from the accident, but for the moment, he was going to have to sit and wait like everyone else.

The deer lay unmoving on the concrete. Rivera was close enough to see the body pretty well, well enough to know that he was looking at just that: a body. The deer's head had been hurled against the concrete floor of the parking lot and blood oozed quickly into the cracks of the pavement.

Wait, he thought. *Why does this feel familiar?*

He almost jumped out of his seat when the shrill, FBI-standard ringtone of his phone went off. Not taking his eyes off the deer—*what was it? What am I feeling?*—he answered using the car system, saying distractedly, "Agent Rivera."

"Agent, this is Melissa Carlton!" Her voice was urgent, clearly panicked.

Rivera immediately pulled his eyes away from the scene and stared at her name on the display as he spoke. "Mrs. Carlton, I want to, but I can't help with the Minx situation—"

"Jesse is missing! Please, I don't know who else to turn to!"

"What?" He had no idea what to do with this information. "Have you tried your house? Or is he missing from the house? What's going on, Melissa?"

"We're on our way there right now. Dr. Bradley says Jesse thinks *he* killed Danny! Something about the night of the accident…skidding on the ice…hitting Danny… Danny getting thrown into the woods. It's all a jumble right now. I have to find him!"

Rivera felt everything fall away. His eyes moved from element to element of the scene in front of him:

A car in a ditch by the side of the road.

A living, breathing creature thrown fifty feet away, its skull probably cracked by the impact of the landing.

Trying to avoid hitting the deer, the car had swerved out of control, hit him and essentially lifted and threw the animal into the air in a way that wouldn't leave a scratch on the car, let alone a dent.

"Agent Rivera?"

I just saw Jesse's accident.

Oh, God. I just saw how Danny Madsen was killed.

"Melissa, I may be able to help explain things," he said. "I just need to think it through a bit more. Meet me at your house." A heaviness filled his chest when he realized that everything had just gotten so much worse. Jesse *had* killed Danny, but accidentally. Danny must have escaped from the bedroom window, been chased by Hastings through the conservation land and reached the road at the same time Jesse was searching for him. *Jesucristo, the odds! Why would God...*

"What do you mean, 'explain things'?" Melissa was crying.

"It doesn't matter right now. All that matters is when you find your husband, you make him realize it's not his fault. That it was an accident. And make sure he doesn't do anything extreme. I don't care if you have to shove him into the garage and lock it. You did hide the gun, right?"

"Y-yes, I did. Do you think he'd try to —"

"I have no idea." He put on his emergency light and rushed around the vehicles in front of him, past the patrol car and accident. "Get hold of the gun and shoot him in the leg if you have to. But stop him now or something terrible will happen."

* * *

Melissa tore through the afternoon traffic to get the three of them back to her house before Jesse arrived. But there was still the chance that if he ran every traffic light, broke the speed limit or both, he could be there already. She had no idea what the man she'd been married to for more than fifteen years was capable of doing in his current state of mind. But all she could do was drive as fast as she could, like a reckless maniac if she had to, as Rivera's words kept spinning through her mind like a tornado. *Something terrible could happen.*

She thought she was driving like a bat out of hell, but the three RPD police cars that whipped by her, sirens blaring and lights blazing toward her neighborhood made her feel like she wasn't even moving. She stepped on the gas and drove in their wake, hoping that following them at eighty miles an hour would keep her moving past all the other cars pulling over for the police.

She kept after the police cars as they turned onto the street before hers. Their vehicles then screamed around the corner to Roseto Street, where she saw two ambulances and a full-size fire truck in front of her house.

She recognized Agent Rivera's car—how he'd gotten there so quickly, she couldn't imagine, but she felt an odd sense of relief when seeing him talking with the other officers. All of them had their eyes fixed on her house and as soon as she screeched to a halt behind the police cars, she saw why.

Jesse was on the porch pacing back and forth in a way that was frantic, almost manic.

And he was holding the gun.

I'm dreaming, she thought. *This is not possible, it can't be happening, I must be dreaming.* But Becky's hand on her shoulder told her she wasn't.

"Jesse!" she shouted at the top of her lungs. "It's me! Stop, please! Listen to me!"

She ran toward the house, but two firefighters held her back at Rivera's urging. "Stay right there, Melissa, I'm asking you. Anything might set him off, including you running up there."

"He's got the gun," she said.

Obviously, everyone knew that, but Rivera just nodded. "We know. That's what I'm saying. Talk to him, but don't approach, okay?"

She nodded, then turned to Becky and Don who were standing beside her. Becky's head was resting on Don's shoulder. She appeared almost too weak to stand.

"Don, I can't take any more," Melissa heard her moan, tears streaming down her cheeks. "I can't lose Jesse *and* Danny. Not like this, not like…"

"Missy!" Jesse yelled from the porch. He waved the revolver at her. "I'm sorry…I found the gun."

The police who had arrived on the scene with her unholstered their weapons. She wanted to yell, to let them know this was her husband, not a killer. One of the officers, holding his gun with both arms fully extended, looked more frightened than skilled at handling the situation. His hands were shaking, and she was about to tell Rivera to have them lower their guns when she heard Jesse's voice.

"I killed him, Missy." Seeing Don and Becky behind her, he cried out like a victim would scream for his life. "I murdered your son! I'm the one! I'm the murderer!"

"No! Jesse, no!" Melissa shouted. She remembered the phone call with Rivera. "It was an accident, Jesse. An accident! You loved Danny!"

"We forgive you!" Don yelled, and everyone on the street froze. Melissa quickly turned to him, astounded that he chose to utter those words that made it sound as though Jesse was guilty. Don returned her gaze and panicked as though he was reading her mind. He shouted so loudly it sounded like his throat might burst. "It was an accident! There's nothing to forgive!"

Don walked past Melissa and then Rivera, toward Jesse. He was halfway across the lawn when Jesse lifted the gun and pointed it at him.

"Stay back!" Jesse yelled. "I said, stay back!"

A shot rang out and Don stopped in his tracks.

Melissa screamed and the onlookers gasped as the gun fell from Jesse's hand.

She turned and saw the frightened officer lowering the weapon he'd just discharged, shaking his head as though confused about what he'd just done.

When she looked back around, Jesse swayed by the front door, his one hand wrapped around the other. She tried to breathe, watching the blood flow down his fingers onto the porch.

Thank God, she thought. *It's over.*

Turning to the officers who stood with their guns pointed at Jesse, Rivera yelled, "Put those goddamned guns away right now or I swear to God, I'll have your badges by the end of the day."

The uniforms holstered their weapons.

Jesse stumbled backward against the house, his haunted eyes now only circles on his face. He picked up the gun with his good hand and tucked it under his arm. "I told you..." he cried, "whoever killed Danny is going to pay with his life!"

He turned toward the door and ran inside, slamming the door and leaving a trail of blood behind him.

"Jesse!" Melissa screamed, starting to run toward the house.

Becky and Don followed, but Rivera and the other officers jumped to hold them back. "Missy—Becky—Don—you can't go in there. It's too dangerous. He could kill any or all of you. Stay right here while I talk to the shift captain—"

And then it happened.

As Melissa was pulling away from Rivera's grasp and Becky and Don were running up the porch steps, a gunshot sounded. Every single person at the scene recoiled at the intensity of the sound.

Melissa had seen the flash. It came from the window of their bedroom. Her mouth moved, but no sound came out. Finally, in an almost silent rasp, she said, "Jesse."

"Goddammit!" Rivera yelled. He looked toward Melissa and then calmly said, "It's okay. It's okay, he could have just fired it into the wall or ceiling."

"No, no, no, no, no, no..." Melissa sobbed, staring at the house.

Melissa ran past Rivera and the other officers up to the house where Don and Becky were waiting for her to unlock the door.

They moved aside as she fumbled with her keys.

She screamed again, "Jesse! No, baby! Jesse!"

Melissa tried to stop shaking long enough to fit her key into the lock. Rivera's voice grew louder behind them as he approached, but she was able to unbolt the lock and run inside, Becky and Don following her toward the staircase.

"Jesse! Baby!" she continued to shriek as she climbed the steps and stumbled through the doorway.

Her shriek stopped with a choked sob of shock. The wail escaped her, spiraling throughout the house and to the dozens of people standing in the street.

Becky and Don came in behind her. Becky screamed, hugging Don as she turned away.

"Oh my God," Don choked on his words, trying to breathe.

When Rivera caught up to them and entered the room, he hung his head. "No."

On the bed was the bloodied body of Jesse Carlton. His hand still holding the gun.

There were two wounds, the one in his hand caused by the officer outside and the other, the fatal shot, in his right temple. Melissa fell to her knees. Jesse had finally killed the man he held responsible for Danny's death.

As she stared at his body, eyes blurred with tears, she shuddered in disbelief. In the same handwriting of the message found on the bottom of the rock, on Danny's bat and next to Minx, was a single word scrawled in blood on the wall behind the bed.

MURDERER.

A Word From Rob

I hope you enjoyed reading "A Broken Reality" as much as I enjoyed writing it! I'd love to hear your thoughts about the book, the characters and anything else you liked (or didn't)!

You can always write an Amazon review or contact me anytime at Rob@AuthorRobKaufman.com

Also, if you liked "A Broken Reality", I'm sure you'll enjoy reading my other books. Learn more about them at Amazon by using the links below...

One Last Lie
In the Shadow of Stone

Thanks again for reading "A Broken Reality"!

To receive emails about my new books, events and news, sign up for my mailing list at www.AuthorRobKaufman.com.

Made in the USA
Las Vegas, NV
09 February 2022

43530067R00187